thrillers and courtroom dramas. Absorbing."
- *The Orlando Sentinel*

"If there's anybody who can mount a challenge to John Grisham's mantle...Buffa's the most sure-footed guy to do it. A crisp, first-rate read...a tightly wound thriller. A richly textured cast of characters."
- *Edmonton Journal*

"D.W. Buffa continues to show great intelligence and erudition. There's nobody else like him."
- *San Jose Mercury News*

"Littered with plot twists and land mines that explode when least expected...A novel with wide appeal. A fast-moving tale that jolts and veers enticingly off track, but also stays comfortably in sight of the main objective. Well-developed characters and a rich milieu add depth to this excellent thriller."
- *Publishers Weekly*

The Defense
"A gripping drama...made up of not just one but several exciting trials...More satisfying still, it ends with a couple of twists that are really shocking. And it leaves you wanting to go back to the beginning and read it all over again."
- *The New York Times*

"An excellent legal thriller."
- *USA Today*

"Stunning legal reversals...fine, flowing prose...[a] devastating impact."
- *The New York Times Book Review*

EVANGELINE

D. W. Buffa

BLUE ZEPHYR

EVANGELINE

CHAPTER ONE

No one spoke, no one moved, the only sound a muffled cough that made the silence more profound. In the crowded solitude of the courtroom everyone waited, as much worried about what this trial might tell about themselves as about the man who was charged with the crime. Their solemn, troubled looks told you that, deep down, they wondered whether they might not have done the same thing- and whether it was really a crime at all.

At the far left, opposite the jury box, a wooden door flew open. Gray eyes blazing, the Honorable Homer Maitland moved quickly to the bench. He cast a long, thoughtful glance at the crowd and then, with a slight nod towards the clerk waiting obediently below, instructed her to bring in the jury. Judge Maitland greeted the six men and six women with a stern formality. It seemed to serve notice, as if any notice were needed, that this was not an ordinary trial, not the kind heard dozens of times each month. This was something different, something that none of those involved were ever likely to forget. He turned away from the jury. The narrow creases at the edge of his mouth spread along his jaw as he studied the two lawyers at the tables set side by side at right angles to the jury box.

"Mr. Roberts," he said in a voice as rough and weathered as his hands.

"Your Honor?" replied Michael Roberts for the prosecution.

"Call your first witness."

It was there for just a second, a brief confession of reluctance, and something more than that: a doubt whether any of this was wise. But Roberts was not there to show doubt or hesitation; he was there to construct a case which, when he was finished, would leave no room for doubt that a crime had been committed and that the

1

defendant- and no one else- was guilty of it.

"The People call Benjamin Whitfield." Everyone turned to look. They had never met him, but they all knew who he was. Even before what had happened, everyone had known his name. Whitfield took the oath in a voice that, though steady, seemed to lack conviction.

"Would you please state your name for the record," Roberts began as he took a position at the side of the counsel table, only a few feet from the jury box.

"Benjamin Whitfield," replied the witness.

Roberts struck a languid pose, his arms crossed in front of him, one foot crossed over the other. "You are the registered owner of a sailing vessel, the Evangeline?"

"Yes, I am. Or, rather, I was."

"Of course. Would you describe that vessel for us, Mr. Whitfield?"

"She was a double-masted sailing ship, the finest of her kind."

"And it was registered in the United States?"

"Yes."

"Did you purchase it new?"

"I had her built. She was finished a year ago. She was in trial runs for several months. This was to have been her first real voyage."

Roberts moved across the front of the courtroom to the clerk's desk. "Would you be kind enough to identify these photographs?" He handed the witness a large folder. Whitfield removed half a dozen photographs, examined each in turn and passed them back.

"They're photographs of the Evangeline. Two of them were taken the day she was christened; three of them while she was undergoing her first sea trials."

Stepping away so everyone could see, Roberts held up the sixth and final photograph. "And this photograph, Mr. Whitfield? When was this one taken?"

With a grim expression, Whitfield stared down at his hands. "The day she left."

Roberts stood next to the railing in front of the jury

box, waiting until Whitfield looked back.

"The day she left Nice," Whitfield explained in a distant, hollow voice. "The day she started her last voyage."

"The day the Evangeline left the South of France to sail out of the Mediterranean, past Gibraltar, down along the west coast of Africa, around the Cape, back up the eastern coast and through the Suez?"

"Yes, that was the voyage she was on, to sail around Africa. It was meant to be a vacation, a way to get away from everything and just spend time with friends."

"And how many of your friends were on board the day the Evangeline left the harbor in Nice?"

"Nineteen."

"Was it your plan to sail the boat yourself?"

Whitfield shook his head emphatically. "No. I could have done it; not by myself, you understand, but with a crew. But I wanted this to be a time when I didn't have to do anything, when I had no responsibilities at all. That's why I hired Vincent Marlowe; so that everything would be taken care of, so that the boat and everyone on her would be in good hands." Whitfield bent forward and stared at Roberts. "I still believe that."

"You still believe...?"

"That Vincent Marlowe was the best choice I could have made. I would trust him with..." Whitfield suddenly stiffened; a shudder passed through him.

"You would trust him with what, Mr. Whitfield? Your life? You trusted him with a lot more than that! You trusted him with nineteen of your closest friends and the other seven members of the crew," said Roberts in a voice that, as it fell lower, became harsh and implacable. "Twenty-seven human beings, Mr. Whitfield- and how many of them are left?"

"Objection, your Honor," cried William Darnell, lifting himself halfway out of his chair. It was unmistakable, that voice. It came clothed in the indefatigable cheerfulness of a man who had lived long enough to know that every day might be his last, and who found in that otherwise depressing fact one more reason to love each day he was alive.

"If I still have any memory left, I could swear I heard the prosecution call Mr. Whitfield as a witness. I'm pretty sure I didn't call him. Which leaves me- and perhaps the court as well- a little confused about why my good friend Mr. Roberts has decided to subject him to cross-examination?"

Homer Maitland lifted one of his gray eyebrows. "Mr. Roberts? He is your witness, isn't he?"

"Yes, your Honor," said Roberts without expression. "Sorry, Mr. Whitfield. That was unfair of me. But to get back to your testimony: you hired the defendant, Vincent Marlowe, as the captain because you wanted to spend time with your friends?"

"Yes. As I say, Marlowe is a very experienced sailor." Whitfield darted a glance past Roberts to the defendant, who was sitting next to Darnell.

"But something happened, and this trip, this voyage around Africa, went on without you. What happened? Why didn't you go?"

Benjamin Whitfield began to rub his hands together as he leaned forward. He was looking straight at Roberts, but staring at something only he could see. "Would it have made any difference if I had gone? I keep wondering what I would have done- what anyone could have done..."

Roberts clutched the hard, varnished railing of the jury box with his right hand and shoved his left hand into his pocket. "Why didn't you go?" he asked.

The question brought Whitfield out of the strange reverie into which he had fallen. He shook his head. "My father had a heart attack. I had to get home."

"I'm very sorry. And did your father...?"

"The doctors could not save him. He died in the hospital a few days later."

"But you were able to spend some time with him? You had the chance to say your last goodbyes. And he died surrounded by his family. He-"

"Your Honor?" objected Darnell. "We're all very sorry for Mr. Whitfield's loss, but I'm not quite certain that I see the connection between the manner of his father's death and the charges brought against my client."

Judge Maitland gave Roberts a cautionary glance. Roberts returned a brief, formal nod and, without moving from his place next to the jury box, went on to his next question. "Mr. Whitfield, there were nineteen passengers and eight crew members on board. What precautions had been taken for their safety? Let's begin with the question of life preservers, or, as I think they are sometimes called, vests?"

"There were dozens of them on board- more than adequate."

"Their number may have been adequate, but were they immediately accessible?" Roberts stared down at the tips of his shoes as he moved one foot slightly in front of the other. There was no reply to his question. His eyes came up first, followed by his head. "Mr. Whitfield?"

"Sorry. Yes, I assume so. They were stored in all the normal places; everything was done according to the standard regulations."

"The life vests- these were the inflatable kind? You put it on, pull a cord, and it inflates itself?"

"Yes, exactly. Everyone knew how to do it. That's one of the first things the crew would have done- shown everyone where the vests were, how to put them on, how to use them. And, you have to remember," said Whitfield, looking towards the jury, "all those people- every one of them- had been on boats before…"

"But always as passengers, never as members of the crew," said Roberts.

"Yes, that's right; but they were familiar with life vests."

Roberts moved his foot another inch forward. "Now tell us, if you would, about the lifeboats that were available in case of emergency."

"There were several inflatable rafts, and two Zodiacs, which are also inflatable but have outboard motors fixed to a wooden board in back."

"And each one could accommodate how many passengers? What I mean to say," Roberts added quickly, "is safely accommodate?"

"The inflatable rafts could probably each handle six or seven; the Zodiacs could carry perhaps as many as nine or ten."

"Certainly enough capacity for the nineteen passengers and eight crew members of the Evangeline," said Roberts with a glance at the jury that was dark and full of meaning.

Darnell bounced up from his chair. An eager smile darted across his mouth. "I'm afraid it's my dreadful memory again, your Honor I know, of course, that Mr. Roberts has now become a witness; it's just that I can't remember him being sworn!"

Homer Maitland drew in his cheeks, forcing his lips forward: the wily expression of a judge who knew the subtle art by which the legendary William Darnell had captivated juries for the better part of half a century.

"Perhaps the clerk had better put you both under oath," he remarked as he studied Darnell through half closed eyes. "Do you have a question, Mr. Roberts? Because if you do, this might be a good time to ask it."

"Yes, your Honor," replied Roberts in a voice that had no humor in it. "Mr. Whitfield, what other precautions were taken for the safety of the passengers and crew? Were the lifeboats adequately provisioned?"

"Yes. I mean, I think so. I mean, the captain, Mr. Marlowe...I'm sure that before they were ever lowered away, he would- the crew would have..."

"What about the communications equipment? There was a radio; there was...?"

"A radio was the least of it. Computers, wireless Internet communication, global positioning, cell phones- the most advanced electronic equipment in the world was on that boat. The Evangeline was one of the most technologically advanced sailing vessels ever built."

Roberts walked back to the counsel table and started to pull out his chair. He stopped and looked again at

Whitfield. "The most advanced equipment in the world- and none of it worked! How do you explain that, Mr. Whitfield? That with all this technology, the Evangeline went down in a storm at sea and for forty days no one knew where she was or what had happened to her?"

With a grim, haunted look, Benjamin Whitfield shook his head.

"How do you explain that, Mr. Whitfield?" Roberts asked insistently.

With an anguished stare, Whitfield shook his head one last time. "They say she went down in less than two minutes. No one on her would have had a chance to do anything."

CHAPTER TWO

When he was not on his feet objecting, William Darnell sat in his chair, his arms hanging limp over the sides, staring at the ceiling as if he were either bored by every word the witness said or had fallen asleep with his eyes wide open. He had done it often enough before, taken advantage of the long winded testimony of a witness for the other side to catch up on his sleep. He had done it at least once in every one of the hundreds of trials in which he had appeared for the defense. And when he had not actually done it, he had made certain to pretend that he had. It was part of the legend that had grown up around him: the brilliant eccentric who, if he slept at all during a trial, slept not at home in bed but in his office, fully dressed, able to make up for what he had missed with a short nap in court.

The prosecution had finished with its first witness. The judge had inquired whether the defense. wished to cross-examine. Darnell had not opened his eyes. His small head was tilted back, his mouth hung slightly open. Homer Maitland bent forward, about to rouse him with a louder voice.

"And so, you planned this trip around Africa as a way of spending more time with a few of your favorite friends?" Darnell's eyes were still closed, his head still thrown back. He might have been talking in his sleep. "But then your father, who, if I'm not mistaken, had a long history of heart failure- this wasn't his first heart attack, was it?- was put in hospital, and for that reason you flew home and the others went ahead without you?"

Darnell's eyes flew open. In a single, fluid motion, he spun out of his chair and moved to the precise spot in front of the jury box from which Michael Roberts had conducted the majority of his direct examination. "May I inquire, Mr. Whitfield, why you did not simply postpone the trip?

"You had been planning it for some time, isn't that true? You testified, if I remember correctly, that the boat had been built to your rather exacting specifications; that it had completed all its trials; that it was a quite wonderful two-master, capable of sailing anywhere in the world. And her maiden voyage- the one you had planned for, the one you had dreamed about, the one on which, at an expense some might think exorbitant, you were bringing nineteen of your friends-"

"Your Honor!" Roberts objected, "I seem to recall something about a witness testifying without first being sworn?"

Homer Maitland drew in his cheeks the same way he had before. A look of sly amusement danced in his eyes as he waited for Darnell's reply. But Darnell stared down at the floor and, with his small hands clasped behind his back, rose up on the balls of his feet and rocked slowly back and forth.

The jurors close to him could see, if they were looking sharply, a smile at the corners of his mouth. Then, suddenly, it was gone. His head jolted up and he staggered forward, planted his feet firmly on the floor, and fixed the witness with a piercing stare.

"Question: You had been planning this trip for some time- correct?"

Startled, Whitfield scratched his head.

"Planning it for some time?" Darnell repeated as he took a step forward.

"Yes."

"Question: The Evangeline was built to your specifications?" He took another step.

"Yes."

"Question: It had completed all its trials?"

"Yes."

"Question: It was capable of sailing- of sailing safely- anywhere in the world?"

"Yes, it was. I just testified that it had all the newest, best equipment, the-"

"Question: You had dreamed about making this

voyage, planned it for years, isn't that correct?"

"Yes- but not just this voyage. We were going to go everywhere, see everything. There was no limit to what we could do with her."

Darnell had taken another step forward and was now close enough to touch Whitfield. At this last answer, he stood straight up and looked back at the jury. Then, with a puzzled expression, he moved across to the counsel table. Both hands on the back of his empty chair, he fell into a long, thoughtful silence. 'She was that good, the Evangeline? There were no limits to what she could do?"

"Yes, that's right," said Whitfield eagerly, "she was perfect. She could...No, I see what you mean. There was a limit, wasn't there? She sank, so there must have been a limit- even for her."

Darnell motioned to the clerk, a plump young woman with a pleasant face. "Would you please hand the witness what has been marked Defense Exhibit 17?

"Would the witness be kind enough to identify the document he has just been handed?"

Whitfield glanced at the cover sheet of a thirty-page document. "This is the report of the sea trials of the Evangeline."

"Yes, yes," said Darnell, flapping his hand as he turned to face the jury. "Would you please turn to page six? Now, would you read the second paragraph from the top? Just the highlighted portion, if you would."

"During the sea trials, after one day of heavy weather, water began to leak through the aluminum hull. A crack was discovered below the waterline."

"Yes, thank you, Mr. Whitfield. That's enough. Now, let me confess to you," he said as he wheeled around and looked at him directly, "I have seldom ventured out in a sailboat anywhere except here on the San Francisco bay. I know very little about them and nothing at all about their construction.

"I have, however, been told by people whose business it is to know these things, that if that happens- if there is a crack in the aluminum hull, and if the aluminum plates begin to pull apart- and especially if it happens in the kind of dreadful storm in which the Evangeline suddenly found herself- the only question is how quickly she is going to sink. In your considered opinion, is that a fair statement of the case?"

"Yes, but that problem was dealt with."

"Dealt with? Yes, I remember; the shipyard investigated. One of the welding rods was used improperly. Isn't that what they found? Something about a welding rod that should have been used to weld a stainless-steel fitting on the rudder was used instead on the aluminum plates of the hull?"

"The problem was identified and fixed. It was just one worker, just one weld. The crack was fixed," replied Whitfield.

"Yes, the crack was fixed- the one you knew about- but did anyone bother to check if there were other, similar failures? Wouldn't the safest thing have been to X-ray all the seams, make sure that all of them had been properly welded?"

"There was no need for that," insisted Whitfield.

"No need?" Darnell's eyes narrowed into a penetrating stare. "You can say that now, after she went down like that, after all those lives were lost?"

"They found the crack; they determined the cause! The people who built her were convinced that everything was perfect!"

"But the question, Mr. Whitfield- the question that I have been asking myself ever since I first read that report- is why, if they thought it was "perfect", did they also offer to check every weld and every seam?"

He looked at Whitfield almost apologetically. "The only point I wish to make is that the shipyard was prepared to conduct a thorough investigation into the safety of every part of that aluminum hull, but the decision was made not to do so. Isn't that correct?"

"Yes, I have to admit that it is."

"We are still left with the question, though: Why,

when you found out that your father was ill, when you found out that you had to fly back home, why didn't you simply put off the maiden voyage of the Evangeline?"

Perhaps not even William Darnell himself could have said whether he had deliberately begun his cross examination as if he were an enemy, calling the witness a liar, so he could convince Whitfield now, when it counted, that he was- if not a friend, at least sympathetic- willing and able to understand that none of the things that had happened later were his fault.

"The reason you did not postpone the date of departure for the Evangeline is because none of your guests could have waited. Isn't that the reason, Mr. Whitfield? The people you invited to go with you on this voyage were not the kind who could be asked to wait a week or even a few days. Isn't that true, Mr. Whitfield?"

"I didn't know how long I was going to be away. I couldn't ask them to wait."

"Because there was a date by which everyone expected to be back in Nice, and they had other commitments, calendars full of places they had to be."

"Yes, they all had other things to do."

"Indeed. The invitations to your guests had gone out nearly six months in advance. I assume that is the kind of notice people who move in these circles require, because of all the other demands on their time?"

"It had been planned well in advance, yes."

Darnell nodded and for a moment stared down at the floor. "That was the reason, then," he said, slowly raising his eyes, "that you could not afford the time it would have taken to have all the welding seams examined- because you had to have everything ready by the date the voyage was scheduled to begin- correct?"

"No, it was because the only repair that was needed had been made! The last thing I would have done is jeopardize the safety of my boat and crew and the passengers on it!"

Darnell listened intently. The Evangeline had been

doomed the day she left port and everyone knew it.

"You testified that these people you invited knew their way around a sailboat." Darnell turned his back to the witness and stared at his own empty chair. "Would it not be more accurate to say that they knew their way around a yacht?"

"I'm not sure I know what you mean."

Darnell's gaze lingered on the empty chair, and then on Marlowe, who wore a strange, impassive expression that had become a kind of permanent mask. Darnell looked back over his shoulder.

"They were used to being taken care of; they were not people who had to do much for themselves."

"I don't think I would go that far," replied Whitfield with a slightly disconcerted look. "They were all successful; they all had money, but-"

"When they showed up that morning, the day the voyage was to begin, how many of them drove their own cars?" asked Darnell as he turned with a jaundiced look to the witness.

"I don't imagine any of them did, but I don't see-"

"How much food and drink was put on board? How many cases of champagne?"

"I don't know, I-"

"And cases of caviar? There was a chef on board- correct? The chef of a five-star restaurant, hired at a cost of...Well, we can get into that later, perhaps. But no one on that boat was going to have anything to complain about in terms of comfort, were they?"

"I wanted everyone to have a good time."

"No one on board was going to have to lift a finger; but that was only what they would have expected. That is the life they were used to, wasn't it, Mr. Whitfield? A life of luxury- and what some might call self indulgence."

Roberts was rising from his chair.

"Yes, I have a question," said Darnell, smiling, "if you'd just be good enough to let me ask it."

Roberts's hands were still on the arms of his chair.

Bracing himself, he sat back down.

"Tell us this, Mr. Whitfield: of those people you invited on this sailboat cruise around Africa, how many do you think had ever pulled an oar?"

Whitfield shifted his weight from one side to the other of the witness chair. "I don't know. I assume some of them must at some point have rowed a boat somewhere."

"Rowed a boat somewhere, ""' repeated Darnell with a dark look. "Let me then ask you the question this way: if you were going to be marooned in a lifeboat, Mr. Whitfield- if your survival and the survival of everyone else were at stake- which of those guests of yours would you have chosen to be there with you? Which of them do you think could have helped you to survive?"

Whitfield tensed; the color drained from his face.

"These people you invited, these close friends of yours, they were all independently wealthy, weren't they? And, as it turns out, the least independent people on the planet. They were useless, most of them, weren't they? When it came right down to it, when everyone's lives were at stake…?"

"I wasn't there! I don't know what any of them did!" Whitfield protested.

Darnell took a step forward. "But Marlowe was different, wasn't he? He knew how to do everything, didn't he? You would not have trusted any of your rich and famous friends if you had been one of the survivors- abandoned in a small boat in the high seas, where no one was likely to find you- would you? But you trusted Marlowe, didn't you?"

"Yes, I trusted him."

Darnell searched Whitfield's eyes, determined to get at the one thing the jury had to know. "And after everything that has happened, after everything you know, you would still do it, wouldn't you- hire Marlowe to be in charge?"

"Yes, I would."

CHAPTER THREE

It was perhaps the least- expected invitation Michael Roberts had ever received. Prosecutors and defense attorneys might be civil to one another in court, but they seldom spent time together. It was difficult to be friends with someone you were trying to beat. But there was more to it than that. There was almost an element of distrust, a belief that what they did on the other side was not quite right. Roberts could count on the fingers of one hand the number of times he had had a cup of coffee with a lawyer defending someone he was prosecuting for a crime; he had certainly never agreed to drive forty miles on a Sunday afternoon to see a defense. attorney at his home.

The directions were meticulous, precise; given over the telephone with the casual ease of someone who knew every turn by heart. When he arrived, the gate at the bottom of the vineyard stood open. At the end of a long dirt driveway lined with gnarled gray olive trees, William Darnell, an old straw hat pulled low over his eyes, greeted him with a pensive smile. "You're right on time. Have any trouble finding it?"

"No, your directions were perfect." Roberts took a deep breath of the country air and looked out over the narrow vine-covered valley.

"This is the valley inside the valley," explained the older man as he pointed towards the low-lying hills half a mile away. "If you keep going along the road, follow it around a few miles, you come out into what the world knows as the Napa Valley. Not many tourists come back here."

They stood on a patio in front of the house, a comfortable contemporary with wooden beams across the ceiling and glass everywhere. A stone chimney towered above the roof.

"Have you had it long?" asked Roberts as he followed

15

Darnell inside. The wooden floors, polished to a hard finish, glimmered in the yellow October light.

"A little more than thirty years. My wife designed it; built it, really. She was an architect, one of the best."

He removed the straw hat and wiped his brow with the back of his wrist. The threadbare polo shirt he wore was damp with sweat. "A few things needed pruning back," he explained.

He gestured towards the blue sofa in front of the bookcase in the living room. "Let me get you something to drink. I could use something cold, myself. Soft drink all right, or would you rather have a beer? I have wine, too, of course."

"Do you make any of your own?"

"No, too much work. But we have ten acres, and that used to qualify us as a grower, which meant we could buy from all the wineries in the valley at cost. That was before it became big business. Have you ever noticed that the more money people make, the less generous they become? But we still have a lot of what we bought years ago." Darnell's eyes lit up. "Yes, that's a good idea. Let me open one of the bottles we got back then. Sarah would approve. I'll just be a minute."

A photograph on the wall across the room caught Robert's eye. "You were on a carrier?" he asked, when Darnell returned and handed him a glass three-quarters full.

Darnell turned to look at the large black-and-white photograph and moved closer. "Everyone I knew was on a ship."

"The war?"

"Yes, the war," said Darnell, his eyes coming back around. "Death was everywhere then. I think we all assumed we would not come back, that we would end up dead. Perhaps that's the reason I never felt more alive."

He looked across at Roberts, sitting on the sofa on the other side of the brightly lit room. He raised his glass. "To your health. And thank you for humoring an old man and coming all this way on a Sunday afternoon. But I thought we ought to talk, and I thought you might prefer we kept it private."

Roberts began a half-hearted objection.

"No, I understand," Darnell assured him. "We tend to look on each other as the enemy. But perhaps in this case we have more in common than opposing lawyers usually have. Your father was in the navy, too, wasn't he?"

"Yes. How did you know...?"

"I read it somewhere. I like to know something about the people I'm going to trial against. Your father was in the navy. He was lost at sea. My ship was sunk, and I was saved."

"That's why you said what you did the other day- that the only sailing you did was around the bay."

"For a very long time I would not do even that. I'm sorry about your father. A lot of brave men died in the war."

"I didn't know him. I never had the chance. I was just a baby when he died."

Darnell sank back in his chair. "He died in the service of his country; a decent, honorable death. Most people now think that there is nothing worse than death, but that isn't true, is it? How you die is rather more important than how long you live. But I'm sorry that you didn't have the chance to know him. It must have been difficult growing up without a father."

"My mother was a remarkable woman," Roberts replied, and then quickly changed the subject.

"You were rescued at sea. Is that why you took the case? Because of what happened to you?"

Darnell shook his head. "Not because my ship was sunk and I spent a few hours floating in the ocean. There were ships and planes all around; it was one of the great battles of the Pacific. I might get killed, I might get picked up- but whatever was going to happen, it was going to happen before that day was over. I had the certainty of that, which is more than Marlowe ever had.

"No, it was not what happened to me then; it was what happened to my wife." Darnell got up from the chair and opened the sliding glass door next to the stone fireplace. A warm breeze brought in the rich, earthy smell of the vineyards below.

"We started coming up here in the late sixties. We bought the land and planted the vineyard before we built the house. You live in the city and you notice the weather and the way it changes; you live out here and you watch the seasons and the way life moves through an endless cycle of birth and death and birth again.

"My wife, Sarah, died after a long illness. She kept reminding me that it was the natural order of things, that everything that comes into being goes out of being, and that you ought to understand that as a gift and not a curse- but it still broke my heart when she died. I watched my wife die and I know I'm not that far from my own death. It isn't at all remarkable if, at my age, I find that many of my thoughts are a kind of meditation on death and dying. That's one of the reasons I took this case: if it is about anything, it is about death and what it means and under what circumstances it is to be preferred."

"And who has the right to make that decision," added Michael Roberts in a solemn voice.

"Yes, precisely," Darnell agreed, moving back to his chair.

"The right- and perhaps the obligation. There's no precedent for what we're doing. Did you think of that when you decided to charge him? There has never been a trial like it- not in an American courtroom, anyway." It was not an accusation, and Roberts knew it, but he still did not like the question. There had not been any choice, not after the details of what had happened began to come out.

"That's not quite true," he replied, a slight trace of irritation in his voice. "There was one."

"The Holmes case is more than a hundred and fifty years old," replied Darnell. "What does that tell us? That things like this never happened after that? That no one did what Marlowe was forced to do between then and now?"

"Forced to do?" asked Roberts with a troubled look. "Isn't that what we have to decide?"

"What difference will it make what we- what a jury decides? There are some things that decide themselves. I understand that people want him punished, as if he hasn't suffered enough- as if anything could be worse than what he has to live with every day. But how can anyone, sitting in the safe comfort of a courtroom, knowing that they are only a few minutes from the safe comfort of their homes, know what it was like out there? Can any of us say we would have done better? Can any of us say we would have done as well?"

"There is nothing I can do," replied Roberts with a plaintive glance. "Even if I agreed with you, it's too late- unless you want to talk about a plea. We offered before. Are you saying he's changed his mind?"

Darnell shook his head. "No, he hasn't changed his mind. From the first day I met him, he wanted to go to trial. As near as I can tell, that's the only thing he wants." Lifting his eyebrows, Darnell stared into the middle distance. "To go to trial and be convicted."

"What?" Roberts sat forward. "He wants to be convicted?"

"I don't think there is any question. I think it would come as a relief, a kind of redemption, if you will; a penance paid for his sins. Not the sin of what he did, but the sin he was born with, that we were all born with, the original sin that meant we all had to die. He did what he thought he had to do, but that was not any choice at all. Yes, I think he wants to be convicted. It's the only way he can rescue himself.

"I can't tell you what he said to me; I can't break his confidence. But I can tell you that he has never told me anything about what happened. God knows, I've tried; but the only response I ever get is a silence as profound as anything I have ever seen. It was that silence, the depth of it, that made me realize that beyond everything else that had happened out there, he had lost that connection with other human beings, that sense of being a part of what we all assume to be normal life. He was an outcast, an exile, and the only way he could get back was to pay the price that civilization demands when someone breaks its law, even though he was so far from civilization that, in a real sense, there was no law to break."

"If he just wants redemption," said Roberts, "if he just wants to pay the price for breaking the law, why didn't he take the offer, plead guilty, and be done with it? He could have done it when he was first arraigned. Why does he want to go to trial?"

"For his confession; but confession to what, I'm not sure. He knows something, though. I can see it in his eyes."

"Something worse than what we know already?"

Darnell looked away. "We shouldn't be doing this, putting all of this on trial. No good will come of it, none that I can see. We're in the same situation as Marlowe, you and I. Neither of us has any choice: you have to prosecute a man who wants you to convict him; I have to defend a man who does not want to be saved. We all do what we have to; but then, that's the point, isn't it? What we have to do, what we have no choice but to do."

"The law says- and not just the law, every moral code-that no one can take the life of another human being."

"There are exceptions," replied Darnell.

"Defense, or the defense of others; but they only allow you to kill someone who is trying to kill someone else."

"And the case of necessity."

"But in Holmes, remember, the defendants were convicted," replied Roberts.

"Yes, but the cases are not the same. Even if they were, it was a hundred and fifty years ago. Remember when you started law school, almost the first thing they talked about in criminal law?"

Roberts nodded in recognition. "When causing another's death is not a crime. A mountain climber falls, the others above him can't hold the rope. If they cut the rope, he dies; if they don't, he takes all of them to their deaths. They sacrifice his life to save theirs. But the difference is that he was dead either way; the only question was whether they were going to die, too."

"That isn't that far from what happened here, is it?"

Roberts put down his glass. "Those law school examples were always so glib. They didn't allow for shades of gray Mountain climbers on a rope, the one at the bottom falls, the others can't hold him. But how hard did they try? Did they wait as long as they could? Did they try everything they knew to save his life? Doesn't that make some difference- how far they were willing to risk their own lives to save his? And what about the one hanging there, holding on- isn't there some choice in all of this for him? Doesn't he at least get to decide to cut the rope himself, to die so the others can live? Doesn't that make all the difference in the way we think of his death? And doesn't it teach us something important about how we should live?"

"That is what you're going to have to argue, isn't it?" asked Darnell. "That there is something more important than our own survival. The strangest part of this case is that Marlowe agrees with you. He believes that more than anything. He would have given his own life to save any one of those people, but what was he to do? It was not just his survival at stake. There were others, and what was he supposed to do about them?"

"The law is going to lead us to perdition if it teaches us to think like that," insisted Roberts. "Human life reduced to a question of mathematics. Someone has to die so others can live. Where do you think that ends? We can't start trading lives."

Darnell rose from his chair and began to move about the room. It was almost as if he were still in court, arguing to a jury. "What does that tell you about the anguish of Marlowe's soul? The awful courage- the unforgivable courage- of what he did, what he had to do?" Darnell looked back at Roberts.

"Was he right to do what he did? Of course he was. Was he wrong to do what he did? Yes, he was that, too. And damned forever because the choice between good and evil was never the choice he had.

"We're going to ruin a lot of people's lives, you and I.

And just like Marlowe, there is nothing we can do to stop it. That's why I asked you to come here today, to tell you that. This is my last case. There won't be any trials after this. But you have quite a few years left. Whatever happens, whether Marlowe is convicted or the jury lets him go, walk away from it when it's over. Don't let this case ruin you."

"Ruin me?" asked Roberts, touched by the old man's concern, and puzzled, too.

"I had a case once, years ago, when I was just starting out. I knew he was innocent, but I could not save him. I had to watch his execution. There has not been a day I haven't 'thought about that, not one! You have to learn to live with the knowledge that sometimes, for all our questioning, we'll never find the answers."

CHAPTER FOUR

Homer Maitland took his place on the bench, looked around the courtroom, as crowded as it had been every day since the trial started, and instructed the prosecution to call its next witness. Michael Roberts made a half turn towards the double doors at the back.

"The People call Thomas Balfour."

Thomas Balfour had broad, burly shoulders and a face burned red by the sea. He walked with his feet wide apart, a habit become instinct even on dry land.

"You're the captain of the freighter, the White Rose?"

"Yes, I am," the witness replied in a British accent that had been dulled by thirty years' contact with other languages and other races around the globe.

"Were you on a voyage last July that took you into the south Atlantic?"

Balfour's face was large, with heavy lips and a thick nose, all of it framed by a gray close-clipped beard. His blue eyes, set well back behind heavy lids, had a shrewdness about them that seemed deliberate, as if he had trained himself to judge things by a standard more rigorous than a native tendency to take the world as it came. "Yes, we had left Punta Arenas on our way back to Bordeaux."

"Punta Arenas? Could you explain to the jury exactly where that is?"

Balfour bent forward at the waist, his thick-fingered hands clasped together. When he shifted his weight you could almost hear the leather chair crack. "Punta Arenas is in Chile, on the western shore of the Straits of Magellan. It's the most southerly port in South America. We had brought out a cargo of French manufactured goods; we were taking back a load of copper tubing."

Roberts, wearing one of the handful of striped ties he regularly wore to court, walked to an easel that had been set up midway between the bench, where Maitland sat, and the two counsel tables, three feet apart from each other.

"That would be here," he said, using a wooden pointer on a map that included South America and the Atlantic.

"Yes, that's right."

"On your way back to Bordeaux?" He drew an imaginary line from the tip of South America to the coast of France. "And what happened- after you left Punta Arenas?"

Balfour craned his neck to get a better view. "Out there, not quite a thousand miles east of Rio de Janeiro- 990 miles, to be exact; our position was 24 degrees, 28 minutes South and 27 degrees, 22 minutes West- that's where we found them."

"Found who? Could you be more precise?" asked Roberts as he stepped away from the map.

"The survivors- what was left of them." A look of disgust swept across Balfour's nearly hidden eyes.

If Roberts felt any emotion, he did not show it. His face was a blank sheet on which an observer was free to write anything he wished, and no doubt all of it wrong. "You're referring to the survivors of the Evangeline?"

"Yes, that was the name they told me, the name of the boat that went down some forty days before we found them- those that were left- nearly dead."

"Just stay with the facts, if you would, Mr. Balfour," said Roberts, suppressing a moment's irritation. "Tell us how you happened to find them. Was there some kind of signal?"

"No, nothing like that," replied Balfour, shaking his head.

"How did we happen to find them, you ask? Chance. That was all, chance. If we had passed that spot an hour later, after the sun was down, we would not have seen them; and if we had not seen them, probably no one would have. That part of the ocean isn't traveled much."

Roberts turned towards the jury and was about to ask the next question.

"We saw them; they did not see us. Or perhaps they did, but they made no sign. They were too far gone for that."

Roberts wheeled around, but Balfour was not about to be stopped.

"Close to dead, they were; a couple of them out of their heads with hunger and thirst. It made you wonder if they were really human, the way they looked," he added with a shudder. "Hope to God I never seen anything like that again."

"Yes, I'm certain they were all in a deplorable state. But tell us this, Captain Balfour, if you would: exactly how many survivors were there? How many people did you rescue from the sea?"

"Six. There were six still alive."

Roberts raised an eyebrow. "Six still alive. Do you mean you found some who were not alive?"

"Yes."

Roberts waited, expecting more. Balfour, with a look that almost seemed a warning, retreated into silence.

"How many?" Roberts asked with quiet insistence.

"One."

Again Roberts waited, and again there was no response beyond that bare minimum one-word answer.

"Captain Balfour, I realize that you come to this with a certain reluctance, and that you may have opinions of your own about what happened, but you're here to tell us what you know. All we are trying to do is get at the truth."

Balfour raised his chin. He looked hard at Roberts. "The truth? The sea has a truth of its own. You can't judge it from here. Marlowe there," he said, nodding with a kind of formal respect towards the counsel table where the defendant sat next to William Darnell, "he knows it, and so do I."

Roberts knew better than to argue the point. He let Balfour's words echo into the courtroom silence and then started again.

"Would you please describe for the jury the condition of the dead body you found?"

"The condition? There was no condition."

"What was left of the body?" asked Roberts, losing all patience. "Did it have a head?"

"No, sir, it did not. Nor hands, nor feet either."

Roberts gripped the jury box railing. He peered intently into Balfour's eyes. "The hands, the feet, the head—had all been severed?"

"Yes, sir, so it appeared."

"What was left of the trunk? And what was the condition of that?"

"Sir?"

Roberts clenched his jaw. His eyes narrowed into a warning of their own. "You're under oath, Mr. Balfour. Answer the question."

Balfour glared at him, and then relented. He nodded his head slowly, as if he had resigned himself to playing a part in a game he despised. "It had been cut open from the sternum to the navel, disemboweled."

Roberts walked the short distance from the jury box to the counsel table. He picked up a black folder and removed a three-page document. He asked Balfour if he recognized it.

"It's the list of what was found in the lifeboat. The names of the six survivors and..."

"And the other name, the name that went with what was left of the body you were just describing?"

"I wouldn't know that. No one told me."

"No one told you? I see. Look at the list again, if you would. In addition to the names of the survivors, you also list the other things you found. How much food did you find on board?"

"Food? There was no food. I mean..."

"And water? How much water did they have left?"

With a grim expression, Captain Balfour shook his head. "There was no water, not a drop."

"No food, no water. And no clothing, either, I assume—except what they wore?"

The two men stared at each other. The silence was ominous, profound.

"There was clothing other than that."

"Extra clothing they had brought with them?"

"No, I would not think they had time to bring anything

except what they wore. It belonged to the others, the ones who did not make it."

Roberts blinked his eyes, nodded quickly, and looked away. "You've listed it there," he said, gesturing with his hand as he began to pace back and forth. "There was clothing for how many people?"

"It would appear there were eight."

"Eight?" said Roberts, as he stopped in mid-stride. "Eight who did not make it? What kind of clothing?"

"I don't understand."

"Men's clothing? Women's clothing? Which?"

"Both. Five jackets that, from their size and style, belonged to men; three coats that belonged to women."

"And what purpose did they serve?"

"You mean to the survivors? It's bitter cold at night in the south Atlantic, especially that time of year. July is winter there."

Roberts was thinking of something else. "There were six survivors, and clothing for eight others. Fourteen people were in that lifeboat- fourteen!- but only six survived. And you found no food and no water- no provisions of any kind?"

"No, sir."

"How long had they been out there? How many days again?"

"We picked them up the twenty-ninth day of July. From what I gather, the Evangeline went down the nineteenth of June. Forty days."

"Forty days in a lifeboat...What was the capacity of that lifeboat, Captain? How many people was it supposed to hold?"

"Eight; ten at the most. How he kept her afloat with fourteen, in seas like that, I'll never know."

"Yes, but there were only six left when you found it- and the remains of one other. You're aware that the Evangeline went down off the coast of Africa. You've been advised of the general location. What is the approximate distance from there to where you found them, Captain Marlowe and the other survivors?"

"A little more than a thousand miles."

"In forty days. Roughly twenty-five miles a day, in an open boat, during winter in the Southern Hemisphere. And you found no food, no water, but the clothing of eight other people, all of whom- or, rather, all but one of whom- seem to have disappeared without a trace.

"Do you think they each of them decided to take their own lives, end this ordeal of hunger and thirst and exposure to the elements by jumping into the sea, but out of consideration for the others did it naked so their clothing could be of some use?"

"Objection, your Honor!" William Darnell had risen slowly to his feet. "There must be a question in there somewhere, your Honor, but I'm afraid I can't find it, and I doubt the witness can either."

Roberts reddened. "I'm sorry, your Honor; perhaps I got a little carried away. In a case like this, it's difficult not to."

He exchanged a glance with Darnell, remembering what they had talked about in private, before turning back to the witness. "No one wants to be here, Mr. Balfour. But there isn't any choice. Let me ask the question this way: do you have any doubt that there were fourteen people in that lifeboat and that eight of them are dead?"

"No."

"Do you have any knowledge as to how they died?"

"Direct knowledge? No, none; I was not there."

"But you do have direct knowledge of how one of them died. You saw the body; the head had been cut off. Isn't that correct?"

"That isn't how he died."

Roberts had just turned to the jury. He immediately looked back. "Then you do know how he died?"

"No, only that he was already dead when the head was taken off."

"And why would anyone do that?" he asked, eyeing him cautiously. "Someone dies, but instead of throwing the body overboard, to make more room for the others, the body is left there- but the head is removed, and the hands and feet as well. Why do you imagine that was done, Captain Balfour? What purpose would it serve?"

Balfour tensed. His eyes drew back until a bare glimmer of their bluish light could be seen. "I could not rightly say. All I know is what I found."

"And just to be sure that we have not misunderstood, what you found were six survivors, what was left of a seventh, and the clothing of the deceased and seven others. And there was no food and no water. When you say that, Captain Balfour, do you mean that there was no sign that they had ever had any?"

"No, when they started out- when they were first in the lifeboat- they had a little water and they had some food. Not much: a few tins of beef, a gallon or two of water. The empty containers were still there. They used them to catch what rainwater they could."

"Given what they had, was it your impression when you rescued them that they had just run out?"

"What they had might have lasted a few days, a week at most."

"Fourteen people?" asked Roberts, his voice filled with skepticism.

"Fourteen, no. The water might have lasted, depending; but the food- a few tins like that- probably not. Although you never know what you can get by on until you have to. And then sometimes you can get things from the sea, and-"

Roberts stopped him with a look. "They had only enough food and water for a few days at most; seven people missing and the disemboweled body of another. Isn't it true, Captain Balfour, that at least one or two of the survivors told you how they did it, what they had to do to stay alive?"

The silence in the courtroom became eerie, profound. This was why they had all come, why there was such intense interest in the trial- to find out if the rumors were true, the rumors that had begun to circulate almost from the day the survivors had been found.

"As I said before, they were delirious, out of their

minds. They said a lot of things; none of it made sense," insisted Balfour with a wrathful look. "What would you have me say?"

"The truth, Captain Balfour; what you're sworn to say- just that!"

"The truth is what you want? The truth of what they said? Well, one of them- that woman, Mrs. Wilcox- kept talking about the two angels that swept down from heaven, one of them with a crystal glass filled with the finest thing she ever drank; while the other one hung in the air above her, beating his wings, waiting until she was finished drinking so he could give her food."

Balfour glared across the courtroom at Roberts. "That, sir, is the truth- the true account of what I heard her say. I'm a God- fearing man, myself. Why shouldn't I believe her? But you, I take it, would rather believe what someone else might have said, though they were not any more in their right mind than she may have been?"

"You're under oath, sir!"

"I know that, sir!"

"Then answer my questions. When you saw what was left of that body, when you say that they had no other food- you knew what that body had been used for, didn't you?"

Balfour looked at him with scarcely concealed contempt.

"Never mind. Tell us this instead: what did the defendant, Vincent Marlowe, tell you about what had happened?"

Thomas Balfour looked from Roberts to Marlowe, and only then turned to the jury. "He said he did what he had to do, that he had not had any choice."

CHAPTER FIVE

"Mr. Darnell, do you wish to cross examine the witness?"

Reclining in his chair, William Darnell watched the ceiling as if he were outside, tracing the movements of the stars.

"Mr. Darnell...?"

"Forty days, you say? That in itself is an extraordinary achievement, wouldn't you say, Captain Balfour? To stay out in a lifeboat that long, and at the end of it still have five other people alive?"

Darnell had not moved, had not looked at the witness. His eyes were still fixed on the ceiling. With sudden energy, he lurched forward and, with his elbow bent beneath him, studied Balfour as if he, the witness, was the only one who could really know what the question meant, what it was like to be out there, all alone, lost at sea.

"In all your years as a seaman, have you ever known of anything more extraordinary than that?"

The answer of Thomas Balfour was immediate, exact. "No, sir. I have not."

Nodding emphatically, Darnell swept his legs out from under the table and got to his feet. "A thousand miles, you say; a thousand miles from where they started to where you found them. A rate of twenty-five miles or so per day, east to west- isn't that what you said?" he asked, his eyebrows raised as he waited.

The reserve, bordering at times on barely suppressed hostility, by which Balfour had attempted to keep the prosecution at a distance, had all but vanished. It was clear that all his sympathies were with Marlowe, a man he had never met until the morning he plucked him out of the ocean; but there was more than that to the way he responded to Marlowe's attorney.

He liked Darnell, liked everything about him, and had known it the moment he first saw his eyes: honest, open, determined and fair, the eyes of a man who could see past the shifting illusions of the world into the heart of things. Balfour did not meet many men with eyes like that among those who lived their lives on land.

"Yes, that would have been the rate: twenty-five miles on average, though some days faster, and some days none at all."

Darnell caught at the last phrase as if it hid a depth of meaning. "When there was no wind, no current; when they were "becalmed"?"

"Yes, right that is. And they had days like that, I know."

Darnell nodded his agreement, as if they were two old friends remembering things they had done together. "A thousand miles like that, twenty-five miles a day ...But they didn't just drift, did they?"

"No, that's right; they did not. They had a sail."

"Had a sail?"

"Marlowe rigged it up. Used an oar- two of them, lashed together."

"I understand. But what about the sail? What did he use for that? The canvas covering, the one that was used to keep the lifeboat dry- he used that, did he not?"

"Yes, sir, he did. It was fairly ripped to pieces by the time we found him, but it had got them as far as they had come."

Darnell's fingers grazed the edge of the counsel table. His other hand clung to his lapel. "What was the point of doing that, of going to all the trouble to rig a mast and sail? They were in the middle of the Atlantic, what difference did it make what part of the ocean they were on?"

"That might have been what other men would have thought," said Balfour with an earnest look.

"Give up all trying and just wait for whatever might happen. Marlowe put up a sail so he could head for land."

Darnell feigned surprise. "They were a thousand miles

from where they started and, when you picked them up, a thousand miles east of Rio de Janeiro. Are you saying that he was heading for South America, two thousand miles from where the Evangeline went down?"

"That's exactly what he was doing."

"But they could not have been more than a few hundred miles from the west coast of Africa when they started. Why didn't he simply head there?"

"That time of year, the winds all run southwesterly, and run with force. The only chance he had was to run with them, and that meant sailing west."

"But why sail at all? Why not wait where they were, closer to where the Evangeline went down, close to where anyone looking for them would look first?"

Balfour hunched forward, his thick neck sunk on his shoulders. His eyes, narrowed tight, nearly shut, seemed to calculate the odds. "From what I gather, there had been a failure of the equipment, and the navigation system had gone out. And then the storm, the storm that sank her, had driven them God knows how far off course.

"Who knew how long it might be before anyone would discover they were missing? And there was not much chance that anyone would find them by accident in that part of the south Atlantic. They had a good- no, a better chance being picked up if they tried to make land on their own. And if no one did, then at least they were doing everything they could to save themselves."

"Among the things you found in the lifeboat, I don't recall any mention of a sextant or any other navigational devices?"

"They had nothing. Marlowe used the stars."

"The route you sailed, Captain Balfour- was that within the normal sea lanes?"

"Yes."

"So the course Marlowe navigated brought him into the path where a ship crossing the Atlantic might be encountered?"

"Exactly."

33

"So whether or not he reached South America, he would, by taking the route he did, improve the chance that some ship would find them?"

"And it worked, too, didn't it? If he had not done what he did, none of them would have survived," said Balfour with great emphasis.

A pensive expression on his face, Darnell lowered his eyes and stared down at the floor. "And he knew how far they had to go, and how long it would likely take?" he asked as he slowly raised his eyes to Balfour's waiting gaze.

"He would have known that, yes; within an approximation, because, as I say, the storm- the one that sank her- had blown her off course and all the navigation was by the stars. But yes, sir, in response to your question, he would have known that he had as much as two thousand miles of open sea between him and any hope of land."

"Two thousand miles across the south Atlantic; and, as you explained, it was winter down there, isn't that correct, Captain Balfour?"

"Winter, and bitter cold."

"And the weather generally, that time of year- pretty bad?"

"The seas can be terrible rough."

"And yet you said a few minutes ago that the sea could be as smooth as glass- no wind, no current?"

"It's what happens sometimes between storms. There are times it's so bad you can't see three feet in any direction: the sea is all around you. Other times, when it's still, every way you look you see the sky, close enough to touch."

"And they were out there forty days in an open boat with a makeshift sail, sometimes in weather so bad they did not know where they were going; other times not knowing if they were going to go anywhere at all. Would that be a fair statement of what it must have been like for them?"

Roberts was on his feet, lodging an objection, but without heat or animosity. "The witness was not in the life-boat. He cannot know what they did or did not encounter," he said in a civil voice.

Homer Maitland stroked his chin. "No, I'll allow it," he said after a short pause. "The witness has direct knowledge of the weather conditions. He can testify to that." Maitland looked down at the witness. "Go ahead, Mr. Balfour: answer the question."

"Yes, that's true. The weather is changeable, and just when you think it's bad, it gets worse."

Darnell twisted his head to the side as if the next question had an especially important significance. "In those conditions, Captain Balfour, would you imagine that they had to think that each day was likely to be their last?"

Roberts was on his feet with another objection, but this time there was passion in his voice, and this time Maitland, without hesitation, sustained it.

Darnell moved immediately to another question. "Mr. Roberts gave you a document that listed the contents found in the lifeboat. You drew up that list from memory, didn't you?"

Balfour gave him a puzzled glance.

"What you remember having seen in the lifeboat. You didn't keep any of those objects- the empty tins, the plastic water containers...the extra clothing- did you?"

"I see what you mean. Well, the answer isn't either yes or no. I didn't make the list after the fact, but while I had it all in front of my eyes. Then we cut the lifeboat loose. I didn't see the need to keep any of it, and we were hard-pressed for room with six new people on board- in their condition."

"You kept none of the clothing?"

Balfour's massive head seemed to draw back. His eyes- those narrow slits wedged into his skull- became forbidding.

"No."

Darnell had begun to pace. He stopped and, with an intense look, began to study Balfour. That one-word answer concealed a secret the captain did not want to share. All Darnell's experience, everything he had learned about what it took to win at trial, told him to take the answer and move on to something else, that what Balfour did not want to reveal would only help the prosecution. But there was something else at work, an instinct that this case was so different that the old rules did not apply, and that to do what he had done before was to guarantee defeat.

"No won't quite do it, Captain Balfour. The question is why? The empty containers might have no further use, but what about the clothing- why get rid of that?"

"It was not usable," said Balfour after a pause.

"Why was it not usable?"

"It was torn, some of it."

"Some of it? What else made it unusable, Captain Balfour? Don't think you're doing Vincent Marlowe a favor by holding anything back. Tell the truth: that's the best any of us can do."

"There was blood on a lot of it."

Darnell looked at him as if he had expected the answer and, not only that, found it immensely helpful to the defense. "There was blood on the clothing, but you have no knowledge about how it got there, do you?"

"No," replied Balfour, watching closely everything Darnell did.

"The clothing- by the way, you assumed that it did not belong to the six survivors you rescued, isn't that correct? It's my recollection that in response to a question put by Mr. Roberts, you offered the opinion that the clothing must have belonged to other people- people who, as you phrased it, 'didn't make it'.

"Because- and again I'm relying on my own memory- the survivors would not have had time to take with them any additional clothing when the Evangeline sank? But you have no direct knowledge of what they did, or did not, have time to do when the Evangeline sank, do you?"

"No, I don't."

"So it's possible that some of them might have grabbed anything they could to protect themselves from the elements in what was, by all accounts, a terrible storm?"

The reply was tentative, circumspect. "It's possible."

Darnell shoved both hands into his suit jacket's pockets. He fixed the witness with a determined look. "You hesitate. Is it because you have been told what happened- then and later- by some of the survivors?"

Balfour did not move and did not speak. His eyes were steady, remote.

"And those survivors, as you reminded us, were all nearly out of their minds when you found them, isn't that true?"

"All nearly dead," said Balfour, shaking his head at what he had seen. "Their bodies were emaciated beyond anything I had seen, like living skeletons they were; except that their feet were swollen up something fierce, like they were ready to burst. Their faces were horrible, with hollow eyes and sunken cheeks; their lips burned black, all cracked and raw- more like scabs than skin; and the skin they had, stretched like dried paper, all blistered and peeling off. It was even more horrible than that; great gaping wounds on their necks and arms, and one of them with a leg all dead flesh and gangrenous."

"I read the report you wrote, the one you filed when you first got to port," said Darnell. His voice, though not much more than a whisper, could be heard clearly in the deathly stillness of the courtroom. "In addition to everything else, some of them were crippled?"

"They were forty days out there!" cried Balfour with a shudder.

"Forty days. Forget the weather, the hunger, the thirst- forty days shoved up together in that small boat, no room to move. Imagine being forced to sit in a small cage for more than a month. They could not stand up, some of them, after we got them off; some of them could not lie down. None of them could do anything without excruciating pain. Not one of them could walk a step without someone holding him up."

Darnell had moved across to the jury box. He lay a hand on the railing. "There were other injuries as well, weren't there?"

"There were indeed."

"One of them lost a foot?"

"Because of how cold it was at night, and the fact he could never get dry, he got frostbite. There was hardly anything left of his foot. It had to come off."

Darnell began to walk back towards the counsel table.

"That wasn't all," Balfour added. "One of them had a broken ankle; another a broken wrist. Two of them had broken ribs."

Darnell placed his hands on the back of his empty chair. "Yes, and more than what happened to them physically was what happened to them mentally.

Let me quote you exactly," he said as he searched inside a file folder for Balfour's report. "'Two of them were quite out of their minds. Another one would not speak: he would only shake his head and moan. One of the women- the younger one, Ms. Grimes- scratched the eyes of the first mate when he tried to lift her out of the lifeboat. The other woman, Mrs. Wilcox-"

Darnell looked up, "the one who talked about the angels that had come from heaven to help her- ?

"'could not stop crying once we had her on board.'" Darnell stopped reading. The page dangled in his hand. "They had all been driven crazy, Hadn't they, by what they had been through?"

"They weren't human; they had lost all reason- that's the God's truth of it. Except for Marlowe, who looked as bad as any of them, maybe worse. He looked me right in the eye and said, "'Thank God. It's over.'"

"'Thank God. It's over.'" repeated Darnell. "Thank God you found them, is that what he meant?"

Balfour raised an eyebrow. "That, and something more than that, was what he meant."

Darnell nodded and then pulled out his chair, ready to sit down. "One other question, Captain Balfour. The body- what did you do with that?"

The lines in Balfour's craggy brow deepened and spread further out. "We wrapped it in a cloth and gave it a burial at sea. We said a few words over it. That was all we could do."

"You know that the defendant, Vincent Marlowe, is on trial for murder. Did you see any evidence that the person whom you buried at sea had died from anything other than natural causes?"

Balfour shook his head. "I saw no evidence of murder."

CHAPTER SIX

William Darnell watched from the window. He did not need to check his watch to know that it was four o'clock in the afternoon; he knew it when he heard the car turn into the drive from the road below. Some people- most people, perhaps- were never quite on time; and in most cases a few minutes one way or the other didn't matter.

In a court of law a different rule- a double standard- applied: judges, blaming schedules, were notoriously unconcerned about making others wait; but lawyers had better be there when the judge finally made his way to the bench. Darnell had almost never come to court late; but outside the courtroom, he was often too preoccupied, too lost in thought, to remember where he was supposed to be next. He had always been at war with time, losing track of it, running out of it, feeling trapped by it. He had once grown irritable and impatient at the way the hours dragged when he wanted them to pass more quickly; now he regretted the way time sped by when he wanted more than anything for it to stop. The days moved faster, as if the days he had left were conspiring to shorten themselves. Time only slowed down on Saturday afternoons, an hour or so before four.

There was a mathematical precision, a strict proportion, between how much he looked forward to her visit and how long it took for that last hour to pass. From the moment he heard the car until the moment she left, he did not think about time at all. He wondered if she ever did. She was always on time, never more than a minute early or a minute late. It was not, as far as he could tell, either a discipline to which she had trained herself or one to which she had been forced to comply. She was the most organized person he had ever known, a woman who had to do dozens of things every day without any way of knowing exactly how long each of them would take, and each of them had to be done in the proper order and without delay. It was, he had decided, a gift she had been born with, a gift that somehow allowed her to make time belong to her.

Summer Blaine parked the ancient Mercedes in front of the garage. She seldom drove it more than a few miles a day, but had it washed every week. She gave it a quick inspection, frowning at the dust, and then threw a mock evil glance towards the window where Darnell stood watching, to let him know that he really ought to pave the drive. With a bag of groceries in her arms she pushed on the open door with her shoulder and let herself in.

"Tell me everything about the trial," she said as she started to put things away. "But tell me first about you."

Her hand was on the cupboard door. She looked at him and smiled. "How are you, Bill? Is everything all right? Are you taking the medication?"

Darnell tugged at his chin, as if he could not quite remember.

"That means you are. That's good. You have to, you know," she said with a breezy air, moving from the cupboard to the refrigerator. "We'll eat about six, is that all right?"

"Wouldn't you rather go out? I thought we might go up valley, to that place you like. We have to go out anyway, and I thought that after…"

"You eat out every night in the city- if you remember to eat at all. Tell me the truth…No, don't tell me that," she said, laughing quietly. "I know enough already. Did I ever tell you that you're the worst patient I've ever had?"

It made Darnell smile, the way she looked at him when she said it; the girlish, high-spirited sound of her voice that made him think that time had run backward and he was only half his age.

"If I was a better patient, you might stop making house calls."

A shy smile floated over Summer Blaine's wide and rather fragile mouth. "Then Saturdays would be wasted and I wouldn't have anything to do."

They looked at each other with affection, grateful

that they still had each other, mourning gently the past they had not shared. They had known each other from the earliest days of their marriages, first through the death of her husband and then, a few years later, the death of his wife.

"Come into the living room," she whispered after she had kissed him on the side of his face and, for a fleeting moment, clung to his neck. He sat in the easy chair across from the sofa.

Unbuttoning his shirt-sleeve he rolled up the faded, threadbare sweater that was as old as her Mercedes. With a physician's clean efficiency, Summer Blaine pumped the blood-pressure cuff.

"Not too bad," she said. "Bend forward."

It was a known routine. He pulled the shirt and sweater up over his back and leaned on his knees. The stethoscope felt ice-cold against his skin.

"Now back." He leaned back in the chair, exposing his frail chest. When she had finished listening, she folded the stethoscope and put it back in her bag.

"This is your last trial, remember- we agreed. You've had two heart attacks already, and the way you're going I can't promise there won't be a third. Your heart may not be strong enough to take that. Do you understand what I'm telling you?"

Darnell got to his feet, tucked in his shirt and adjusted the sweater. He grinned defiantly and bounced up on his toes. "There's nothing wrong with me," he insisted.

"This case may kill you," she insisted with a worried look.

"This case may keep me alive. I would have been dead years ago if it weren't for the work. That's when people die- not when they're working, but when they don't have any more work to do. It's a law of nature."

It was false bravado, but that was not the reason he immediately regretted the remark. She had lost her husband; he had lost his wife. Work, or the lack of it, had had nothing to do with either death.

"Sorry," he said, touching her arm. "But there is some

truth to it. I have to stay active; I can't give up. And if I have a heart attack and die...what of it? Better that way than what happened to Sarah."

"And to Adam, too, perhaps. Though I'm not sure how much better it is to go too quickly. At least we were able to say goodbye. The point is, I don't want to lose you, and your heart isn't what it used to be. I want you to be careful. And you did agree, remember?"

"That this would be my last trial. Yes, I suppose..."

"Suppose? You're incorrigible. I should know better than to rely on a lawyer's promise."

"A lawyer's promise?" said Darnell, a sparkle in his pale gray eyes. "A lawyer who knows what a promise is, would be more like it. A promise, to be enforceable, has to be supported by a promise in return. I promised this would be my last case, but what promise did I get in return? Are you going to stop the practice of medicine? Give up your blissful sixty-hour week and spend the rest of your days puttering around the garden with me? Remind me, but I don't remember any promise like that."

"Better bring a jacket," she told him, shaking her head. "It's November now. I don't want you catching cold."

He did not think he needed one, but she worried about him and he liked that she did. If he would not yield to her in the larger questions of his life, he did not mind doing what she asked in the smaller ones. He threw on a corduroy jacket and caught up with her at the car.

"And how was your week, Dr Blaine?" he asked as she drove. "I envy you a little, able to help people without harming anyone else."

He watched the houses set far back on the hillside slip by, neighbors he scarcely knew. "That would have been a good life, never having to choose. Although I suppose it must happen sometimes, mustn't it? When you have two people dying and you don't have time to save them both. That's what intrigues me so much about this case: the moral ambiguity of everything that happened. I keep wondering what I would have done if I had been in Marlowe's place."

She kept her eyes on the twisting road, but her gaze, or so it seemed to Darnell, became more intense. "You can't always help. Sometimes the best thing you can do is not to help at all."

"I've thought about that, too," he replied, staring out the window at the familiar scene, the route they traveled together the first or second Saturday of every month. "Doctors who let their patients go; the ones who decide that the only life left is pain and suffering, and that to prolong the agony makes medicine a kind of evil.

"It must happen every day, but no one would ever admit it because life- existence- is the only standard on which anyone can agree. That is what I keep coming back to: that there are certain things that should never be made public. I'm a lawyer, and there are rules. If you start making exceptions, arguing that in certain instances the rules don't apply, then it isn't long before everything is an exception and the rules don't exist. And so we insist that everyone follow the rules even when we know there are times when that might be the worst thing anyone could do.

"Marlowe should never have been charged with murder, and yet charging him with murder was the only thing the prosecution could have done. What happened out there should have stayed a secret, but there were too many survivors for that. It was not enough that they were alive, they wanted absolution, too. This is both the greatest case I have ever had and the worst. The law wasn't made for this," he said, growing more energetic.

"It's too far out of the common experience." Summer parked the car and from the back seat retrieved two small bouquets. She gave one of them to Darnell. Holding hands, they walked up the path that led between the rows of headstones until they were at the very top of the cemetery.

"A few minutes," she said. With a wistful glance, she let go of his hand and, while he headed in one direction, she went in the other. When Summer Blaine reached her husband's grave, she looked back over her shoulder, waiting until Darnell had gone the farther distance to where his wife lay buried. He did not turn around to look at her; he never did. She smiled to herself, then bent down and replaced the old flowers, withered with age, with the new. She was waiting for him at the path when he returned.

"Did you have a good visit?" She took his arm and held it tight, afraid he might fall, as they moved down the narrow, uneven trail to the car. The scent of burning leaves floated in the air. The soft November sun left a burnished glow on her cheek.

"I talk to her now in ways I never talked to her when she was alive. That's the trouble with words, I think- they always get in the way. They never quite come out the way you want. When I come here it is not so much a conversation as a meditation, a sense that she shares whatever thought I have. It's a kind of catharsis, I suppose; but it's more than that: it's the way she always makes me better than I am. Death does that, doesn't it? It puts things in the right perspective, gives you a sense of what is important and what is not."

Under the darkened shelter of an oak tree, they sat together on a wooden bench. Summer nestled close, keeping hold of his arm.

"You were lucky to have her. There aren't many men who married the first girl they ever loved. I don't talk to Adam when I visit his grave; I didn't talk much to him when he was alive. I suppose I come here because I was married to him and it doesn't seem right he should just be forgotten.

"We were never any good together. That wasn't his fault, it was mine. Sometimes I try to remember what things were like, in the beginning, before things got bad. The truth, though, is that if he had lived- if he hadn't gotten sick- we would have divorced and I doubt I ever would have thought, or tried to think, about how things had been at the beginning. But he died instead, and I feel this responsibility. The dead go on living, don't they? They're alive in us."

Darnell pulled his jacket close around his throat.

"You're cold. We'd better go." She drove him home and, while he sat at the kitchen table reviewing some material for the next week in trial, she made dinner.

"Did I tell you that yesterday morning I delivered Olivia Ceballos' baby? A girl, seven pounds, eight ounces."

Darnell looked up, a blank expression on his face.

"The second generation," she said, reminding him of what she had told him before. Darnell's eyes lit up.

"Of course! You delivered Olivia- twenty years ago."

"Yes, and her mother came, and afterwards we had a photograph taken: three generations and me."

"Twenty years from now, you can have another picture with four."

"And I suppose you think you'll still be trying cases," she remarked as she brought their plates to the table.

"I wonder what kind of world it will be then." Darnell lifted a glass of red wine to the level of his eyes, studying it with a strange fascination. "On the surface, no doubt, even more artificial than this."

"Artificial?"

"You see it every day," he said, as he put down the glass. "What we all believe; that with all the new advances, all the things that science will soon be able to do, we will live longer, better, more productive lives. Every week in the papers I read how the normal life span will become a hundred and fifty years, maybe more. As if that were any great achievement; as if by some small delay death could be defeated!

"That is what has everyone so fascinated with this case. It shows how artificial we have made- or tried to make- the world. Feel bad? Take a pill. Have a problem? Suffered a loss? See a counselor who can teach you how to cope. It is the narcotic of the modern age, a way to try to forget that we're as much a part of nature as everything else that is born and dies. But out there, in that lifeboat- without food, without water- what good was all our modern science to them? What difference would it have made whether life expectancy was measured in terms of centuries instead of years to people who did not know if they would live another day? That is what has everyone on the edge of their seats: this knowledge that all the things we take for granted have made us forget what it really means to be alive!"

But Summer's mind was on a question she was almost afraid to ask. "What happened to the others? There were other lifeboats, weren't there? There were twenty-seven people on the Evangeline. What happened to the other thirteen?"

A strange, distant look came into Darnell's eyes. It was a look Summer Blaine had seen before, seen on the faces of her patients when she had to tell them they were dying and that there was nothing she could do. The look faded away, but it left behind a sense of something somber, troubling and profound.

"What happened in those first few minutes? What happened in that first hour? When that comes out, I'm afraid that no one will understand Marlowe then."

He looked at Summer Blaine, a question in his eyes. "If there really is nothing more important than life, why is it that I feel so much more sorry for the living than I do for the dead?"

CHAPTER SEVEN

Joshua Steinberg did not understand the question.

"The reason, Doctor; the reason why you found it necessary to hospitalize the survivors of the Evangeline?"

Bent over the counsel table, examining a medical report, Michael Roberts looked up. Tall, thin, with the gaunt look of the long- distance runner, Dr Joshua Steinberg sat on the side of his hip, two long fingers stretched along the side of his jaw. He had dark, intelligent eyes and a fine, sensitive mouth. He had none of the arrogance of his profession.

"There were different reasons for each; but if you want a statement that encapsulates their condition, I'd have to say the effects of exposure and exhaustion."

"They were hospitalized here, in the same hospital where you first examined them?"

"That's right. They were brought by ambulance from the airport, as soon as they arrived from Brazil. Benjamin- Mr. Whitfield- made all the arrangements."

"Would you describe what, if any, medical attention they had received before you saw them?" Roberts closed the file, but did not move from the counsel table. "I assume they had not been in a hospital."

"No, not in a hospital, but they had been given medical attention. A doctor in Rio de Janeiro examined them. He set- or, rather, reset- some of the broken bones. Some of them had been set originally when they were still in the lifeboat; the rest on the freighter that picked them up."

"The White Rose? Captain Balfour's ship?" said Roberts to make sure the jury understood. "Was there a doctor on board?"

"No, apparently not. It was a freighter, not a passenger liner. Some of the crew had the kind of first-aid training you would expect, and they did have medical supplies. Captain Balfour did an admirable job with what he had. I don't think there is any question but that at least two of the six survivors would have died within days if he had not taken care of them the way he did."

"Dr Steinberg, I'm going to read you a list of six names. Would you tell us, please, if these are the people you treated at the hospital?"

Nodding after each name, Steinberg agreed with the list. Roberts then went back to the beginning and asked what had been the condition of each.

"James DeSantos- would you describe for the jury his physical condition at the time you examined him?"

Steinberg gestured towards the table. "May I refer to the records?"

Roberts brought him the document. Steinberg glanced at it a moment and then held it on his lap.

"Broken ankle, three broken teeth. Suffered temporary blindness. He had severe ulceration."

"What about his mental condition, Dr Steinberg?" asked Roberts, moving to a crucial element in the prosecution's case. "Was he lucid? Was he, as we laymen might say, in his right mind?"

"Yes, very much so. He was fully alert and in command of his senses."

"So he was not delusional? He knew where he was, what was happening to him, he could answer all your questions? In other words, Dr Steinberg, he was normal?"

Joshua Steinberg was not someone's paid witness, brought in to give expert testimony for a fee. Roberts's question posed a dilemma. "Normal?" he mused aloud.

"No, I would not think to call him that; not after what he had been through. I understand your question," he said as Roberts started to ask the question a different way. "Yes, he was lucid, rational; he could answer my questions; he knew where he was. But he was not right, and I doubt he or any of the others will ever be again."

"Yes, but my question is really much more narrow than that. What is important for us to know is whether he had suffered the kind of mental deterioration- whatever the cause- that would make it impossible for him to give an accurate account of what transpired between the time the Evangeline sank and the time they were rescued. Was he delusional, was he insane, is the question- and I take it from your answer that he was not. Is that a fair interpretation of what you said?"

"During the time I examined him, during the time he was my patient in the hospital, I saw nothing to suggest that he lacked the capacity to think clearly."

"And what of the others?" asked Roberts.

"Well, perhaps we'd better go through each one in turn. Let's start with Hugo Offenbach. What can you tell us about him?"

Steinberg smiled to himself and shook his head. "I saw him play, here in San Francisco, ten years ago: the greatest violinist in the world."

Everyone knew who Hugo Offenbach was. The fact that he had been saved, rescued from the sea, had been seen as a miracle- but then, as the rumors started, it seemed to intensify the shock. Normal people, driven to desperation, might do such things, but someone like him? No one wanted to believe it; there had to be some other explanation.

"Mr. Offenbach was in the best condition- and in the worst condition- of all."

"I'm afraid that is more of a riddle than I can solve."

"He had nothing broken; no injuries of that sort what-soever. And though he was the oldest, he did not seem to have suffered quite so much as the others from exposure. Of course, he had lost a lot of weight; they were all barely skel-etons. God knows what they looked like when they were first picked up. I have the sense, given Mr. Offenbach's age, that he was looked after by the others in a way they did not- or could not- look after anyone else. He could not possibly have survived what happened to him otherwise."

"And what was that, Dr Steinberg? What happened to Hugo Offenbach?"

"He had a heart attack; a minor one, but bad enough. It happened during the storm, when they had to abandon the

Evangeline. He felt the pain running down his arm. He lost consciousness. Someone must have carried him to the lifeboat; he certainly could not have reached it on his own."

"I assume that he was not delusional, or irrational, during the time you observed him?"

Dr Steinberg lifted his chin. His eyes seemed darker than before. "Hugo Offenbach may be the most rational man I have ever met."

"And what about Aaron Trevelyn? Other than his physical condition, did he suffer any mental impairment, anything that would make us doubt his ability to remember what happened or to render a clear account?"

Steinberg gave Roberts a look that bordered on incredulity. The physical condition of Aaron Trevelyn was the worst of all of them. "His wrist was broken, and he lost his foot."

"Frostbite?"

"Yes, I'm afraid so. He'll be crippled for life. I'm not really sure about his mental condition. He may have suffered some memory loss."

Roberts had taken two steps towards the jury box. He looked back at the witness. "You're not saying that Mr. Trevelyn doesn't remember what happened, are you?"

"When I examined him, he seemed vague, confused- but whether it was because he could not remember or did not want to, I can't really say."

"But you could say the same thing about the others, couldn't you? Wouldn't it be quite reasonable- given what they went through- to have a certain reluctance to talk about it?"

"Yes, I suppose, but Mr. Trevelyn..."

Roberts seemed in a hurry to move on. "There were three other survivors- the defendant and two female passengers: Samantha Wilcox and Cynthia Grimes. Beyond what they suffered physically, did either of them exhibit any symptoms that would prevent them from recalling the events that transpired before their rescue at sea?"

"I don't think so, but I can't be completely certain.

Mrs. Wilcox appeared to be a deeply religious woman, but
how far that might affect her ability to perceive events,
I'm in no position to say. With regard to the other woman,
Cynthia Grimes, I can't even tell you much about her physical condition. She left right after the ambulance brought her
to the hospital."

"You never saw her?"

"She refused treatment. She did not say why. She was
not a patient, and we couldn't hold her against her will."

"No further questions, your Honor," Roberts
announced as he crossed in front of the jury on his way back
to the counsel table. Once he had taken his chair, Roberts
clasped his hands under his chin, awaiting with more than
usual interest the next move of the defense. Most lawyers
were predictable, asking the same questions in the same
ways, but you could never be quite certain what William
Darnell would do on cross-examination. There were times
when he did not cross-examine at all. He would just flap his
hand in a petulant show of impatience, as if the witness had
already wasted too much of the jury's time. But this time
Darnell shot to his feet. Then, as if he had suddenly changed
his mind, he sat down again. Maitland started to turn
towards Dr Steinberg to tell him he was excused.

Darnell jumped up again. "That bracelet, the one you
wear on your wrist," he said with a puzzled expression.

"What exactly is that? It's one of those medical things,
isn't it? Identifies you as a donor, so that if something
happens to you someone else can receive the benefit. Am I
right?" he asked, raising his chin with an air of expectation.

Joshua Steinberg held the metal bracelet between his
fingers. "Yes, that's right. It means I'm an organ donor."

"But why wear a bracelet, if you have it in your will?"

Steinberg was not sure that Darnell was serious. If
it had not been for a look of intense and almost obstinate
ignorance on the lawyer's face, he would not have thought
it necessary to answer. "Because it could be days, or even
weeks, before anyone would know what was in my will."

Darnell continued to profess his ignorance. "But if

you'll forgive me for putting it like this, Doctor- dead is dead, isn't it? What difference does it make when anyone finds out that you are willing to have your organs used by another?"

"If the organs deteriorate, they can't be used."

"I see, I see," said Darnell, stroking his chin.

"Then the organs themselves don't die, not all at once. There is still life in them, for at least a short while, after we're dead? Is that a fair way of putting it?"

Roberts understood immediately where this was going. There was at least a chance that the rules of evidence did not allow it. "Your Honor, I'm not sure I see the relevance of this line of questioning. That Dr Steinberg is an organ donor is no doubt laudable, but the connection to this case seems a little obscure."

Darnell turned around and for a moment searched Roberts's eyes. "Do you really think so? I wonder."

Roberts was left with the uncomfortable sensation of having done something wrong and, worse yet, of having lost a battle before it had even begun. "Relevance, your Honor?" he asked in a voice that seemed forced and hollow.

Darnell took away even this. Instead of leaving it to Homer Maitland, he decided what would happen next. "A few more questions, that's all I'll need." Then he turned back to the witness.

"You wear the bracelet because it is important that the transplant be done right away, is that correct?"

"Yes, precisely."

"And I assume that you would encourage others to do the same- to make those kinds of arrangements so that people who need these transplants can have them?"

"Yes, of course. Thousands of lives are saved every year. There is a tremendous need."

"In other words, Dr Steinberg, there is no objection to the use of other bodies? In fact, if I understand you correctly, the lives of thousands of people depend upon it?"

"Absolutely."

"Very good," said William Darnell with a sidelong

glance at the jury. "And in fact, Doctor, there are cases where to save the life of one person, the organs of another person are taken while that other person is not in every sense of the term quite dead- isn't that true?"

There was an audible murmur in the courtroom, the expression of a collective doubt, an instinctive disapproval.

"What is the medical definition of death, doctor? When the heart stops beating- or when there is no more activity in the brain? Isn't that when a heart is taken, a heart that can save another life? Because if you wait much longer, it can't be used; because if you wait much longer, it won't have the gift of life..."

"Yes, but I-"

Darnell shook his head. "It doesn't matter. Forgive me, Doctor, I got a little ahead of myself. What I need to ask you about is the condition of those you examined. And I have just a few follow-up questions from what Mr. Roberts asked."

Darnell stood next to the counsel table, glancing down at his notes. "James DeSantos was the first person Mr. Roberts asked about. He is the well-known movie actor, isn't he?"

"Yes."

"He was rather seriously injured, was he not? I believe your testimony was a broken ankle, broken teeth, ulceration and even blindness?"

"Yes, but fortunately the blindness was only temporary."

"So his vision is fully restored?"

"No, not quite. He still has partial blindness in his right eye. He can see out of it, but his vision in that eye is blurred."

"And his ankle? I don't think you mentioned it- I noticed Mr. Roberts did not ask about it- but that was a compound fracture, was it not?"

"Yes."

"Meaning...?"

"The broken bone punctured the skin. With that kind

of break, if it is not set properly at once, it won't heal right."

"Which will affect the way he walks?"

"Yes, but with physical therapy..."

"I understand. Do you know how his ankle was broken?"

"He said it happened when he jumped into the boat. He landed on it, and it twisted under his weight."

Standing at an angle to the witness so he could see the jury, Darnell lifted an eyebrow and nodded slowly. "An accident, then. No one broke it for him. And what about his teeth? Another accident?"

"As far as I know."

"As far as you know. Yes, of course. One other question about Mr. DeSantos: his wife was on that voyage with him, was she not?"

"Yes, according to what I've read."

"You didn't examine her, though, did you?"

"No, she was not one of the survivors."

With a rapid stride, Darnell went across to the counsel table where he appeared to study a page of longhand notes.

"Aaron Trevelyn," he said, his eyes still on the page. He looked up, a strangely pugnacious expression on his smooth, round face. "May have suffered some memory loss? He was a member of the crew, was he not? Or is that one of the things he has managed to forget?"

"I'm just reporting what I observed," said Steinberg, stiffening.

"What you observed? Or what Mr. Trevelyn claimed?" asked Darnell with a wrathful look that changed almost immediately into an apologetic smile. "You may be wondering why both the prosecution and the defense. have concerns about what Mr. Trevelyn can or cannot remember. I'm afraid that will have to remain a mystery a little while longer. But so we're all clear about one thing: I take it you found no physical damage to his brain, no physical trauma that would explain this alleged partial loss of memory?"

"No, the CAT scan was normal; but there are other kinds of trauma."

"Oh, indeed, Doctor; and perhaps few as severe as what those poor people suffered during their long ordeal. Did any of the others- and you examined all but one of them- claim any loss of memory?"

"No, but I could not go so far as to state categorically that none of them didn't suffer some loss, or some distortion," he explained in a slightly hesitant voice.

"Are you saying that some of what they saw, some of what they experienced, may have been so traumatic that what they remember of it may not be entirely accurate?"

"We have all done things we later regret, and sometimes, perhaps to ease our conscience, we begin to shade the truth, to see it in less vivid colors- to make it appear, even to ourselves, that it was not really as bad as we had thought at first. Sometimes it's more dramatic than that. When a memory is too painful, we try to forget it- and sometimes the mind will do this, so to speak, on its own. It pushes that memory into the subconscious and replaces it in the conscious mind with something more palatable, something that gives a different shape to the same event."

"Mrs. Wilcox, for example?" asked Darnell. "I believe you testified that she appeared to be a "deeply religious" woman. Another witness testified that she claimed two angels came from heaven to help her. Is this the kind of thing you're talking about, Dr Steinberg? The way the mind reinterprets reality to make it easier for us to live with something that has happened?"

"I shouldn't like to comment on anyone's religious experience, but yes, it's possible."

"Just one or two questions more, Dr Steinberg. The other woman who was rescued- Cynthia Grimes. She refused treatment? She left the hospital?"

"Yes."

"You don't know where she went? Whom she saw?"

"No, I'm afraid I don't."

"But you had seen her before, hadn't you? She wasn't a complete stranger to you, was she?"

"What do you mean?"

"You're the chief of staff of the hospital, and Benjamin Whitfield, in addition to being a member of the board, is the largest single contributor to the hospital's endowment. He is also- is he not?- a man you consider a close friend."

"Yes, that's true. Benjamin Whitfield and I are friends."

"Then surely you knew that he and Ms. Grimes had been involved? And isn't that the reason she left, to avoid having to face any questions about what she had been doing on the Evangeline in the first place? To avoid, I imagine, the embarrassment of having to explain her relationship with one of the country's most respected men?

Yes, well, never mind," he remarked, before Roberts was out of his chair with an objection.

"It doesn't matter. Let me see...Hugo Offenbach. Yes, I saw him play here, myself. You say he had a heart attack- correct?"

"Yes, a mild one, but-"

"A mild one that would have killed him if someone had not taken care of him. Do you happen to know who that was?"

"Mr. Offenbach told me that Mr. Marlowe saved his life."

"Did he, now? Did he say that? Well, yes, I imagine he would say that. One last thing, Dr Steinberg," said Darnell, peering intently at him from the end of the jury box. "You examined the survivors of the Evangeline- all but one of them- and you did this how long after they had been picked up by Captain Balfour and the crew of the White Rose a thousand miles east of South America?"

"Nearly a week."

"During which time they had been given food and water and at least some medical care, to say nothing of a dry bed and plenty of sleep?"

"Yes, that's true."

"Would it be fair to say, then, that Captain Balfour, though he is not a doctor, had a better opportunity to observe the mental condition they were in at that time than you had?"

"Yes, of course."

"So when he said that they were all nearly dead and that some of them were quite deranged, you would not contradict that?"

"No, I would not."

"And finally, Dr Steinberg, let me ask you about the one person you examined that Mr. Roberts did not ask about. What was the condition of Vincent Marlowe when he first arrived?"

"Physically exhausted, emotionally spent. He had lost more weight than any of the others. He had a broken shoulder and two broken fingers. He was the one I was most concerned about. I knew the others would all survive. I was not sure about him."

"Because of his physical state?"

"No, because I don't think he wanted to survive; I think he wanted to die."

CHAPTER EIGHT

The prosecution, as it was required to do, had given the defense. a list of the witnesses it intended to call. Darnell knew the names, but could only guess at the order in which they would be summoned to the stand. He had guessed correctly so far, but that had not been difficult. In selecting his first three witnesses, Michael Roberts had followed a strict chronology. He had led with Benjamin Whitfield for the obvious reason that it had all started with the owner of the Evangeline. The voyage had been his idea, and the boat had been built to his specifications. Who better to give the jury a sense of the enormous contrast between what was expected at the beginning and what had happened at the end?

The second witness, Thomas Balfour, was the logical sequel to the first. Whitfield had seen them off, the smiling passengers and crew, on a sun-drenched morning in Nice; Balfour had seen them next, or rather what was left of them, the six survivors he rescued from the windswept ravages of the south Atlantic. He had found them all half dead, some of them out of their minds.

The third witness, Joshua Steinberg, was able to establish that those who survived were now all well enough to be in command of their senses- whatever may have happened to them during their forty-day ordeal- perfectly capable of telling what they knew.

Those three witnesses had been enough for Roberts to give the jury a broad outline of the story. A sailing vessel, the most advanced of its kind, had left for a luxury voyage around Africa. The boat had gone down in a storm so violent that there had been no chance to communicate with the outside world and very little time for even one lifeboat to get away. Only fourteen people out of twenty-seven had managed to escape the Evangeline, and forty days later only six of them were left alive. Without food, without water, they had traveled nearly a thousand miles in an open boat, six people barely alive and what was left of one dead body.

But the only thing the testimony of those three witnesses had proved was that the Evangeline had left Nice in the third week of June with twenty-seven people on board and that six of them had been found a thousand miles east of Brazil at the end of July. There were only six people who could be called to testify about what had happened after the Evangeline went down, and one of them, Vincent Marlowe, could not be forced to say anything unless he chose to testify for the defense. That left five witnesses, and until the day the trial started, only one of them had agreed to talk to anyone connected with the case.

"There were five other people in that lifeboat and none of them will talk to me. Five witnesses and only one of them has spoken to anyone. Why? Was there some agreement made before you were rescued- or while you were on the White Rose- that you would all maintain your silence, that none of you would reveal what happened out there? Has Trevelyn now broken that agreement, broken his word to save himself?"

William Darnell leaned back in his leather chair. He had spent so much of his life in it that it fitted him like a well-worn glove. He waited while Marlowe thought about his answer. There was always a pause, a silence, while Marlowe took in fully everything you had said. Darnell was convinced that he had unusual powers of concentration. In the months they had known each other- or rather, because that implied a degree of openness, of candor, that didn't exist, in the months in which they had had occasional conversations- Darnell could not remember a single instance in which he had been asked to repeat something he had said. There was something slow and steady and reliable, something you could trust, about Marlowe. But beyond that, there was something deep and impenetrable about him. He would never lie, but there were things about him, secrets, at which you could only guess.

"We had no agreement among us," said Marlowe. "None that was ever spoken."

Marlowe reached across his chest to tug the lapel of his thick tweed coat. He had been in Darnell's office at least half a dozen times before, but each time, shortly after he settled into the chair on the other side of the lawyer's desk, his eyes moved around the room and the same quiet smile broke the even line of his mouth.

"Outside- where the others work- it's bright as day, and at every desk there is a computer and everyone is busy all the time. But in here, it's dark and quiet and I've never seen a machine. All I see are books, thousands of them, and here and there a picture, a photograph, nothing else."

Darnell nodded towards the wall. "That one has been there since the day I started practice: my class photograph. We looked older than law school graduates look now. In part because we were- most of us had been in the service before we started. The other reason is that in those days we all wore suits. There were nearly two hundred in that class, and only five of them women. All of the women, and nearly all of the others, are now either retired or dead, a distinction without a difference, it always seemed to me."

Marlowe nodded in agreement. "I never could understand why anyone would want to stop what they did, just to sit around and watch the years slip by. I like this room. It's like a ship: quiet, dark, out of the way."

"Out of the way?"

"Of other people and what they do."

"Is that why you decided to spend your life at sea?"

Marlowe rose from the chair and walked over to the bookshelves that, from the floor to the ceiling, covered every wall but that which faced the street below. "I might have been a lawyer if I'd been any good at school. I like to read. It's what I do when I'm on a ship at night and I don't have the watch. It's the way I spend most of the time I have in port- find the library and if I don't know the language, try to learn it. I read whatever I can find that I think might improve my mind."

Marlowe picked at random one of the thick volumes of reported cases, the appellate opinions that interpret and decide the law. He held it in his large hands with the reverence of a serious reader, the respect owed to written words meant to last. "They didn't think I could learn anything when I was a boy in school. I was always falling behind the others."

Marlowe thumbed through a few more pages, intrigued by the division of the text into double columns. "I could never get it into my head that you had to move on to the next thing before you had completely understood the thing on which you had started." He closed the book and carefully put it back in place. "Time is the trouble- always is. Everyone else was studying the next bunch of problems, while I was still trying to understand why I had gotten a couple wrong on the math test we had had the week before. In the sixth grade, I got tired of it and quit."

William Darnell gazed out the window. A shaft of sunlight cut through the thick morning fog. From a few blocks away came the mournful racket of a cable car, tolling its bell, as it jolted its way up California Street to Nob Hill. He thought about how Marlowe always had a book in his hand, or stuffed in his pocket, and that he read Pushkin and Dostoyevsky in Russian. And Marlowe had not even finished the sixth grade.

"How did you come to leave school so early? Why did your parents allow it?"

Marlowe went to a second window that looked down on Montgomery Street. It was a few minutes before eight. The morning traffic was a bedlam of muffled noise and light.

"My father was a boilermaker. Worked in the ship-yards in Seattle. He used to take me with him, days when he worked on some freighter. They came from every place imaginable and there was always someone on board who liked to tell stories to a boy. It fed my imagination- not just the stories, but the strange dialects, and even stranger looks, with which they told them. My father died in an explosion; left my mother with nothing but a small widow's pension and two children to raise."

For a long time Marlowe stared down at the floor. When he finally raised his eyes he met the waiting gaze of Darnell. "I was twelve, but big for my age. There were always freighters coming in and out. My father had worked on a lot of them. There was a ship from Singapore; the captain had known my father, took me on as a cabin boy. Was the best thing that could have happened to me: got me out of school and all its useless drudgery. The sea became my education."

Marlowe gestured towards the book-lined shelves. "And this was yours? Reading all those cases, decisions made by the courts?"

A smile, close to nostalgia and not far from regret, slipped across William Darnell's soft, almost feminine mouth. At the beginning, and for a long time after that, he had read them all. Now everything was on a computer, as Marlowe had remarked, easy to access if you knew what you were looking for and why. For his part, however, William Darnell did not think he had lost anything by being forced to carry his library around in his head.

"And every case adds something new," he said, nodding to the empty chair so Marlowe would sit down. "Now tell me what you can about Trevelyn. You have to do at least this much. You haven't told me anything about what happened…"

"I've told you that I'll testify and that I'll tell the truth," Marlowe objected.

Darnell leaned against the arm of his chair. He studied Marlowe intently. "You'll tell the truth at trial, but you won't tell the truth to me. That is a very strange way of proceeding, one without precedent in my experience. I never represent anyone who doesn't tell me everything I need to know."

But he was doing it this time, even though Marlowe's refusal had been made plain at the beginning. "I assumed it was the condition you were in at the time, the shock of what you had been through, and that when you were back on your feet, fully recovered…I didn't press you for details at the beginning, because I didn't need them then. Your sister told me you would not hold anything back, that you always tell the truth. Can't you trust me when I tell you that I'm only trying to do what is best for you?"

"But I do trust you. I knew you were a decent man the first time I sat in this chair and looked you straight in the eye. And I have told you the truth. I told you that it wasn't my idea to hire you, to hire anyone. My sister wanted that. She is the one who hired you; she's the one paying your fee. I didn't want a lawyer because I don't need one. I did what they say I did: I'm guilty, plain and simple. I killed. I did it for a reason, but no reason can bring a dead man back. I'm guilty and the trial will prove it. Whatever the others say, I'll still say I'm guilty, because it's the truth- and the truth, or some part of it, has to be said. Don't you think we owe that much to the dead- to tell the world why they died?"

"And will Aaron Trevelyn tell the truth as well?" asked Darnell with a glance full of meaning.

"Is that why, of the six of you, he's the only one who has said anything? Because he thinks he's guilty, but could not wait for the trial to tell it to the world?"

Darnell bent forward, the look in his eye withering in its implications. "There were only two of you- two members of the crew- who survived in that lifeboat. You're charged with murder; Trevelyn isn't charged with anything. Wasn't he just as much responsible for what was done out there as you? Perhaps even, from what I've heard, more? Isn't he the one who first suggested…?"

The same silence that met his every question met this one as well.

"Trevelyn wasn't in charge. The responsibility was not his," said Marlowe finally. There was too much pride, and not enough regret; too much willingness to take every-thing on himself. Marlowe was bound to a tragic sense of life. He, and only he, had been selected by God or Chance or Fate to choose between the death of everyone or, at the price of murder, the survival of at least a few. That had been the most difficult thing for Darnell to grasp- that Marlowe was not ashamed of what he had done and that the only thing that would have shamed him would have been to evade the consequences of the choice he had made. It was no wonder Marlowe preferred to live at sea among other men who had forgotten where they came from. His sense of honor was too rigid, too unforgiving, to live his life among the tolerant men and women of civilized nations.

"Trevelyn may not have been in charge," Darnell persisted, "but by suggesting, by not refusing, by taking part, he would in the eyes of the law be a co-conspirator, every bit as guilty of murder as you. Now, you must tell me: did he first suggest it? What happened out there? Won't you tell me anything to help?"

Silence.

With an air of exasperation, Darnell threw up his hands. "What happened when the Evangeline sank? No, what happened when she sailed? With all your experience, with everything you knew, why did you agree with Whitfield that it was enough to fix that one crack, that it wasn't necessary to examine every welding seam in the hull?"

Marlowe seemed stunned by the suggestion.

"You didn't know? You didn't know about the crack in the hull, the one they found in the sea trials, the one they fixed?" Darnell asked, certain now that he was right. "The people who built the Evangeline took her through her trials. You had only ever taken her out, for a few days at a time, in the Mediterranean. He didn't tell you. And you've known Benjamin Whitfield for how many years?"

"I first started sailing for him four years ago."

Darnell looked at him sharply. "That's why it sank, or at least sank like that, went down that quickly in the storm- because under all that stress, the seams just came apart?"

Marlowe nodded, then got up and began to pace around the room. "I don't know why he didn't get the rest of the seams checked, except the reason he gave in court: that he was told it wasn't necessary and that there wasn't time- not if she was going to set out on schedule."

"But that doesn't explain why he didn't tell you about the problem, does it?" said Darnell, giving him an odd look.

Marlowe shrugged it off. "I worked for him from time to time, sailed his boats different places in the world. He isn't the kind of man spends time talking to ones like me. He only tells people what he thinks they have to know. He's always busy- too many other things he has to do. He was that way with everyone. I never had the feeling he had any real friends, just people he wanted to be around. The girl may have been different, though. She seemed to think so, the way she acted when he said he wasn't going to be able to go."

Darnell threw him a puzzled glance. "The way she acted...?"

"She seemed more upset about it than the others did. They had quite an argument about it."

Darnell tapped his fingers together slowly, a shrewd expression stealing across his mouth. "Trevelyn," he said, suddenly alert. "What is he going to say?"

Before Marlowe could answer, Darnell sprang from his chair. With his hands clasped behind his back he took three quick steps towards the far window and then turned back. "There were fourteen people- fourteen! Did they all...?

"Never mind," he said. "Whatever happened it will all come out- though in God knows how many versions. But if you won't talk about what happened, about what you had to do to save the others- because for some reason that makes no sense to me you'll only talk about it at the trial- you can still tell me what happened when the Evangeline went down. She had plenty of lifeboats on her- the Zodiacs and the other inflatable rafts- but only one got away?"

"No," replied Marlowe without expression. "Two got free."

His mouth half open, Darnell stared at Marlowe. "Two got away? What happened to the other one? There were fourteen people in your boat. How many in the second one? What happened to them?"

CHAPTER NINE

With his jaw set tight and his eyes focused straight ahead, Homer Maitland moved a little more quickly to the bench than he normally did. He was not trying to make up for time lost- the minute hand on the clock was snapping into place as he entered the courtroom- but to get a start on what was certain to be a long day. He had presided over enough trials to know when the prosecution had finished with the preliminary witnesses and was about to enter the most crucial part of its case.

"Bring in the jury," he said with a cursory nod towards the bailiff. While the jurors took their places in the jury box, Maitland studied the witness lists in the court file. "You may call your next witness," he said, raising his eyes to the well of the courtroom below him where Michael Roberts sat waiting on the edge of his chair.

"The People call Aaron Trevelyn," announced Roberts, as he got to his feet. It was difficult not to feel sorry for Aaron Trevelyn as he hobbled into court on a pair of wooden crutches. The right leg of his pants hung in an empty knot where his right foot had been. He was not yet used to the limits of his condition. When he raised his right hand to take the oath, the crutch on that side fell free. With a stricken, mortified look, Trevelyn waited while the clerk knelt down and picked it up.

With hollow eyes and sunken cheeks, Trevelyn, though only thirty-eight years old, had the look of a man whose time was running out. He lowered himself onto the witness chair and set the crutches aside. With a strange, fearful smile he glanced around the courtroom. The crowd was staring at him with an intense fascination, driven by a plainly morbid curiosity. He looked away, but he could not help himself; he looked again, fascinated by the way they looked at him. Slowly, each word spoken with precision,

Roberts asked the questions needed to establish the identity and background of the witness. He then began to ask a series of questions designed to remove any sympathy that the jury might to this point have felt for Vincent Marlowe and what he had done.

"Would you please tell the jury how you happened to be employed as a member of the crew of the Evangeline?"

"It was an accident; it was nothing planned." Trevelyn flushed at the unexpectedly high-pitched sound of his voice. Embarrassed, he stared miserably at his hands. "Nothing planned," he repeated as he shifted uneasily in the chair.

Roberts stood at the end of the jury box, his hand resting on the rail, waiting for Trevelyn to go on. But all Trevelyn did was change position again. He spread his legs apart, the right one dangling free. With his elbows on the curved wooden arms of the brown leather chair, he bent forward, eyeing Roberts with nervous suspicion.

"Nothing planned," said Roberts with a pensive smile as he advanced towards the witness.

"I'm not quite sure I understand what you mean. The question was how you happened to become a member of the crew."

"It was an accident," said Trevelyn, repeating himself with mechanical insistence. "A mistake."

Darnell leaned forward, anxious to hear. Marlowe stared straight ahead, his expression unchanged.

"A mistake?" asked Roberts. "I'm afraid you have me really lost now- and, I imagine, the jury as well." Roberts searched his eyes. "I know this is difficult, Mr. Trevelyn, but it will be much easier if you simply answer the questions you're asked. Now, again, would you please describe to the jury the circumstances that led you to become a member of the crew of the Evangeline? Start this way: Were you hired by Benjamin Whitfield, the owner, or by Vincent Marlowe?"

"Marlowe brought me on, day before we sailed."

"Just the day before?"

"He was shorthanded. Someone who was supposed to go couldn't, or had a change of heart- a premonition maybe..."

"You had not sailed with Mr. Marlowe before?"

"No, never. Had not even met him. But I had sailed a lot in the Mediterranean. I heard they were looking for someone for a trip around Africa, and I was ready for something different. And when I saw the Evangeline it was not hard to decide. I had been on a lot of different vessels- some of the biggest yachts in the world. But the Evangeline! I'd never seen anything like her. She looked like she could fly."

"Was this, then, the first time you had sailed out of the Mediterranean and down the coast of Africa?"

"Yes, and I wish to God I'd never gone! I should have stuck with what I knew."

Roberts shoved his hands into his pockets and began to pace back and forth, two steps one way, two steps the other. He waited until Trevelyn's emotion had begun to subside.

"'She looked like she could fly.'" But she didn't, did she? She sank. What can you tell us about that, about the storm and how she went down?"

"I thought I had been in weather before," said Trevelyn with a shudder. "Weather? I hadn't seen anything. It was like you know what rain is and then you see a typhoon; or you once felt a tremor, a slight shifting of the ground, and then a real earthquake comes and levels a city. Weather? That storm wasn't weather; that storm was pure evil, the end of the world. It was the day of judgment; it was Hell.

"The winds so loud you thought you would go deaf; the seas so high you thought you were buried." His eyes grew distant, remembering with a kind of stupefied wonder the start of the storm and his own dim refusal to believe that it could keep getting worse.

"It was what we expected, that's what we told ourselves. We were in the south Atlantic; you expect some weather that time of year. And to tell the truth, we welcomed it, those first few days as the winds gathered and the swells became heavy. The Evangeline seemed to come alive, to breathe- the way she cut through it, the speed she had. The sun was shining, not a cloud in the sky, that's what it was like at first. Everything was smiles and laughter, people cheering when she broke through a wave and landed with a thump. Because, you see, it was perfect weather, blowing sun and wind. And you could almost taste it in the air, the sense that it was going to be like this, or even better, every day we were out." Trevelyn's haggard face grew tense, his gaze turned rigid. He looked at the jury.

"But it didn't get better. The winds got stronger and the sea got rougher and the sky turned gray. It didn't matter. The Evangeline could sail through anything. We all knew what weather was like." Trevelyn fell into a silence that became a kind of permanent fact, a condition of existence, the only true expression of what lies at the heart of things.

"But the weather got worse," said Roberts, prompting him gently.

"Yes, it got worse. And it kept getting worse."

"But didn't you have warning that it would? Wasn't the Evangeline equipped with all the latest technology? Surely you could track the weather by satellite."

"It didn't work, that's what I was told; some of the equipment had broken down. But it wouldn't have made any difference. Before we knew it we were in the weather, in the middle of the storm. There was nothing we could do but ride it out."

"What happened then?"

"It kept getting worse, and we kept thinking that it was as bad as it could get. And then it happened, sudden like, hit by a wave fifty, sixty feet high. It just ripped her apart. We were taking water, tons of it coming through the companionways. She was getting heavier and heavier, lying deeper and deeper in the water. She was sinking so fast, it was as if the bottom had broken out of her as well. It was the middle of the night, about two, two-thirty in the morning. The passengers- some of them were caught below."

"And the rest? How many of the twenty-seven passengers and crew managed to get to the lifeboats, and how many of the lifeboats got away?"

"One of the Zodiacs…I got to it first; managed to tear away the tarpaulin- it was filled with boxes; there wasn't time to get them out."

"Boxes? In a lifeboat?"

"The lifeboats were never going to be used. It was a pleasure cruise," said Trevelyn, tossing his head in derision. "A cruise down the coast of Africa for a few of Whitfield's rich and famous friends. The boxes were crates of champagne, caviar, all the fine things people like that expect. There wasn't room for all they needed in the galley, so why not use the lifeboats? What other use could they have?"

"Lifeboats? Were more than one of them used like this?"

Trevelyn shrugged. "All I know is about the one, the one I tore my hands up trying to get ready before I found out what it had inside."

"What did you do next, after you discovered that the lifeboat- the Zodiac- was not usable?"

Trevelyn gave Roberts a mocking glance. "I wasn't on some careful search, some examination of what was fit to use and what wasn't. People were screaming, falling all over each other, things were flying everywhere. Every wave that hit her sunk her lower. All you could think about was how you were going to get off the Evangeline before she finally sank. When I saw what was in that lifeboat, I thought I'd never get off, that I was as good as drowned."

"But somehow you got to the other lifeboat, the one where Marlowe and the others were?"

"I must have."

"You must have? That's the lifeboat you were in, the one in which you and the others were eventually found."

"I don't remember how I got there. The Evangeline was heaving up, breaking apart. All you could do was hang on, try to get away. When I was looking inside that lifeboat, the one all filled up- it went straight up in the air. I was hanging on with my hands, my feet below me, those boxes banging all around. Whether I crawled my way to the other boat or was thrown there, I couldn't really say. There is a lot

I don't remember about what happened- then or later," he added with a dark, ominous look.

Roberts pushed his head forward, returning Trevelyn's look with a warning of his own. "There is a difference between not being able to remember and not wanting to."

"I can't remember that much about what happened then. There was so much going on; it's all a blur. Somehow I got off. Maybe I hit my head or something, because I can't remember anything until sometime later, when the storm was nearly over. I was in the lifeboat, with all the others, and Marlowe was there, giving orders."

From the counsel table, Roberts picked up a list of the passengers and crew and began to read the names, asking after each one whether that person had been in the lifeboat. Beyond the five other survivors, Trevelyn identified seven others.

Roberts gave him a puzzled look. "That makes only thirteen. If I'm not mistaken, there were fourteen people in the lifeboat at the beginning."

"He wasn't on the list."

"Who wasn't on the list?"

"The boy- the cabin boy. He wasn't old enough to be a regular member of the crew. He worked, though, he did his part- I'll give him that."

"And do you know this boy's name?" asked Roberts.

"Billy. That was the only name I knew. No one told me his last name."

"What happened to him...?" Roberts started to ask, then changed his mind. "No, tell us first, if you would, how you survived; how fourteen people survived in a lifeboat, lost at sea. In the beginning at least, there was food and water?"

Trevelyn bent forward, scratched his head, looked around and then stared at the floor- concentrating, as it seemed, on remembering correctly and in the right order the things that had happened. "A little water, very little food. Maybe a gallon of water to start; three or four cans of food. That was all we had."

"For fourteen people?"

"We managed to collect some water from the rain, and we had a line we rigged, with a hook to catch a few fish. Then there was the seaweed- we ate that as well. We lived like that for more than a week, all packed together, no room to move. We were going to die out there. No one was going to find us. We knew that."

"Why do you say that? Why didn't you think you would be found?"

"No one knew the Evangeline had sunk. No distress signal had been sent. It happened too fast; and even if there had been time, nothing worked. We made a sail, followed the wind, but we were thousands of miles from anywhere, and we were going to starve to death before we had gone two hundred. And besides, luck wasn't with us."

"Because the Evangeline had sunk? Because the storm had become so violent so suddenly?" asked Roberts in a solemn, sympathetic voice.

"No luck because we could have been found three different times in those first few days and we weren't. Three times freighters passed us. We could see them just a few miles off, riding high on the horizon, but twice they did not see us."

"Twice? But you said three times you saw...?"

"That ship was less than a mile away, and there isn't any chance they didn't see us. Maybe they were carrying some cargo they didn't want discovered- or maybe it was a ghost ship come to taunt us. That was when we gave up all hope of rescue, when we watched that black and red freighter pass right by us as we shouted after her- those of us who still had voices. We watched that bastard ship disappear over the horizon, that long wisp of smoke trailing behind it, dissolving with our hopes."

Trevelyn paused, a bleak expression in his haunted, hollow eyes. "That was when it happened: when the first one died. Wilson..."

"Arnold Wilson?" asked Roberts, checking the name against his list.

"He jumped into the water, started swimming. Thought he could catch her, I suppose; did not last but a few minutes."

"Did anyone try to stop him, to go after him?"

Trevelyn looked at him like he was a fool. "There was nothing anyone could do, we were all so weak with hunger and thirst. No one cared that he was gone. We were all going to die. Some were already sick."

Roberts remembered the boy. "Billy. What happened to him?"

"What happened to him? He was sicker than the others. It was only a matter of time. That's why he was chosen."

"Chosen?"

"Chosen to die, so the rest of them could live, even if it was for only a little while longer. Chosen to die, Mr. Roberts, so they could eat him."

CHAPTER TEN

Lawyers tell other lawyers that you take your witnesses as they come. Like most things lawyers tell each other, it gives a kind of comfort to the evils of the trade. Witnesses are not chosen because they are good and honest people; they are called to testify because of what they know. Michael Roberts did not call Aaron Trevelyn as a witness for the prosecution because he thought a jury would like him; he called him because Trevelyn was the only one of the survivors of the Evangeline who would talk.

The jury despised Aaron Trevelyn. Part of it was the twitching insincerity in his eyes, the way he never looked at anything or anyone for very long. What might have been interpreted as nervousness or fear at the beginning of his testimony yielded to a judgment far less forgiving once they detected the caustic resentment in his voice. Others had died, but he had lost a foot. The others had no meaning to him. They were abstractions, names of the sort we read in the papers; names of people we never knew. Why would he think about them when a part of him was missing? Why would he grieve over anyone else when, for the rest of his life, he would bear the pain and the curse of his own disfigurement?

Roberts had been visibly stunned by Trevelyn's brusque indifference. A boy had been chosen to die, and it was as simple as that? No emotion, no regret, not so much as a passing thought for the tragedy of a life lost at such an early age? The only clear feeling, glaring and almost obscene, vindictiveness about what others had done?

Whether Roberts, with his eyes fixed on the witness, had seen the horrified looks that spread over jurors' faces, he could sense the change of mood. He tried to rescue what he could.

"It must have been awful, what you went through. But

the jury was not there; they only know what you tell them."

"And perhaps not even that much!" exclaimed William Darnell in a loud voice from his chair at the other side of the courtroom.

Roberts shot him an angry look. "Your Honor, I..."

"My apologies, your Honor," said Darnell, rising part way up from his chair. "Sometimes I hear myself talking when I thought I was only thinking something to myself."

With a single glance, Homer Maitland cut dead the laughter that rippled through the courtroom. He peered over his glasses and, with a certain suppressed admiration at Darnell's incorrigible smile, shook his head. "Do not depend too much on the tolerance of the court, Mr. Darnell. You might find the consequences somewhat disagreeable should I find it necessary to give voice to what at moments like this I might be thinking. Are we clear?"

"Yes, your Honor," said Darnell, the smile stretching further across his face. "Crystal clear."

"Good." Maitland looked at Roberts. "You may continue. But, please, Mr. Roberts- ask a question."

Roberts moved to within an arm's length of the witness. "You said the boy was chosen- chosen to die. Who made that decision?"

Trevelyn pointed at Marlowe. "Him. He did. It was his decision."

Grim- faced, impassive, Marlowe had been staring straight ahead. At Trevelyn's answer, his eyes flashed open and his head turned sharply. He seemed to be challenging him to repeat it. Trevelyn lowered his eyes and sank back in the witness chair.

"Mr. Trevelyn?" Trevelyn looked up, his eyes hostile and suspicious. He cast a defiant glance at Marlowe to show that he had not been defeated, but Marlowe had already looked away.

"It was his decision," repeated Trevelyn. "His decision how the decision should be made."

"Explain that, please," said Roberts quickly.

"We had been out there ten days, two weeks... I don't

know for sure. That last ship passed us, and- what was his name? Wilson?- went in after it. We knew it was all over. We were thousands of miles from land. We could catch a little water- not much, a few drops- but we were out of food."

"You had a hook and line- you could catch fish. Isn't that what you said?"

"We did, for a while; but it wasn't much good and then we lost even that. Someone was supposed to watch it, have their hand on it all the time, but in one of the storms…"

"Mr. Trevelyn?"

"Sorry," said Trevelyn, coming back to himself. "What was the question? Yes, I remember," he said, forcing himself to sit straight. "We were out of food, and there were eleven of us left. We…"

"Eleven?" asked Roberts. "There were fourteen, then Wilson drowned…"

Trevelyn shrugged. "Ten days, two weeks- things happened. You would nod off- crowded like we were- wake up an hour later and someone next to you might be gone. Fell in, or went of their own accord rather than face another day of it, I couldn't say. After that ship we saw, after what we saw Wilson do, it was like I said: we were all dead, the only question how we wanted to die."

Pausing, Trevelyn looked around the courtroom, a hard shrewdness in his hollow eyes.

"It isn't like going hungry for a few days, knowing at the end of it you'll be all nice and safe with lots to eat. After a while you start to feel your body start eating itself. We would have died out there, if we hadn't done what we did. It wasn't what they did was wrong, but the way they did it. None of it was fair."

"Before you tell us what you think was or was not fair," Roberts interjected, unable to hide a certain irritation, "tell us first what was done."

Trevelyn turned away from the courtroom crowd, scowling at the interruption. "What was done? I'll tell you what was done! There were ten of us left-"

"Ten?" cried Roberts in frustration. "You just said

there were eleven!"

"Did I call the witness, your Honor?" asked Darnell, perplexed. "Because if I did, when the prosecution is finished with its cross-examination, I should like to have the chance to ask a few questions on redirect."

Roberts had lost all patience with the courtroom theatrics of the legendary William Darnell. He waved off the remark.

"Ten, eleven- which is it?" he demanded.

"Ten, eleven- how would I know?" Trevelyn fired back. "I was as good as dead; so were all the others. What difference did it make who was left? Another day, maybe two, and we all would have died!"

Trevelyn's eyes moved down to the foot that was no longer there. A scornful look passed over his face. "Might have been better if we had," he muttered under his breath.

"Tell us what was done," repeated Roberts with stern insistence.

Trevelyn raised his eyes, but this time he looked at Roberts without animosity. "The boy was dying. There was no mistake about that. He might have lasted a few more days, but that was all. And those few days- none of us would have lasted any longer. That's when Marlowe decided. That's when he decided the boy had to die, and that it could not wait. And that's what Marlowe did. He took his knife- the boy was still alive- and he got behind him, held his hand across his mouth, and tore open his shirt. He plunged the knife straight into his heart. That's how he killed him."

"Stabbed him in the heart! Why?"

"Why? I'll tell you why. So the others- some of the others- could drink the boy's blood, that's why! It was nourishment, that's what Marlowe said. It would keep you alive, that's what he said. And you had to do it that way, while the heart was still beating, because if you waited, if you waited until it stopped, if you tried to do it after someone was dead, the blood coagulated, dried up. It would be useless then. We had to do it- that's what Marlowe said. We had to drink it, or we would die."

"We had to do it?" said Roberts sharply. "You also…?"

"I was out of my mind with hunger and thirst! But I hated myself for doing it. I swear that's true!"

Roberts turned away, perhaps to hide his revulsion. He went to the counsel table and glanced through a file. "And then, I take it, the body of the boy was used as well?" he asked, looking up.

"Yes. The head was removed, and the feet and hands. The same way with all the others."

A tremor ran through the courtroom, a great collective sigh of dismay and disapproval. Some of the jurors looked at Marlowe as if he had been revealed as something not quite human; others refused to look at him at all.

"'All the others?'Do you mean to say that this is how the rest of them died? Ten, eleven- whatever the number left-there were only six survivors. First the boy, then the others? Four, maybe five people died this way?" asked Roberts with a look of incredulity. "All those other people died the same way? Stabbed in the heart while their hearts were still beating?"

"No, one of them was stabbed in the throat."

Trevelyn nodded towards Marlowe, sitting rigid in his chair. "He shoved the knife into her jugular while someone caught the blood that spurted out in one of the empty cans."

"Her jugular? The victim was a woman?"

"The second one, after the boy."

"Was she sick as well? Did she also have only a few days left?"

"That's not so easy to answer. None of us had more than a few days left. We were all dying. The only question was whether we would all die together or one at a time so the ones left could live a little longer. There was one or two who said we shouldn't do it, that it was better to die than live like that, but most didn't see it that way. They wanted to live. Nothing else mattered. Not that it was ever put to a vote, or anything like that. Marlowe made all the decisions. He was in charge."

"Do you know who this woman was? Do you know

79

her name?"

Hunched forward, Trevelyn raised his head. He looked at Roberts as if he was not sure he should answer.

"The name, Mr. Trevelyn. Who was she?"

Trevelyn's closed mouth pulled back to the side as he bit his lip. Roberts kept staring at him, hard, unrelenting.

"She was the famous one, the movie star- the wife of that fool DeSantos."

The courtroom came alive. Heads turned, eyes met; puzzled faces confessed their ignorance and curiosity searched for answers. DeSantos was James DeSantos, the well-known actor. Until this moment everyone had presumed that his wife, the equally famous and infinitely desirable Helena Green, had vanished with the Evangeline. No one had ever suggested that she might have been in the same lifeboat with her husband.

"Helena Green- she's the woman to whom you refer?" asked Roberts, ignoring the murmurs of the crowd which, with a glance of the utmost severity, Judge Maitland reduced to an impeccable silence.

"Helena Green. Yes, she's the one, the second one who died. The second one Marlowe killed."

Roberts moved behind his chair at the counsel table. His hand tightened around the back of the wooden spindle chair. The color drained from his face. "And you and the others- the ones who were left- that was how you lived? On the flesh and blood of Helena Green?"

There was a look of pure contempt in Aaron Trevelyn's eyes, an expression of cruel vindictiveness against the cheap morality that could not ask the question but only dance around it.

"Do you mean, did her husband live off her flesh and blood as well?" Trevelyn's eyes fairly glittered with the pride of evil. "Yes! And more than that, he insisted that, as she was his wife, he get her first!"

Roberts's face turned completely ashen. In the tumultuous noise of the outraged courtroom, he gripped the chair with all his strength.

Maitland pounded his gavel as hard as he could. "This is a court of law!" he thundered in that gravel-rough voice. "Not some sideshow. You're not here to express an opinion or give vent to your feelings. This courtroom will either be silent," he continued, as his voice grew quieter with the crowd, "or, with the exception of those directly involved in the case, it will be empty."

Maitland started to direct Roberts to ask his next question, then he changed his mind. Waving his index finger back and forth, he turned and cautioned the jury. "It may be well to remind ourselves what is at issue here. The defendant, Vincent Marlowe, is on trial on a charge of murder. The defendant, by virtue of certain pre-trial motions made by his attorney, has joined to a plea of not guilty, a notice of his intention to rely on what is called the defense of necessity.

"The issue, then, is not so much whether someone was killed, but whether, in a manner allowed by the law, that killing was necessary. Both Mr. Roberts and Mr. Darnell told you during their opening statements something about the circumstances- and, I would add, the extraordinary circumstances- in which this defense might be available. At the end of the trial, I will instruct you on the law of necessity and how you are to apply it to the facts of this case.

"I will tell you now that part of your task will be to decide what, under all the circumstances in which the defendant found himself, including the responsibility he owed others, were the choices he had- and whether what he did was the only thing a reasonable man could have done. It is no answer to say that it should not have been done, that no one should ever kill. The question- the only question- is whether he had any real choice. The question- the only question- is whether the choice he made was the lesser, or the greater, of two evils.

"Finally, as I instructed you at the very beginning, you are required by your oath to suspend all judgment until you have heard all the evidence. The law gives you no choice in this."

From their solemn demeanor, it appeared that the jury understood everything Maitland said. They seemed relieved that the law would allow them to keep a certain distance from the raw, gruesome facts of death; grateful that they did not have to look too closely into what had been done, and only into why. They did not have to touch the leper, only determine the cause of his disease.

The rest of that day and all the next, Roberts led Aaron Trevelyn through the grim recitals of death and survival. At the end of it, despite Maitland's cogent warnings, it would have taken a rare detachment not to believe that Vincent Marlowe, if not a born monster, had been a man gone mad, driven by hunger, thirst and fear to make a mockery of decency and raise serious questions whether, pushed to extremes, men were worse, far worse, than beasts.

When Darnell left the courtroom at the end of Trevelyn's second day of testimony, he knew he had a long night's work in front of him. He did not mind that. The work made him feel useful and alive. It was nearly quarter to six, but Mrs. Herbert, his secretary was still waiting for him.

"He's here," she said. "In your office."

Darnell was annoyed that anyone should be in his office. "If someone wants to see me, they can make an appointment. No, they can't," he said, immediately correcting himself. "I'm in a trial; I don't have time…"

"You've been trying to reach him for weeks. When he called a little after three and asked if he could see you, I thought-"

"Who?"

"Hugo Offenbach."

"Here?" He turned and walked away, moving anxiously down the long corridor. He stood before the closed door to his own office, adjusting his tie. He knocked before he entered.

"It's a great pleasure to meet you finally, Mr. Offenbach," he said as he shook hands with the famous violinist. "I heard you play once."

"I did not know what would come out," explained

Offenbach in a worried voice that struck Darnell as being at the same time profoundly courageous. "But after what Mr. Trevelyn has said, I thought I had better come to see you."

"You were in court today?" asked Darnell. With a gesture he invited the violinist to take the chair in front of his desk.

"No," replied Offenbach. There was a look of hesitation in his eyes, and then he added, "I don't go anywhere in public now. No, I read in the papers what he said yesterday. That's why I'm here. I thought you might like to know the truth."

They talked far into the night, and when Hugo Offenbach finally left his office, Darnell knew far more about what had happened to the unfortunate survivors of the Evangeline, and more about Vincent Marlowe, than through anything Marlowe had shared. He knew enough to make the cross-examination of Aaron Trevelyn a much more interesting prospect than it had seemed before. When he finally fell asleep, sometime after two, he was already dreaming about the morning and what would happen when it came.

CHAPTER ELEVEN

The court reporter was setting up her machine. The bailiff stood off to the side, stifling a yawn.

"I know what happened out there," Darnell whispered to Marlowe. "Offenbach came to see me. He told me everything."

The last of the spectators squeezed into place. The bailiff straightened up and became alert.

"He asked me how you were doing," Darnell continued when Marlowe made no reply. He pulled away, just far enough to look Marlowe in the eye. "He said if there was anything he could do for you- anything at all- he would. He said to tell you that you were in his prayers."

The stoic shield fell away. Marlowe's eyes filled with emotion, and a slight tremble broke the line of his mouth. The door at the side burst open. Two hundred people rose as one. Homer Maitland, in full stride, hurried to the bench, issuing instructions to first bring in the jury and then the witness. "Mr. Darnell, do you wish to cross-examine?" he inquired after Aaron Trevelyn had been reminded that he was still under oath.

Darnell was already on his feet. The fingers of his right hand drummed on the front corner of the counsel table. An eager, cat-like grin crossed his mouth as he stared down at the floor. His fingers stopped moving; he pulled his hand away from the table and placed both hands on his hips. He rocked forward, peering at Trevelyn as if he could not see him quite well enough at this distance to be entirely certain he was the same witness to whom he had been listening for the last two days. Trevelyn looked uneasy. He shifted position in the chair, returning Darnell's puzzled glance with one of his own.

"I'm confused," said Darnell in a strong, clear voice as he stepped forward. "You've been testifying for the better part of two days- and with some reluctance, if I'm not mistaken."

Darnell seemed to expect an answer; Trevelyn did not know there was a question.

"I say with some reluctance, because you only agreed to become a witness for the prosecution after you were given a grant of immunity. That's true, isn't it? You were given immunity in exchange for your testimony; that is the deal you made, isn't it?"

"I was given immunity. That's true," replied Trevelyn with caution.

Darnell smiled. "So that everyone understands, immunity in this instance means that the government- Mr. Roberts- has agreed not to prosecute you, and he did this because he wants your help in prosecuting Vincent Marlowe. Does that about sum up the case?"

The suspicion in Trevelyn's eyes became more pronounced. He knew Darnell was leading up to something.

"The problem I'm having, Mr. Trevelyn- the reason for my confusion- is that I don't understand why. What possible reason would you have to demand immunity as the price of your testimony if you haven't committed a crime? Why insist on immunity from prosecution if there is nothing for which you could be punished?"

Trevelyn started to reply, but the first word came out a stutter. Darnell did not give him time to catch his breath.

"You did not commit a crime; you did nothing wrong. Unless I dozed off at some point during your testi-mony- testimony which, I must say, certainly answered the purposes of the prosecution- You've insisted that you were nothing more than the unwilling beneficiary of Marlowe's gruesome work."

Trevelyn began to protest that he had not benefited from anything Marlowe had done. Darnell stopped him with a cold, hard stare. "That's right, Mr. Trevelyn, you can't even admit that. You did nothing, did you? You committed no crime, you did nothing wrong. Marlowe murdered the boy, Marlowe murdered everyone. Marlowe, Marlowe- never you!

Or was it that you thought you needed immunity because, though you disapproved of everything that was done, you did nothing to stop it?"

Darnell raised his head as if to study Trevelyn from a different angle, to see him and what he was from a new and more critical perspective. "You did not lift a finger; you did not do a thing. Is that what you feel guilty about? That Marlowe is sitting here, on trial for his life, while you sit there, alive and with nothing more to fear because those things you now claim to find so offensive and immoral were the very things that saved your life?"

"He killed them! I had nothing to do with that!"

Darnell's thin gray eyebrows shot straight up. "Nothing to do with that?" He walked quickly to the counsel table. "You're an American citizen, correct?"

"Yes."

"But you haven't lived in this country for nearly ten years?"

"I travel around, go different places. I don't like to get too tied down," he replied with a restless gaze.

"Married?"

Trevelyn's head snapped up, a look of puzzled suspicion in his eyes. "I was."

"Was? You're divorced?"

Trevelyn stared at Darnell a moment longer, then looked away. "I'm not married anymore," he mumbled.

"I'm sorry, I could not quite hear you. You'll have to speak up."

"I'm not married anymore."

"Then you are divorced?"

"As good as."

"Then you're not?"

"I haven't seen her in years. Last I heard she was living with someone else. Divorced? I don't know, maybe. I never got papers. But then, I wasn't here," he said, folding his hands over his chest and sinking back in the chair.

Darnell seemed to be enjoying this. "You might still be married or you might not. Perhaps you can give a more definitive answer to the question of whether you have children?"

"I have two."

"They both live with their mother, do they not?"

"Yes. As I said, I move around a lot and-"

"And it would not make much difference if you didn't. They live with their mother because the court gave custody to her in that divorce you know nothing about."

Roberts was on his feet. "Your Honor, I fail to see what Mr. Trevelyn's domestic arrangements have to do with...?"

"Credibility, your Honor," Darnell asserted.

Maitland nodded. "Overruled."

"In point of fact, Mr. Trevelyn, you know all about the divorce, just as you know that you were ordered to pay child support. Isn't it true, Mr. Trevelyn, that the reason you left the country in the first place- the reason, as you put it, that you "travel around, go different places"- is to avoid that obligation? You've never paid your wife anything, have you? Not one penny in all these years to help support your own children. I'm afraid, Mr. Trevelyn, that the immunity agreement you have with the prosecution won't cover that!"

"I meant to pay, I did," insisted Trevelyn as Darnell moved from the counsel table to the far end of the jury box. "I meant to, I wanted to. But every time I got a little ahead, had enough to send, my luck seemed to go bad."

"Luck. Yes, I see. It seems to follow you everywhere, doesn't it? That was the reason you were on the Evangeline in the first place, wasn't it? Isn't that what you said? That it was an accident, a mistake?"

"And look what it cost me!" Trevelyn cried as he shoved out in front of him the empty knotted pant leg where his foot should have been.

"And look what it cost some twenty others!" retorted Darnell, an ominous look in his eyes. "You had, if I'm not mistaken, a certain responsibility for what happened to them, didn't you? No, Mr. Trevelyn, don't protest. Just answer my questions and we'll let the jury decide whether you acted the way you should have."

"I'm sure he would answer your questions," interjected Roberts with a droll smile, "if you were ever to ask one."

With a tip of his forehead, Darnell took the point. "An excellent suggestion. Now, Mr. Trevclyn, let us begin with this: you were hired on as a member of the crew, correct?"

"Yes."

"Hired by Vincent Marlowe?"

"Yes."

"Mr. Marlowe explained to you the nature of the voyage and what your responsibilities would be?"

"He did."

"He also explained to you, along with the other members of the crew, the responsibilities that each would have in the event of an emergency? Not only explained it, but put you through regular and repeated drills so that there would be no question of where you were to go and what you were to do if something should happen?"

"We knew the routine; we practiced it."

"And one of the things you practiced as part of the lifeboat drill was to move as quickly as possible to a lifeboat- one of the Zodiacs or one of the inflatable rubber rafts- and make it ready, correct?"

Trevelyn seemed to shrink inside himself. His eyes went blank, his face grew pale. He stared at Darnell and did not answer.

"And not just to any one of them, but the one to which you were assigned. I don't mean assigned as a passenger, but assigned as the crew member in charge- because without a member of the crew, someone who knew how to handle a Zodiac or a rubber raft, the passengers would not have a chance. You had such an assignment, did you not, Mr. Trevelyn?"

Again there was no answer, just that barren stare.

"But you did not do what you were supposed to do, what you had been trained to do. You did not go to the lifeboat you were supposed to take charge of. In your panic, in your fear, you forgot everything except your own survival.

That's why you ripped the canvas off the Zodiac that- as you would have remembered if you had not been scared out of your wits- was filled with cargo and could not be used. Isn't that the truth, Mr. Trevelyn? You panicked and, because of your panic, God knows how many people died!"

"I didn't, I swear I-"

"You were one of the survivors, picked up in the life-boat forty days after the Evangeline went down. But that was not the only boat that got away, was it, Mr. Trevelyn? There was a second one as well- a rubber raft- wasn't there?"

Trevelyn's head jerked back as if he had been struck a blow. His hands curled around the arms of the witness chair, his nails digging into it. His eyes were wild, frantic. "It wasn't panic- I swear it wasn't. There just wasn't time!"

"But there was enough time for the other boat to get away- time that you wasted!" cried Darnell, thrusting out his chin. "Tell us, Mr. Trevelyn, if you would: what happened to that raft, the one that could have held at least eight people, the one that was your responsibility? How many of the people in it survived? How many of them were rescued at sea?"

"None that I know of."

"None that you know of. That raft was never seen again, was it?" As if he had done with the whole thing, finished with the witness, Darnell returned to the counsel table and sat down. He stared at the ceiling, the way he often did when a witness was being examined by the other side.

"There wasn't time," said Darnell, rolling the phrase off his tongue as if it held a meaning deeper than he had originally thought. "There wasn't time to get to the raft where you were supposed to be in charge. But if there wasn't time to go directly to that one, how did you have time to get to the Zodiac? Yes, of course, because it must have been closer. But after you discovered that that lifeboat would not work, you still had time to get to a second one, the one in which you were found. How do you explain that?"

Trevelyn denied it. "I didn't go to any other boat. There wasn't time. The Evangeline was going down. The

storm was awful- the storm from Hell. I was swept overboard, and I don't know what happened after that. I don't
know who it was that pulled me from the sea."

"Yes, I forgot. You don't remember what happened
after the Evangeline sank." Darnell rapped his knuckles on
the table and stood up. "But others do, Mr. Trevelyn," he
said, his voice a warning. "It isn't likely they'll ever forget."

Darnell began to pace back and forth, a few steps one
way, a few steps back, moving more rapidly with each step
he took. "You're under oath, Mr. Trevelyn; this is a court of
law. A man stands accused of murder, a man who saved your
life. This is your chance, your only chance, to tell the truth.
You were in a panic, as afraid as you have ever been in your
life. Everyone can understand that. You made a mistake-
you went to the wrong boat. You expected to find it ready
to lower away; you found it filled with things that had no
business being there. The storm was so ferocious- the wind
howling all around you, the waves as tall as buildings crashing down over your head- you knew you were going to die.
Then you saw it, your only chance, the lifeboat, the one with
Marlowe in it- and you jumped!"

"I was thrown overboard. I don't know who pulled me
out of the water and into the boat."

Darnell stopped in his tracks and shot him a withering glance. "You jumped, which is how you broke your
wrist- you landed on your arm. You jumped into a lifeboat
that already had too many people, a lifeboat that, without
Marlowe's skillful management, would have gone down the
same way the Evangeline had."

"No, I-"

"The lifeboat had too many people, and there were
others, floundering in the water, crying out for help, grab-
bing onto it in a last desperate attempt to save themselves. A
choice had to be made: either everyone was going to drown,
or those trying to get in would have to be stopped and some
of those who had gotten in would have to be thrown out.
That's what you did, Mr. Trevelyn! How could you forget
it? How could anyone forget that, hitting drowning men and

women with an oar to keep them away, pushing others out? You did that, Mr. Trevelyn! Why won't you admit it?"

"We all would have drowned!" cried Trevelyn in mortal anguish. "We had no other choice! Don't you know they would have done the same to us? There were hands and arms everywhere, everyone fighting to get in, trying to force the others out. And the storm raging all around like nothing you've ever seen, the boat thrown so high at times you thought for sure we would all be tumbled out, like water tossed out of a glass.

"There was no telling who was in, who was out, every-one hanging on to anything he could grab. The ones that started, the ones who got there first- don't think they were the ones who were there at the end, when that hellish storm was finally finished with us and those of us still breathing could finally collapse!"

"It was every man for himself, then. Is that what you are saying- now that you can remember?"

Trevelyn sat back with a shudder. "You blame me for trying to forget that awful night?"

"No, Mr. Trevelyn," said Darnell in a stern, unforgiving voice. "I blame you for a good deal more than that. The boy, among other things. Why don't we start with him? You testified that he was sick and that was the reason he was chosen. Is that still your story, now that your memory seems to have in some measure been restored?"

"Sick? He was dying. Anyone could see that. He didn't have more than a few days left."

"He became sick, or rather it became obvious he was dying, some ten days or two weeks after the Evangeline sank?"

"Somewhere around that time, yes."

"I take it, then, that in the first few days at least, he did not appear to be any worse off than any of the others?"

"I suppose that's true."

"And just so we can all be certain about this, this boy we are talking about was not some eighteen or nineteen-year-old, but a young boy- thirteen, fourteen ...something like that?"

"No more than fourteen at the outside. And not very big for his age, either," Trevelyn volunteered.

"So when you describe what happened right after the lifeboats got away as a brutal fight for survival, as 'everyone fighting to get in, trying to force the others out,' that was just a turn of phrase, a mere expression that you did not mean to be taken literally?"

"But I did mean what I said. That's what happened, everyone trying to save themselves," insisted Trevelyn.

"Even the boy, even Billy? This young boy, fourteen, if that, small for his age, fighting off the others in the hope of survival?"

Trevelyn's face grew hot. He slapped his palm on the arm of the chair. "No, of course not. He couldn't have done anything but hang on."

"And what about the women? What of Samantha Wilcox, what of Cynthia Grimes- two of the survivors? But there were more than two women at the beginning, weren't there, Mr. Trevelyn? Or did that fact slip your mind as well? There were four women, Mr. Trevelyn. What about them? Are they to be included in that struggle to the death? Is that how they ended up in that lifeboat, because like you they fought with all the strength they had to keep the others out?"

The eyes of Aaron Trevelyn became a vacant stare. The silence in the courtroom became hot and oppressive, the air thick with blind anger and nameless fear.

"So the boy had not harmed anyone, had not saved his life at the cost of another's- and yet he was the first to be chosen, the first to be sacrificed so that others could live. But this was your idea, wasn't it, Mr. Trevelyn? You were the first to say that it had to be done, that the only way any of you could survive was if someone else died."

"No, I didn't do it! He killed him, not me!" Trevelyn exclaimed, bolting forward to point at Marlowe. "If it was my idea, why would he have done it?"

Darnell nodded, paused, then nodded again. "Yes, you're right, Mr. Trevelyn," he said in a quiet, thoughtful voice. "You did not kill him; you did not put a knife in his heart. Were you surprised when it happened, surprised at what the boy did?"

Trevelyn was confused. "I'm not sure…"

"Surprised that he did not resist?"

Trevelyn tried to dismiss it. "He was dying."

"That was not my question. The boy did not resist, did he?"

"No."

"Which reminds me…You did see it happen, didn't you?"

"Yes. I said-"

"And you did nothing to stop it? Of course, why would you? You were as hungry as the others were. He did not resist, "Darnell went on, raising his voice over Trevelyn's attempt to protest. "He did not resist because Marlowe spoke to the boy, told him what was going to happen, and why it had to be him. Isn't that what Marlowe did?"

"I would not know," replied Trevelyn with a cold eyed stare.

"And isn't that why Marlowe covered the boy's mouth and nose- not to stop him crying out, but to do what he could to ease his passing?"

CHAPTER TWELVE

The prosecution had kept Aaron Trevelyn on the stand for a day and a half; the defense kept him there for two. Working entirely from memory, William Darnell quoted back at the witness answers he had given to Roberts and dared him to try to explain their inconsistency. Even more powerful in its effect was the way Darnell could make the things Trevelyn had not said seem more important, and more damaging, than what he had.

"When you were asked by Mr. Roberts about the first person to die after the boy, you said that she was 'stabbed in the throat?'"

"Yes."

Darnell placed his hand inside his suit jacket, adjusting his tie. "That was Helena Green, the actress- isn't that what you said?"

"That's right."

"And that was Marlowe's decision?"

"He made all the decisions."

"And Marlowe killed her. He 'shoved the knife into her jugular' is how, I think, you put it. Is this still your testimony, that Vincent Marlowe killed Helena Green and that it was his decision to do so?"

Trevelyn tried his hand at logic. "If he killed her, he must have decided to do it."

Ever so slightly, Darnell raised his chin. "Yes, because you also said, 'Not that it was ever put to a vote, or anything like that.' Is that what you meant? That no one else had a hand in that decision, or in any of the other decisions?"

"Marlowe was in charge."

"Yes, I remember you said that too. 'Marlowe made all the decisions. He was in charge.' Very good."

Darnell stood next to Marlowe and put his hand on the other man's shoulder. "Marlowe was in charge. Marlowe made all the decisions. Still, there were discussions, were there not, about what should be done?"

"None that I remember." Trevelyn lowered his eyes and began to fidget with his hands. "None that would have counted."

"Because Marlowe was in charge? Because Marlowe made all the decisions?"

"That's right, he did."

"But you also said- when Mr. Roberts asked whether the reason Helena Green was chosen was because, like the boy, she was sick- that you were all dying. You said, and I think in exactly these words, 'The only question was whether we would all die together, or die one at a time so that the ones left could live a little longer.' Isn't that what you said?"

"If you say so."

Darnell let go of Marlowe's shoulder and moved away from the counsel table until he was almost directly in front of the witness. "I do say so, Mr. Trevelyn. I remember it quite distinctly because it struck me as being in such utter conflict with your insistence that it was Marlowe, and only Marlowe, who was in charge."

Trevelyn's only response was a look of blank incomprehension.

"There were fourteen people when that lifeboat started out, correct?" asked Darnell with a show of impatience.

"Including me."

"Ten days, perhaps as much as two weeks, passed before someone decided the boy had to die?"

"Marlowe decided!" Trevelyn exclaimed with great force.

Darnell held his ground. "Ten days, perhaps two weeks- is that correct?"

"That's what I said."

"Ah!" Darnell sighed in relief. "You do remember! I'm sure we're all quite thankful!"

"Your Honor!" protested Roberts, rising with a much-put-upon expression on his face.

"Counsel's sarcasm wears a bit thin."

"The selective fantasies the witness calls his memory wear a bit heavy," Darnell shot back.

"That will be enough, Mr. Darnell," said Homer Maitland, not amused.

"My apologies, your Honor," said Darnell, who immediately turned back to the witness. "Where was I? Oh, yes- out there ten days, two weeks; dreadful weather, worse conditions; no more food, no more water. There must have been conversations, some discussion, about what you were all to do. Or is it your testimony that thirteen of you, crowded together so close there was no room to lie down, simply waited, mute and uninterested, to hear what Marlowe might decide?

"You're out on the high seas," Darnell went on, working himself to a fever pitch, "and every one of you decided that you would not decide anything, that whatever Marlowe said, that would be all right?"

"I didn't say no one talked about it," replied Trevelyn.

Darnell seized on his words as if they proved everything he wanted. "That's right, you never said that. In fact, what you said was something really quite different. You said, and correct me if you think I have it wrong, 'There were one or two who said we shouldn't do it'- you were referring to the killing of the boy- 'that it was better to die than live like that.' And then you added- immediately afterwards, if I remember right- 'but most didn't see it that way.'"

Darnell cocked his head, a grim, doubtful smile on his lips. "How did most of the others see it, Mr. Trevelyn? Tell us that."

"They thought there wasn't any choice, that it was the only way to survive."

"Yes, exactly. Though when you were answering Mr. Roberts's questions, the way you put it, I believe, was that 'They wanted to live. Nothing else mattered.' Now, the question I have for you, Mr. Trevelyn, is which side were you on? Were you one of the 'one or two' who thought it was better to die, or were you part of what appears to be the great majority who thought it better to live, no matter what harsh measures that might require?"

Under Darnell's relentless stare, Trevelyn looked down at his hands.

"I take it from your silence, Mr. Trevelyn, that you were not among the dissenters," said Darnell, as he turned away and began to pace back and forth, gathering his thoughts. "In other words, Mr. Trevelyn, there were discussions about what should be done, and everyone still alive was involved in them. Isn't that correct?"

"There was talk, yes, but-"

"But it was 'never put to a vote'- is that what you were about to say?"

"We didn't vote on anything."

"But vote is exactly what you did. No, I understand; there was no show of hands, there were no ballots. There was no need. Everyone knew what was necessary, what had to be done if any of you were to survive, and all but one or two of you agreed to do it. Isn't that what happened, Mr. Trevelyn? Was there not an agreement among you that someone had to die so that the others could live?"

"Yes, we all understood that," admitted Trevelyn with a wrathful look. "But that wasn't the same thing as deciding who should die- or who should kill them!"

"Because Marlowe was in charge?"

"Yes, that's what I keep saying!"

"You were the only other member of the crew?"

"If you don't count the boy."

"Yes, the boy," said Darnell. He bent his head at a thoughtful angle. "The first one who died; the first one Marlowe killed." He turned away from the witness and looked straight at the jury. "The one Marlowe killed in full agreement with you and all the others."

"Marlowe chose! Marlowe decided!"

Darnell wheeled around, his eyes blazing. "That isn't what you said a minute ago: you said that there 'were one or two who said we shouldn't do it'. We, Mr. Trevelyn- that 'we shouldn't do it'. Not Marlowe shouldn't do it- we!"

"I said the boy was dying; I said he didn't have more

than a day or two left. He was going to die anyway, no one could save him- but he could save us."

"And that was what most of the others thought should be done? It wasn't just you?"

"I told you from the beginning. It wasn't me."

"Because it was what everyone, or almost everyone, had decided had to be done?"

"Yes, that's the way it was. That was the only choice, that or death."

Darnell scratched his head, and then shoved his hands deep into his pockets and stared intently at the floor. "I want to make absolutely certain that I understand what you are telling us. You had been out there in those dreadful conditions, starving, nearly dead, the boy worse off than the others. You know that you- and by that I mean all of you- can't last another day. You know that there is only one thing you can do, and everyone, or almost everyone, agrees that it has to be done, and that someone has to do it. It was not just your idea; it was everyone's idea. Everyone was in agreement. I'm not trying to put words in your mouth. Is that what happened?"

"Yes, it's what I've said."

"So it wasn't Marlowe's idea to kill the boy? At least, not his idea alone?"

"I never said it was."

Darnell smiled as if they were in complete agreement. He lowered his eyes to watch, as if it were the mirror image of the way his mind worked, one shoe slide slightly ahead of the other. "Marlowe, then, was doing what the others wanted?" he asked, his eyes still fixed on the floor, the smile- shrewd, canny- still on his face.

Trevelyn rubbed his leg as if he were trying to restore circulation to a part of him that no longer existed. "There wasn't any choice- that's what I said," he replied, with a vituperative glance out of the corner of his eye.

Darnell pushed his foot another half inch forward. The smile grew faint, then fell away. He raised his eyes and squared his shoulders. "There was an agreement," he said in the loud, clear voice that announces a fact. "The agreement, made among you all, was that someone had to die; an agreement binding on all of you, however you may have felt. That's true, is it not?"

With a show of impatience, Trevelyn shrugged his shoulders and threw up his hands. "I don't know what you're getting at. I told you we all knew there wasn't any choice, that-"

"Yes, but you also said there were 'one or two who said we shouldn't do it, that it was better to die than live like that'. But they didn't die, did they? At least not then. I see you're still confused. Let me ask the same thing a different way. You've already testified that after the boy was killed the rest of you survived on his blood and flesh, correct?"

"Yes, I admit it. We did."

"All of you- including the "one or two" who had been of the opinion that the boy should not be killed?"

Trevelyn understood. "All of us."

"In other words, Mr. Trevelyn, and the point I'm trying to make is really quite simple, there was a discussion- perhaps not all at once, perhaps spread over days- and then, when things were truly desperate, a decision on the question. Not everyone was in agreement, but almost everyone was, and what the majority decided, the others- the 'one or two' who had been against the killing- accepted. They went along with what the others wanted, as evidenced by what they did after the killing. Isn't that what happened?"

Grudgingly, Trevelyn assented, and as soon as he did Darnell fired his next question. "In other words, the decision was made by everyone, all of you, and not by Marlowe alone?"

"But he's the one who did it! He killed the boy- no one else. He's the one that killed them all!"

"Which brings us to another question you haven't answered, Mr. Trevelyn. Why did Marlowe kill the boy? Why did Marlowe kill any of them?"

"Why did he...?" Trevelyn sputtered with rage. "To live, to survive- he didn't want to die any more than the rest of us!"

Darnell's chin snapped up. "Then perhaps you would be good enough to explain why, when the boy was chosen, Vincent Marlowe- the man you accuse!- tried to take his place? Perhaps you can explain why this man you call a killer, this man who saved your life, was willing to be the first to die?"

There was a kind of silent roar in the courtroom, a sense of outrage at what, if it were true, Trevelyn had withheld.

"It's true, isn't it, Mr. Trevelyn? Vincent Marlowe did not want the boy to die, and he was willing to give his own life to prevent it!"

Trevelyn shouted back, "What he said, what he thought- how would I know what he really meant? He killed him, that's all I know- stabbed him in the heart just the way I said he did. That isn't something I'm ever likely to forget, the way the blood shot out, the way everyone was so desperate to get it."

"Including you!"

"It was that or die!"

"Answer my question, Mr. Trevelyn!"

"What question is that?"

"He was willing to die in place of the boy?"

Trevelyn leaned forward, his forearm resting at an awkward angle on the leg that was still whole. "You're forgetting something," he said with a brutal grin.

"Enlighten me."

The grin cut deeper across Trevelyn's mouth, twisting it into a vengeful scowl. "You're forgetting that he still did it. The boy is dead, isn't he? And Marlowe, he's still here. The boy is the one got killed, not him!"

"But that was my next question, Mr. Trevelyn. Perhaps now you'll answer it. Why did the boy die? Why didn't Marlowe take his place? Have you forgotten?"

The grin retreated. "I just told you," said Trevelyn as he sank back in the chair. "All I know is what I saw. I don't know what he was thinking."

Darnell stared at him, incredulous. "Are you saying- is it your sworn testimony...? No, never mind. Answer this: whether or not Marlowe offered to die in the boy's place, why did he kill him? Why Marlowe and not someone else?"

Coolly belligerent, Trevelyn folded his arms together and turned his shoulder. "Marlowe was in charge. He decided."

"That seems odd, doesn't it?" Darnell waited until Trevelyn's eyes came back to him. "Odd that after everyone, including you, decided someone had to die; odd that after everyone, including you, decided that it should be the boy- odd that, suddenly, Marlowe should be the one to decide who should kill him?

"Odder still, don't you think, that he should employ this newfound power to choose himself ? Is that what you would have done, Mr. Trevelyn, if you had had that power: chosen yourself, instead of any of the others, to kill, to murder?"

"No one wanted to! No one!"

"Exactly Mr. Trevelyn! Exactly! No one wanted to. There you all were, nearly dead, only one way to live and yet no one willing to do what had to be done. And so you chose the only person you could insist had that obligation, the responsibility to do everything necessary to save the rest of you: Marlowe, the captain, the only one who could not argue that it had to be someone else!"

"And he did it! He killed him, he killed them all!"

"Because he had to, because it was the only way you and the others could survive. But tell us again- how was the boy chosen? Why was he the first?"

"He was sick, dying; he didn't have much time left! I told you that! How many times do I have to tell you again?"

"Until you tell the truth! He was dying, you say?"

"Yes!"

"Then why would Marlowe want to take his place? Why would he be willing to die if, no matter what he did, the boy was going to die anyway?"

"You're the one says that's what Marlowe wanted."

"And I have a witness who confirms it, a witness who will testify that you knew it, too. Hugo Offenbach has a rather different story from the one you tell."

Red with anger, Trevelyn nearly bolted from the chair. He held onto the arm of it to keep from falling forward. "Offenbach? I wouldn't wonder," he said, gesticulating wildly with his hand, his eyes gone crazy. "After what Marlowe did for him!"

Darnell hesitated, a thousand questions crowding incoherently in his brain. He had already broken at least a dozen times the lawyer's rule against asking questions to which the answer is not already known. The rules were not made for a case like this. What harm could there be in doing it again? "And just what did Marlowe do for Hugo Offenbach that would make Mr. Offenbach do anything but tell the truth?"

"He took his name off, that's what he did. He wouldn't let him be included. Everyone else was part of it, but not the two of them, not Marlowe and Offenbach- they were safe."

"Safe? What do you mean? Took his name off what?"

"The names of those who could be chosen; the ones who each time we needed to, would be killed."

CHAPTER THIRTEEN

"Stop talking," insisted Summer Blaine in the practiced voice of a physician. "I need to listen."

Darnell laughed in protest, and then submitted.

"Take a deep breath and hold it," she instructed, pressing the cold stethoscope against his skin. She moved it a little lower. "Again."

When she was done, she sat next to him on the sofa, wearing the same look of benevolent concern he had so often seen before.

"Did they teach you that in medical school?" he asked before she could speak. "That warm, maternal look that makes the patient think that, whatever is wrong with him, the doctor can fix it?" Darnell finished buttoning his shirt. He went over to the window of the Pacific Heights apartment where he had lived since the year he and his wife were married, and watched the sunlight penetrate the morning fog.

The Golden Gate seemed to float inside a thick white cloud that rose up from the gray water of the bay. The bridge had almost come to measure his existence. There were not many people left who could remember when it was being built; fewer still who had been living here in San Francisco, watching while it was being finished. Nearly all the friends of his youth were gone now, but the bridge carried him back to a past that seemed all the more vivid as the future became less a question of the things he could still do than of the time he had left.

"You have to take care of yourself," said Summer Blaine, kindly and without reproach for his repeated failures to follow her advice. Darnell heard her words, or rather the sound they made, the sweet inflection of her voice. He heard the words, and behind them the hope, the wish, that he take those few precautions that might grant them the time to do some of the things they wanted. And behind the wish, he grasped the warnings in the half- worried looks and the soft, whispered reminders about his medication and the need for sleep. He did most of what she asked, or tried to, not because he believed it would make any great difference- he was too old to believe much in medicine or science- but because it was one of the few ways he had to indulge her need to feel useful.

"I'm glad you were able to come in for the weekend. There are too many things going on with this trial for me to leave the city, but I know how much you have to do, and…"

"When you said you couldn't come home…" She put the stethoscope back in the black bag and took out a syringe.

"Do I really have to?" he asked as she pushed up his sleeve and, with a cotton swab, briskly rubbed a spot of alcohol on his arm. She laughed as he grimaced, laughed as she called him a coward, laughed again when, with boyish defiance, he bravely admitted it.

"I always hated that," he muttered, wincing at the way it stung. Glad it was over, he pulled down his shirtsleeve. "And you promise that with just one injection a week I'll have the virility of a twenty-year-old?"

"We have a pill for that now."

"There seems to be a pill for everything now," he muttered to himself. His eyes narrowed into a shrewd, thoughtful stare. "Except how to solve a moral dilemma."

She knew he meant Marlowe and the trial. It was all he had thought about, all he had talked about, for months. "The papers say you were brilliant."

"I'll tell you how brilliant I was. When I started the cross-examination of Aaron Trevelyn, the jury hated Marlowe; by the time I finished, the jury hated them both. I'm not sure that should be counted as much of an achievement."

Darnell plopped down in an easy chair next to the fireplace. The living room was enormous. Three sets of French doors led out to a balcony with a view that stretched all around the bay. Persian rugs were scattered over the gleaming hardwood floor. A painting by Manet hung above the fireplace, a wedding gift from his wife's mother. The carpets, the paintings, the furnishings- none of it had been changed, none of it had been moved, in the years since his wife's death. The room had the shabby gentility of a happily remembered past.

"It's a strange business, the law. You remember that famous line of Dickens's? 'The law is an ass.' A more acute observation would have been, 'The law is a fraud.' Aaron Trevelyn is the prosecution's main witness, the only one of the six survivors who talked, the only one who told Roberts what he knew. Leave aside for the moment whether his testimony- what he said on direct- was accurate; leave aside all questions of bias and distortion. What was almost the first thing I did with him? How did I set about to raise questions in the mind of the jury about his honesty and credibility? I did what any young lawyer- or for that matter any third year law student- would have done: impeach the witness out of his own mouth; have him say something you can then show to be a lie."

With a distant look, Darnell shook his head. "He lied about his divorce; he lied about child support. But all that means is that he has a legal debt that he has not paid. And from that everyone assumes he must be a liar and a cheat, someone dishonest. But what do we really know about him?"

Darnell looked at Summer, who had taken the chair opposite. "What do we know about his wife? Did he come home one day and find her in bed with another man? Did she tell him that her children- the ones he now has a legal obligation to support- were fathered by someone else? There are a thousand reasons why he might have run off to Europe and tried to start a different life, but all the jury knows is that he has not done what a court said he had to do and that he tried to lie about it."

"You sound like you feel sorry for him- but, like you said, he's the prosecution's main witness. What choice did you have?"

"There wasn't any choice, I know that; no choice

because everything is limited by the rules, which is why this case is so damn confounding. We are in a court of law, trying a case to a jury, bound by the rules of evidence, rules which allow me to show that Trevelyn lied but do not allow him to show why he might have had a good reason not to tell the truth. Which is another way of saying," cried Darnell as he sprang from the chair and, with a burst of energy, began to walk around the sunlit room, "that he isn't allowed to tell the truth, because whatever the law says, the truth sometimes has to conceal itself in a lie."

Throwing open the French doors, Darnell listened to the sounds of the city drifting up from below. Somewhere out on the bay, out towards the Pacific, a steamship headed into the broken fog, its whistle blowing a mournful lament for the journey that lay ahead.

"But do I feel sorry for Trevelyn? I feel sorry for them all, the living more than the dead. And not just the survivors- I feel sorry for all of us, everyone involved. This is a terrible case, even worse than I had imagined. I knew it the moment I saw the jurors' eyes."

With her legs curled under her, Summer Blaine lay her head back in the warm luxury of the overstuffed chair. She watched him with a languid gaze, marveling at the sharp acuity of his mind and the way that, even now, at an age when most men would have been long since retired, this case had become his sole obsession. All their talk of an idle retirement was a sweet narcotic, a harmless lie that let them both pretend to want the kind of normal lives that would have bored them silly. She asked him questions, not because she had any great interest in the answer, though the answers were often interesting enough, but for the simple pleasure of listening to him talk. The voice that had seduced who knew how many juries, had long ago seduced her.

"What about the juror's eyes? What did you see in them? Something you had not seen before?"

He leaned against the open doors, watching as the Golden Gate became each minute more luminescent. "When I started out, all those years ago, juries were more easily shocked. In the first murder case I tried, the prosecution passed around photographs of the victim, a woman who had been shot. She lay face down in a pool of blood. Several of the women on the jury had to force themselves to look; none of the jurors, man or woman, would look for very long.

"Those photographs were all in black and white; there was nothing that by today's standards would be considered the least bit graphic. It was not just what they saw that they found shocking and offensive: it was the fact of death, the fact of death by violence that upset them. It was the very idea that a woman had been murdered that made some of them refuse even to look at the defendant until much later in the trial.

"All that has changed. It is practically what we live for now: death, murder. It is not enough that someone dies; we have to see the way it happened, we clamor for all the grue-some details. Sex and violence- we're a nation of voyeurs. That's what I saw in the eyes of those twelve otherwise decent people sitting in that jury box: the descriptions of what happened out there, how those six survived, the stories of death and cannibalism- they're mesmerized, entranced; they can't get enough of it. That's what I saw in their eyes: blood lust."

Darnell turned from the Golden Gate and the fog that was dancing away back to Summer Blaine and the smile that, when he saw it, made him feel suddenly self conscious "I'm always trying this case, aren't I? That must have sounded like a summation."

"No," she said with a laugh. "But you can't stop now. Tell me what you've decided."

"Decided?"

"Everything you ever see in a trial makes a difference in what you do. If I've learned anything, I've learned that. If the jury is enthralled with the story of what happened, if we're all the voyeurs you think we are, you're not just going to regret what we've become- you're going to use it. How?"

He nodded with a kind of dutiful smile, as he often did when he heard her tell him what he really thought, and

then teased her with his eyes. "I have no idea," he admitted
with a candor. that was both abrupt and disarming. "No idea
at all. I know a great deal more than when the trial started-
mainly because of what Hugo Offenbach told me- but it isn't
enough. I'm still feeling my way, guessing at a lot of it."

At the mention of Hugo Offenbach, Summer's eyes
flashed with curiosity. "What was he like...after everything
that's happened? Will he ever play again? The papers say
he's become a total recluse. He doesn't go out anywhere; he
doesn't see anyone."

"Will he ever play again? In public? No, I don't think
so," said Darnell as he moved across the room to the chair
where she sat waiting. He touched her forehead and felt
better for the warmth. Then, driven by some restless urge, he
began to walk around again. "Trevelyn has finished testifying. Now he's going to get rich. Every publisher in New
York wants his story: the cannibal with a clear conscience. A
movie deal can't be far away."

"A nation of voyeurs," said Summer Blaine, repeating
Darnell's earlier observation, agreeing with it.

"Trevelyn feels the need to justify himself before
the world. Offenbach knows he can't. He may be the most
remarkable man I've ever met," said Darnell, growing more
intense. "He's grateful to Marlowe for saving his life, but
he would have been more grateful had Marlowe left him for
dead.

"He knows what Marlowe did and, more importantly,
he understands why he did it. In his judgment, and it's a
judgment with which I cannot disagree, Marlowe is both
tragic and heroic. He admires Marlowe's strength of character, his will, his moral courage- all the things that made
Marlowe think that whatever else he did, he had to save
Offenbach's life- but now Offenbach has to live with the
shame of what he, Offenbach, did not want done."

A look of irritation, directed not at Summer Blaine,
but at himself, filled his eyes as he wandered aimlessly
from one place to another until he suddenly stopped, looked
straight at her and threw up his hands. "Life is full of splen-

did ironies, isn't it? Marlowe and Offenbach, the only two who were willing to die, the only two Marlowe made certain would not be killed.

"Yes, what Trevelyn said is true. Marlowe was willing to let all the others die, willing to kill them himself, but not the two of them: Offenbach because he is a genius, Marlowe because he was the only one who could save the others. That is what is so remarkable, so extraordinary. Offenbach understands it, understands Marlowe's motive, but how am I supposed to convince a jury that what Marlowe did was right?

"It's easier to make the case that Marlowe had to live. No one else could control that boat; no one else knew what to do. Trevelyn, the only other member of the crew, had a broken wrist and was in constant pain. No, Marlowe had to live: without him none of the others stood a chance. But Hugo Offenbach? He was an old man compared to the rest of them, frail and in ill health. He had just had a heart attack; he might have died at any minute. Even if he had been in perfect health, even if he had been twenty years younger, why should his life be spared? Why should his name have been kept off the list of those who might die so the others might live? Because Hugo Offenbach is a genius, the greatest violinist in the world. That was Marlowe's reason. It is the one thing he seems proud of, the only thing that brings some light into his eyes- that he saved Hugo Offenbach and what Offenbach does for the world."

Darnell shook his head in wonder. "Poor Marlowe. All the world will see is a criminal failure to treat everyone the same, equally entitled to the same chance. Marlowe has lived his life at sea; he never suffered the disadvantages of a formal education. All he sees is the gift that Offenbach brings, a gift so rare that only a coward or a fool would fail to do whatever he had to do to save it. I'm afraid all the jury will see is someone who thinks that some lives are more important than others."

"Offenbach knows this?" asked Summer Blaine when Darnell fell into a long silence. At first he did not hear her as he thought about what seemed a hopeless dilemma. He noticed that the last wisps of fog had vanished from around the Golden Gate and that the sounds from the street below seemed sharper. "He knows this...?" She repeated in a gentle reminder. Darnell nodded slowly.

"You can't tell by looking at him, you won't hear it in his voice- but Hugo Offenbach knows his life is over. He was revered by everyone, and now...he knows what they think. He'll never play again- I'm sure of it. I suspect the last time any of us will see him in public is when he testifies at the trial. He's determined to do that now, to tell the truth about what happened- to do what he can to save Marlowe's life. It may be the only hope Marlowe has. I suppose I should say the only hope I have, because Marlowe doesn't seem to care."

Sitting down, Darnell began to talk about where they might go that evening for dinner. Aware that what he had said must sound depressing, he made an effort to break the mood, to bring things back to normal, but a few minutes later he was talking about it again.

"What happened out there, what's happened to all of them, but especially Marlowe and Offenbach; the way that after the Evangeline went down everything else that happened seemed almost foreordained; the sheer necessity by which each thing followed another; the way all of it has ruined their lives- only someone like Melville could describe it all."

Summer Blaine twisted her thin, angular face to the side and asked with her eyes for an explanation.

"When I started this case, I read everything I could get my hands on about shipwrecks and survivors and what they did to stay alive. The most intriguing story, and the one that offered the most interesting parallel, was the sinking of the Essex, a Nantucket whaler, sunk by a sperm whale in November of 1820. That was what Melville used, the idea of the ship sunk by a whale, when he wrote Moby-Dick. But he did not use the rest of it. Three of the whaleboats got away. One of them disappeared, but in the other two, bodies were eaten. Eight people had been killed, each of them chosen by a method similar to the one used by Marlowe and the others. Eight people killed and only two survivors. There is another parallel, more eerie than the first. The captain of the Essex offered to take the place of one of the victims, a boy, but the boy refused."

CHAPTER FOURTEEN

In the most important part of its case the prosecution had led with its strength, Aaron Trevelyn, the only survivor willing to talk. But whom would Michael Roberts call next? He could not call Marlowe- only Darnell could do that- and after what the defense had claimed about Hugo Offenbach during Trevelyn's cross-examination, there did not seem much likelihood that Roberts would call him. There were only three other survivors, only three other eyewitnesses to what Marlowe had done: the actor, James DeSantos, whose face was known everywhere, and two women, whose names had only become famous because of the trial. Cynthia Grimes had disappeared, gone into hiding somewhere in Europe. No one had heard from her; no one knew exactly where she was. That left DeSantos and Wilcox.

Which would Roberts call first? If you have three witnesses, you put the weakest one in the middle because the things that come at the beginning and the end are what most people remember. Roberts had started with Trevelyn and the jury had hated him; there was a chance that the jury would not have any greater love for DeSantos. Better to call him next and then finish with a woman who, whatever you thought about her religious beliefs, seemed not to have forgotten what it meant to be civilized. Trevelyn, DeSantos, Wilcox- that was the order Darnell would have done it. But Roberts did something else: he called Samantha Wilcox. Darnell wondered what Roberts knew that he did not.

There was no doubt that Samantha Wilcox was a devout Catholic; she had been educated in some of the best Catholic schools in Europe. With a husband she seldom saw, and then only on occasions which can best be described as ceremonial, she let herself be loved by other men- but always with the knowledge that divorce was unthinkable. Darnell was intrigued by her, and somewhat disconcerted by his own reaction. The claim that angels had come to her rescue, an idea he would have dismissed as a crazed delusion had it been made by some redneck Southern Baptist, carried a certain persuasive charm when it came from the mouth of an intelligent, mainline Eastern Catholic. Tall and elegant, her every movement graceful and at times almost artistic, Samantha Wilcox had the well bred habit of pausing before each answer to make certain there was not something Roberts wanted to add to the question.

"Could you tell us, Mrs. Wilcox," asked Roberts delicately, "what you remember about the decision that was made- the decision that someone would have to die so that the others could live?"

Her voice was magical, a whispered breath that entered your mind like the memory of a lost romance, the girl you always wanted, the one you knew you could never have. For a moment Darnell had the uncanny feeling that he was looking at someone he used to know.

"I remember that no one really wanted to, that it only happened when there seemed to be no other way." Samantha Wilcox looked at Roberts, her gaze steady, unwavering, unafraid of the truth.

"Was everyone in favor of doing this, or did some of you oppose it?"

"Some of us opposed it- that's true."

"And what about you, Mrs. Wilcox? How did you feel about this? Did you oppose it?"

A look of despair came into her eyes. With her right thumb she began in a slow, methodical way to rub the back of her other hand. "I was against it, yes."

"Could you tell us why? Wasn't everyone near death from thirst and starvation? Did you think it better that all of you should die than that one of you be killed?"

A smile, rueful and forgiving, crossed her fine, straight mouth. She raised her chin. "I thought everything should be left in God's hands. Whether we lived or died, whether we were rescued or abandoned to the sea- that was God's decision. No, I didn't think anyone should be killed; I didn't think we should do anything that we shouldn't."

Roberts nodded sympathetically and moved quickly to the next question. "Did you, or did anyone except Vincent Marlowe, kill anyone?"

She seemed shocked by the suggestion. "No, I couldn't have...Did any of the others? No, I don't think so, I..."

"You don't think so? Are you saying it's possible that someone other than Vincent Marlowe killed some of the people whose bodies...?"

"I didn't see anyone- Mr. Marlowe or anyone else- kill anybody. I couldn't have watched a thing like that. I didn't. You don't know what it was like out there," she added with a shudder.

"I could barely keep my eyes open; I could barely move my arms or my legs. All I could do was pray, and most of my prayers were that God would take me next."

With a searing, anguished look, she added, "My first prayer, when it started, was that He take me first. But instead, He took the boy. To spare him any more fear and torment, I suppose."

Roberts was confused. "But the boy was killed because he was about to die anyway."

"No, Mr. Roberts, the boy was killed because that's the way it came out."

"The way it came out?" asked Roberts, more confused than ever. She seemed surprised that he did not know. Then she understood that none of them knew, that no one sitting in that courtroom knew. Or almost no one. She looked at Marlowe. He had not forgotten the grim ritual they had gone through together.

"I didn't think we should do it; I didn't believe we had the right to decide who should live and who should die. God, in His infinite wisdom, takes us when and how He pleases. We didn't know what was going to happen next. There might be a ship just over the horizon, about to come into view. Mr. Marlowe believed that, too. He kept telling us not to give up hope, that the worst thing we could do was stop believing that somehow we were all going to survive, that somehow someone would find us. He kept us alive, Mr. Marlowe did. If it had not been for him, there would not be a trial, because all of us would be dead."

"But you were against it," Roberts quickly reminded her. "You did not think anyone had to be killed, or should be killed. No one could know when a ship might appear."

She gave him a dark look. "But we know now, don't we? We know that the ship that finally came, the ship that rescued us, wouldn't have found anyone alive if..." She stopped herself. "You asked about the boy. He was chosen in the same way as the others. I didn't want it to happen- I told you that- but once it was decided, we had to let God choose who it would be. There were some who thought we should choose, that we should make that decision ourselves, but Mr. Marlowe agreed that if it were going to be done, there was only one way to do it. It was done by lot, Mr. Roberts, that was how it was decided, that was how that boy was chosen: we drew straws. I hoped- I prayed- that I would go first."

"So it was a drawing? A matter of chance who was selected, who the next victim would be? But then why would one of the other survivors say that the boy was chosen because he was sick and dying?"

"Trevelyn?" she said with contempt. "Is that who you mean? I imagine because he would like everyone to think that so long as the boy was going to die anyway, it was not really a killing, that it was not really a sin- when he's the one who first suggested that some of us should die so the others could live. What he meant, of course, was that others should die so he could live. He told Mr. Marlowe- I heard him say it- that the members of the crew had to stick together, that the passengers were expendable, that without the crew to handle the boat none of the passengers could survive anyway. Mr. Marlowe would not hear of it."

Roberts seized on this. "Would not hear of it for Trevelyn- only for himself!"

"That isn't quite true in any sense, Mr. Roberts, and in one sense it isn't true at all. When the boy was chosen, Mr. Marlowe wanted to take his place. No, it's true- I swear it!

You didn't see the awful look on his face when it happened. I did, and I can assure you, Mr. Roberts, that I'll never forget it. He would have taken the boy's place, all right- there isn't the slightest doubt- and done it gladly. Why he didn't, I'm not quite sure I understand. The boy wouldn't let him, but that wouldn't have been enough to stop him. I think perhaps, despite all the encouragement he kept giving us, that he had given up, that he didn't believe that there was any chance of rescue, or that any of us would survive. Perhaps he decided finally that he should spare the boy more suffering. I don't know. What I do know is that Mr. Marlowe was not afraid of death."

"Whatever Vincent Marlowe did or did not think," said Roberts, eager to move on, "this drawing you described- was this the method used each time someone new was selected?"

"Yes, it was."

"And you drew along with the others?"

"Yes, but each time I lost."

"Lost? Oh, yes, you wanted to die," said Roberts in a voice that seemed troubled and remote.

"I wasn't brave like Mr. Marlowe and some of the others," she said with a modest, faraway glance. "All I could do was pray for deliverance."

Roberts stood at the end of the jury box. The fingers of his right hand rested lightly on the railing. He looked at Samantha Wilcox as if he owed her an apology. "I have to ask you something that I know will be difficult. The last time this was done, the last time another person was chosen- how long was that before the White Rose came? How long before you were rescued?"

There was no response. The silence became profound. With each passing moment she seemed to slip further away, vanishing inside herself to a place where no one could follow.

"Mrs. Wilcox?" said Roberts gently.

"One day," she said finally.

"We drew lots the day before."

"And would that person- the one chosen- have lived another day and been rescued with the others?"

"Yes, I imagine he would have been."

Roberts stared at the floor, nodding solemnly. "Nothing further, your Honor," he said, and then walked slowly to his chair at the counsel table.

Homer Maitland peered down from the bench. "Mr. Darnell, do you wish to inquire of the witness?"

With his legs stretched straight out in front of him and his chin sunk on his chest, Darnell appeared to be making up his mind. "Mrs. Wilcox," he said, his eyes still fixed on a point somewhere on the floor between them. "At the risk of laboring the obvious, you had no reason to believe on the day before your rescue that the White Rose or any other ship would suddenly appear the next day- or, for that matter, any day- did you?"

"No, of course not." Darnell's gaze slid across the floor

"So the fact that you were rescued a day later changes nothing about what would have appeared to a reasonable person in those same dreadful circumstances to be what necessity required, does it? It was no different- except for what, after the fact, appears to add just one more lamentable dimension to what everyone admits is the tragedy of the Evangeline- than what was done, what had to be done, each time before?" he asked as his eyes finally met hers.

As soon as she agreed, Darnell got to his feet. "Each time this was done, each time another person was chosen by lot, you had to have hoped- you all had to have hoped- that it would be the last time; that before you were once again reduced to starvation, rescue would come?"

"Yes, of course. We all prayed for that."

Darnell nodded his belief that she was right, that everyone had done what she said, as he moved around the counsel table and came closer. "Mr. Roberts did not ask you, so I will," he said as he stopped in front of her. "Captain Balfour- I'm sure you remember him- testified that you said two angels had come down from heaven and that you had been rescued by them. Is that true, Mrs. Wilcox? Is that what happened?" There was not the slightest skepticism in his voice, certainly none of the scorn of the unbeliever. Darnell was simply providing her the opportunity to give her own account of what she had seen.

Samantha Wilcox was more than willing to offer testimony to her faith. "I know that many of you don't believe- that you think that it was just an accident that we were rescued, that the White Rose just came along by chance. But just what chance is there that in all those thousands of miles, in all that trackless sea, that ship- any ship- would find our small boat, a speck on the horizon, nothing more? I believed; I'm alive. There is a reason- there has to be. There is a meaning in all of this.

"Yes, I saw two angels, radiant in the sun. Did I see them the way I see you, a physical presence in front of my eyes, or did I see them only in my heart? Does it matter? Are you going to tell me that only one sense is real? "There is a meaning in all of this, if you'll only grasp it. We are more than just animals; we're not just part of dumb creation. We died for each other out there. We drew lots- we let God decide. But we did it willingly- or they did, the ones who were chosen to die for the others

"Doesn't that tell you that there must be something god- like in each one of us, each one of you?" Her face glowed with an inner light that conjured up visions of things cloistered and medieval. Only someone as lost and bitter as Trevelyn would have doubted that she had meant it when she said she had prayed each time that the next one chosen would be her.

Darnell held her gaze in his own, taking comfort from it and trying to give some comfort back. "Would you tell us please, Mrs. Wilcox, something about the boy? Do you remember him from before the storm- what he was like while he was working on the Evangeline?"

"Yes, I remember him. He was fine, intelligent- quick as a whip. He seemed to idolize Mr. Marlowe. He followed him everywhere, just waiting for whatever Mr. Marlowe asked him to do next. That isn't so surprising; a man who knows what he is doing, a man everyone admires. That is who boys are drawn to- men they want to be like. Poor Mr. Marlowe! When the boy was chosen…I've never seen a look like that."

"Could you explain to us why, if he was willing to allow the boy to die- a boy for whose life he would have given his own- he would not let Hugo Offenbach be included among those whose names were drawn?"

She looked at him as if she was not sure whether he was serious. "It was not just Mr. Marlowe. Mr. Offenbach kept us alive." She quickly corrected herself. "No, Hugo Offenbach gave us a reason to live."

"I'm afraid I don't quite understand. Mr. Offenbach- in his condition- what could he do?"

She gave him another look of incredulity. "What could he do? The greatest violinist in the world? He played, Mr. Darnell- he played! Every day, for hours, whenever there was not a storm. That's when I lost whatever doubts I may have had that we were all in the hands of God: when I heard that music. It was like angels singing."

"He had his violin?" asked Darnell, astonished. "But it was not with him when he was rescued; it was not found in the boat."

Darnell shot a glance at Marlowe, hoping to find the answer in his eyes. Marlowe stared straight ahead, his face as enigmatic as a sphinx.

CHAPTER FIFTEEN

Despite her own obvious sympathies, the testimony of Samantha Wilcox had been devastating to the defense, and no one knew it better than Darnell. This was a case that hung on perceptions as much, or more, than it did on facts. The defense of necessity was the only defense Vincent Marlowe had, and the jury had now been told that the last survivor killed would have been alive with the rest of them had his death been postponed by even one day.

The point that Darnell was quick to make, the question he had immediately put to the witness- that no one could have known when, or even whether, a ship would arrive- might, as he later came to understand, have actually worked to Marlowe's disadvantage. It seemed to raise in a new and doubtful way just how narrow were the range of circum- stances that could ever be thought to justify the taking of one life to save the lives of others. Forget what Marlowe knew, or thought he knew; forget how little life the others still had in them- they surely could have held out one more day. But if that were true, if they could have gone one day longer, there was no necessity for what Marlowe did, and what he did was murder.

The only hope Darnell had was to make the jury see things through Marlowe's eyes, feel what Marlowe had felt, try to face the same intolerable and inescapable deci- sion to do what had to be done to save what lives he could. Each time he cross-examined a witness for the prosecution, whatever else he tried to do, he tried to do that: give the jury another glimpse into that primitive state of nature in which Marlowe had been forced to live and act.

The day after Samantha Wilcox testified, Darnell was back in court, getting ready to do it all over again with what might be the last witness the prosecution would call. James DeSantos would not have been called at all if he had had anything to do with it. From the moment he took the oath, glaring at the clerk, he did everything he could to give vent to his displeasure. Roberts tried to begin with a question that would put him at his ease. It did not work. Asked to describe to the jury why he and his wife had decided to sail on the Evangeline, DeSantos exploded.

"I told her it was a stupid thing to do! I told her that it was crazy to spend that much time away!" His dark, handsome eyes burned with more than anger; unaccountably, in light of what had happened, it was something close to hatred. "I don't know why I bothered- you could never tell her anything! She did what she wanted, no matter who it hurt. This time, it hurt her."

His eyes had wandered all around the hushed, crowded room. Now he looked at Roberts with a hostile, penetrating stare. "What do you want from me? Why did you bring me here? Haven't I been through enough?"

"You were brought here to answer questions, Mr. DeSantos," said Roberts with a steely glance. "You were brought here to tell the truth about what you know."

"What I know is that my life is over-ruined, because all she ever thought about was herself. She had a contractual obligation, a picture that was to start shooting in a couple of weeks. She didn't care if they had to wait, if hundreds of people had to sit on their hands, if the studio lost millions of dollars. She just wanted to have a good time! Sail around Africa- how romantic!" he exclaimed, his eyes wild with rage."Sail around Africa and look what happened! Look what happened to me! Look what I was forced to do! And if that wasn't bad enough, look what's happened since."

"What's happened since?" asked Roberts, stunned by the violence of the outburst.

DeSantos ignored him. For the first time, he turned to the jury, a ghastly smile on his face. "What do you think of me now, after what You've heard? What is the first thing that comes into your mind? The movie star idol, the box-office sensation? Or the pathetic survivor, the ghoul who lived off dead people, including his own wife?"

His eyes, brutal and triumphant, darted back to Roberts. "That's what has happened since. I've become a pariah, an outcast. No one will have anything to do with me; no one returns my calls. The pictures I was scheduled to make- cancelled; the offers that used to come in by the dozen every week- withdrawn."

Roberts would have none of it. As forcefully as he could, he reminded DeSantos once again where he was and what was at issue. "This is a murder trial, Mr. DeSantos. A man is on trial for his life. Your wife was killed. We're not much interested in what may or may not have happened to your career!"

DeSantos jumped forward to the front edge of the witness chair. A caustic grin shot across his mouth. "My wife? Helena Green? Yes, I remember- we were married once. I seem to remember something about the ceremony, though not much about her being a wife after that. Married? Let me think. Yes! I guess we were. Two years, in which we may have spent all of two months together. Married? Not even enough to warrant a divorce. So why did we go on that ill-fated voyage, isn't that what you asked?

"The question is misleading, Mr....? Yes, Roberts. Misleading, because it suggests that it was something we decided on together."

"Yes, I understand," said Roberts, taking advantage of a pause to get things back on track. "You said in so many words that it was her idea. Now, let me ask..."

"Her idea that she go. It was not her idea that I come along. I knew you didn't understand. She was going, and nothing was going to stop her, but she had a thousand differ-ent reasons why I shouldn't come along. The real reason, of course, was that she wanted to be with someone else. That's right: my wife, Helena Green, wanted to sail around Africa sleeping with someone else. And no, he didn't survive either."

It seemed to serve as a kind of catharsis, that public acknowledgment of his wife's infidelity, that harsh indict-ment of her betrayal. They were both dead, his wife and her lover, but he was still alive. For the moment that seemed sufficient satisfaction. He looked at Roberts with an air of weary resignation, as if he had said everything he cared to say on the subject.

"There is really only one point we wish to understand, Mr. DeSantos. It has to do with your wife and the way she died. Was she or was she not killed by the defendant, Vincent Marlowe?"

DeSantos looked at Roberts and then, as if he had just become aware of his presence, looked at Marlowe. His whole demeanor changed. His eyes became serious, thoughtful and introspective. The last trace of anger and defiance left his lips. His voice was quiet and subdued. "I don't know how she died."

Roberts went rigid. Standing next to the end of the counsel table, he pressed his fingers hard against it to keep his hand from shaking. "You're under oath, Mr. DeSantos," he warned. "I will ask you again: did Vincent Marlowe kill your wife? Did he kill Helena Green?"

DeSantos did not blink. "And I'll tell you again: I don't know."

"Sir, we have a witness who has already testified that you saw Vincent Marlowe do it; not only saw it happen, but were the first to... to make use of her blood as a means of survival. Do you deny this?"

"What do you mean, "make use of her blood"? Is someone saying...? Is that what that liar Trevelyn said? That I drank her blood so I could stay alive?" he demanded.

"That's exactly what he said. And more than that, that you insisted on your right to do so first because she was your wife."

DeSantos stroked his chin. "I wonder if that is true, if I really did? I wonder what any of us did out there?"

"I beg your pardon? You're saying you don't remember what happened? That you don't remember what was done?"

"No, I remember some of it. What I don't remember is how much of it was real, and how much of it was some kind of hallucination. What I remember mainly is the smell:

the rotting flesh, the open wounds, the urine- did you know, did Trevelyn tell you, that we drank it, after the water ran out? Drank our own urine because we were driven mad by thirst? The smell, the stink, relieving ourselves in what we wore. And then the rest of it," he said, his voice dying in the stunned silence of the crowd, "the bodies, the blood..." He looked up at Roberts as if he had forgotten where he was.

"And what about the blood?"

"It made them crazy," said DeSantos in a distant voice. "The sight of it, the taste of it."

"It made them crazy? Who? Who did it make crazy?"

"All of us, everyone- almost everyone. That's why it happened."

"Why what happened?"

"The first time, the first time flesh was eaten- no one would take much, only what they had to. But then, when we got hungry again, all anyone wanted was more and warmer blood. It made them crazy- that's what I said- the taste of blood. They could hardly wait to draw lots so they could taste it again."

"Your wife was the second victim, wasn't she? The second person Marlowe killed?"

"Marlowe was against it," said DeSantos sharply, the dazed expression gone. "He was against it from the beginning."

"Are you saying that he did not kill your wife? Are you saying that he did not kill anyone?"

"I'm saying that whatever he did- and I don't know that he did anything- he only did because the others said he had to."

"For the last time, Mr. DeSantos: did you or did you not see Vincent Marlowe kill your wife?"

"I don't know what I saw. I was like the others: half dead and out of my mind. For all I knew I was dead, dead and sent to Hell. And you want me to tell you what happened? We suffered, all of us, like nothing you can imagine; and we did things, most of us, that can't be forgiven. But did Marlowe do something he should not have done? He may have been the only one who did not."

To DeSantos' surprise, Roberts seemed to agree. "Certainly some of what he did was admirable, if what other witnesses have said is true: that when the boy was chosen to be the first to die, Marlowe tried to take his place. That's really quite hard to believe, though, isn't it? That someone would be willing to do that?"

"It's true, though. That's exactly what he did, but the boy- how brave he was!- would not allow it."

"Would not allow it?" asked Roberts with a skeptical eye.

"He said that it wouldn't be fair and that he didn't mind so much as long as Marlowe did it."

"You saw all this? You heard it?"

"I won't ever forget it!"

"You saw the boy die? You saw what Marlowe did?"

"I couldn't watch; I turned away. I saw Marlowe slide his hand down over the boy's eyes, and then I couldn't look."

Roberts nodded as if he understood what DeSantos must have gone through. "And did you then follow Marlowe's example?"

DeSantos looked at him with a blank expression. "His example?"

"Yes. Marlowe offered to die in place of the boy. Did you offer to die in place of your wife?"

They stared at each other, locked in silence. Roberts, with a swift movement of his chin, wheeled around and faced the jury. "You remember quite vividly everything that happened to the boy, and you remember nothing about what happened to your wife. Some people might find that a little difficult to believe!"

"Believe whatever you like!" DeSantos shouted back. "What difference could any of that make to me now? Don't you understand anything about what happened out there? We were all dead! It wasn't a question of who was going to survive; it was a question how best to die. You think that lottery we held, the way we all drew straws, was some pact made with the devil to decide who would go on living? It was more like a covenant we made with God to let us ease our suffering.

"There were some, like Trevelyn, who would have killed us all, done anything to stay alive, but that was not true of most of us, not after the boy died. That was the example that stayed in our minds: the brave acceptance, the undaunted courage, with which he greeted his fate. It was hard to be a coward after that. He made death seem so simple.

"Everyone, except for the likes of Trevelyn, wanted to die, and we would have, if Marlowe had let us. But he seemed to think the boy's death taught a different lesson: that death had meaning only if it helped those it left behind. That's why we went on like that, doing what we had to do, what was necessary, to stay alive, playing that ghastly lottery to decide who died and who lived.

"There were a few who thought we should not do it, that it was better that we each die when our time came, rather than kill each other just to live a little longer when, at the end of it, having murdered all the others, only one of us would be left and that one left to die alone."

"But Vincent Marlowe decided what you all should do? And Marlowe did the killing?"

"Marlowe killed the boy because the boy said it was the only way he knew he could be brave enough. Who killed the others? They killed themselves. They died by their own agreement."

"But Marlowe performed the act?"

"I wouldn't know," insisted DeSantos with a solemn, determined look. "We were all out of our minds, delirious, barely alive, delusional. All I know for sure is that without Marlowe all of us would be dead."

Roberts gave him a stern look. "Including the last one he killed, the day before you were rescued?"

Darnell was out of his chair shouting an objection.

With a dismissive glance at DeSantos, Roberts withdrew the question. "No further questions," he said as he took his chair.

Homer Maitland leaned forward. "Mr. Darnell?"

Darnell shook his head and started to sit down. "Well, perhaps just one or two questions," he said, rising again from his chair. He looked at DeSantos with a puzzled expression. "You said that the boy- his name was Billy, correct?"

"Yes."

"Do you happen to know his last name?"

"No, I just knew his first."

"He asked that Marlowe do this thing? It wasn't Marlowe's idea?"

"Marlowe's idea? He wanted to take his place."

"Yes, I understand. My question, though, is whether he asked that Marlowe do it because he was under the impression that, if he didn't, someone else would instead?"

"I'm sorry, I don't..."

"Mr. Trevelyn testified that the boy was chosen first because he was closest to death, that he would not have lived much more than another day."

"That is a lie! He wasn't any closer to death than the rest of us."

"I understand. So he was chosen by lot- like the others would be. But that only explains the method by which the one to die was chosen; it doesn't explain the method- if there was a method- by which the one who had to kill them was selected. Mr. Roberts seems to want to suggest that all of the deaths were caused by Marlowe and that Marlowe did it solely of his own volition."

"Trevelyn was the one who pushed for it, who insisted it was the only way to survive. He would have killed the boy- I know he would have- if Marlowe had let him. If it had been Marlowe himself to die, instead of the boy, I think he would have insisted Trevelyn do it, to make Trevelyn take the responsibility for what he wanted done. But he never would have let him touch the boy."

"But before that- before that first drawing- what had been decided about who should do it?"

"A second drawing, so that everything would be decided by chance: who would die and who would kill."

Darnell nodded to himself and then tilted his head to the side. He looked at DeSantos with the utmost seriousness and respect. "You know that Marlowe killed your wife. He is going to admit that, along with everything else he did, when he testifies. And while I understand why you might want to protect him by being less than truthful about what you know, you cannot help him with a lie. What we need to know- what we need to know from you- is why, after the boy was killed, it was Marlowe, and not someone chosen by that process of random selection you just described, who killed the others? Why wasn't there a lottery to choose the one who would kill your wife? Why did Marlowe do it?"

"Because of what happened to the boy. Because you knew how much it hurt him, how deep it went. Because you knew that you could trust him to make it as painless as he could. Because you knew that if he had to take your life, it wasn't because he wanted to save his own."

CHAPTER SIXTEEN

Homer Maitland wanted to see both attorneys in chambers. The word suggested something exquisitely Victorian, a room cluttered with ponderous furniture, thick littered carpets and heavy draperies, with a constant fire against the bone-chilling fog of a London December. The reality was rather more prosaic: a small rectangular room with a gray linoleum floor, two metal bookcases of standard dimension and a nondescript desk with a cheap wooden veneer. There was a window, but no view.

"DeSantos was your last witness?" he asked as Roberts and Darnell settled into the two chairs in front of his desk. A thin, shrewd smile stole across his mouth. "Or was DeSantos the first witness for the defense?" This was not condescension, nor was it second guessing. Homer Maitland understood the chances a lawyer sometimes had to take. "It's a strange case when the defense lawyer insists that the prosecution's witness provide the testimony that the pros- ecution could not get from him. That's why you called him, isn't it?" he asked Roberts directly. "To testify that he saw Marlowe kill his wife, Helena Green? Never mind- that isn't something I should ask."

"It doesn't seem to matter why I call a witness," said Roberts with a modest, self-effacing smile. "By the time Mr. Darnell..."

"Bill," insisted Darnell.

"By the time Bill finishes with them on cross exami- nation, I've lost more ground than I've gained."

A quick, hard grin cut across Maitland's mouth. "I wouldn't be too surprised if Bill doesn't think the same thing after you finish with the witnesses he calls for the defense."

He looked from Roberts to Darnell and back again. "You were right, both of you, in your opening arguments. This is the most unusual case any of us will likely ever see. I've been on the bench thirty years this April, and I've never seen anything like it. I'm not sure that the wisdom of Solomon would be enough to decide this one."

There was a long silence in which each of them wondered what the chances were that anything close to that measure of wisdom might be found among this or any other jury.

"Perhaps they'll draw straws to decide whether Marlowe lives or dies," said Darnell finally.

"Isn't there some way to resolve this before it comes to that?" asked Maitland. He turned to Roberts. "Is there any way to negotiate a plea?"

"He wouldn't plead to manslaughter. There isn't anything lower than that except dismissal."

"And the first thing he would ask me is whether he could fight it," said Darnell to Maitland's astonishment. "Marlowe won't plead to anything; he wants this trial, not to prove his innocence, but to prove his guilt. What you said a moment ago is truer than you could have known: the best witness for the prosecution is likely to be the defendant himself."

"So you are going to put him on the stand?" asked Maitland, just to be sure.

"I can't stop him; and at this point, I'm not sure that I want to. He needs to get it out, to make his confession. It might send him to prison; it might cost him his life. That doesn't matter to him- it might even be his incentive."

"So we go on with it, then," said Maitland with a sigh, "and let the jury decide."He looked at Darnell closely. "I'm sure you've explained to him that in a case like this the court has no discretion. If he is convicted, it will be either death or life in prison."

"Marlowe is quite aware of that."

"Unless they should find him guilty of manslaughter as a lesser included charge. We would not oppose that instruction," offered Roberts.

"Yes, I've thought of that; but even that carries time in prison." Darnell tapped his fingers on his knee. "The jury may not be looking for a way to be lenient. After what Marlowe tells them, I wouldn't be too surprised if they want to hang him."

"Who would ever believe it?" said Maitland after a brief and troubled silence. "A case in which the prosecution wants leniency and the defense rejects it!"

Maitland got back to business. He asked again whether the prosecution had called its last witness. Roberts said he had. "In that case, the defense can begin its case in the morning. Other than the defendant," he asked Darnell, "how many witnesses do you plan to call?"

"All the survivors; or rather, the ones Michael did not call."

Maitland had his pencil. "And those would be?"

"Other than Marlowe- Hugo Offenbach...And perhaps the other woman, Cynthia Grimes, if I can talk her into it."

Roberts raised his eyebrows. "You found her? You've talked to her?"

Darnell responded with a playful frown. "Yes and no."

"Yes and no?" asked Roberts, laughing.

"Yes, I talked to her; no, she did not talk to me, at least not at first. Our first conversation went as follows: 'Hello, Mrs. Grimes? This is William Darnell, the attorney for Vincent Marlowe.' Then I heard a click." Darnell paused for a moment before he added, "No, I don't think I've left anything out."

"And you're calling her anyway?"

Darnell was on his feet. "I will if I can. But I can't force her to come, and, so far at least, she has made it quite plain that she does not want to."

Maitland made a check mark next to each of the three names on the witness list in the court file. "Anyone else?"

An impish smile crawled across Darnell's mouth. "Yes."

"That's half an answer," replied Maitland drolly. "Give me the names and you've got it all."

"I'm going to call the naval architect who designed the Evangeline. I've forgotten his name at the moment, but

Mr. Roberts has it- the one who signed the report, already introduced into evidence, about the sea trials and the repairs that were done."

"Anyone else?" asked Maitland when Darnell appeared to hesitate.

"There is a chance that I may call one of the witnesses already called by the prosecution."

"Which one?" asked Roberts, intensely interested.

"The first one: Benjamin Whitfield."

"But why? What more can he add to what he has already testified?"

"I could not tell you that, even if I knew. I have a feeling, that's all- let's just leave it at that."

A feeling was all it really was, and perhaps even less than that: an unsupported hope. He confessed that night at dinner that he did not think he had any choice, that he had to take a chance, throw away all the rules, all the tried and tested principles on which experienced courtroom lawyers depend for their success.

"It started to crystallize itself in my mind while I was listening to the testimony of Samantha Wilcox, something she said about everything being in the hands of God."

Summer Blaine put down the menu, wondering at the useless habit that made her glance at the list of dishes she had long since learned by heart. They had been coming to this same Fillmore Street restaurant from almost the first time she had come into the city to spend an evening or a long weekend at the apartment in Pacific Heights. It was odd the way a habit could become a custom, a part of your practice, something that gave shape to your life. There was a strange fear that to give it up was to risk the unknown, that even the smallest change might, like the first crack in a foundation, lead to the destruction of everything else. The menu was a totem of her own invention, and she knew it, but that did not make it any easier to risk her luck. When she scrubbed for surgery, she always washed her right hand first.

"There has to be some cause, some reason for the things that happen," Darnell went on, growing more animated as he spoke. "Especially when it is something truly awful. It was fascinating, what she said about why they drew lots to choose who would die: that it had to be left to chance to make sure it was God's decision. What a powerful belief that is- that nothing happens by chance, that everything has a meaning, that everything is part of some larger design!"

With a last, almost surreptitious glance at the menu, Summer Blaine ordered what she usually did; and then, because he was too wrapped up in what he was saying to pay attention to what he wanted, she ordered, as she often did, for Darnell as well. The small restaurant was quiet, nearly empty, the way it often was at the late hour they came. It had become a private joke, the familiar greeting repeated each time they walked in, that it must be almost time to close. That was part of the habit, too- the custom by which Darnell held himself to the rigor of the schedule in which he worked through the evening, took an hour or two for dinner, and then, while nearly everyone else was asleep, worked into the early hours of the morning. It might have killed a younger man, but he insisted, as he did about most of the things to which Summer Blaine objected, that it kept him alive.

"Do you believe in God?" he asked, bending his head to the side the way he did when he was particularly interested in the answer.

"Yes, but it doesn't mean I believe in heaven." Her answer did not surprise him. Nor did it seem to confuse him.

"The God who creates the world and then leaves it to its own devices?"

"Yes, I suppose- something like that. I've been a doctor too long to believe that something as intricately organized as the human body is just the chance result of simple cells organizing themselves. I've helped bring too many children into the world- delivered too many babies- to believe that higher things just happen to evolve out of lower ones. If you know a building is made from bricks, and that the bricks are all the same weight and size, that still doesn't really tell you much about how Chartres or Mont-Saint-Michel were built. There has to be some intelligence, something that

133

makes us what we are."

"But nothing after death?"

"Just the memory we leave behind."

"Death is final, absolute?"

Summer Blaine picked at a green lettuce salad. She was not quite certain what she believed and was too honest not to say so. "Isn't that the real mystery of existence- that we're here at all? So many people worry about what will happen to them after they die. I don't hear many of them worrying about what happened to them before they were born. We accept the fact that we did not exist. But then, how could there be anything like life eternal? Eternity does not just mean that there is no ending: it also means that there is no beginning."

She pushed the salad plate aside. In a teasing parallel, she bent her head the same way he bent his. "Now that I've solved the problem of the universe, why don't you tell me what you were going to tell me about the trial? What was it about what Samantha Wilcox said that made you think you had to throw out all the rules? Which rules do you mean?"

Darnell's gray eyebrows became expressive half circles. "In the vast majority of murder trials, the defense is really quite simple: either the evidence is not sufficient to prove the guilt of the defendant, or the evidence, no matter how powerful, could just as easily be used to prove the guilt of someone else. If the defendant had a motive to kill the victim, there were others who had an even stronger reason to want him dead. It is all perfectly straightforward; it only gets complicated when there is no serious dispute about the facts. Let's take you as the killer."

She laughed when she saw the mockery of melodrama in his eyes. "Me? I'm the villain? Who am I supposed to have killed?"

"Not supposed to have killed- you did it. And there isn't any doubt about it: you confessed."

"And was my confession voluntary or was it beaten out of me?"

Darnell waited while the waiter cleared away the salad

plates and served the main course. "You confessed to killing several patients, each of them in terrible pain, none of them with any chance of survival. You killed them because it was the only way to end their suffering. The prosecution says that doesn't matter; whatever reason you claim to have had, it's murder. The defense says that it not only matters, it is the only thing that does. You had it in your power to ease their suffering. A law that says you should not do that is barbaric and should not be obeyed."

"Can you say that? Can you make that argument in court? Tell the jury that in some cases the law should not be obeyed?"

"No, I can't. But that doesn't mean a jury can't decide on its own to ignore the narrow requirements of the law. But there isn't much chance they'll do that unless they think there is someone else who is more to blame for what happened." Darnell paused to sample the food in front of him. With the fork dangling in his hand, he leaned towards her, his eyes filled with cheerful malice as he told her how she might be saved.

"You killed these people because you could not stand to see them suffer. But why were they under your care in the first place? Why were they in the hospital, going through such torment? Suppose that it was not because of some normal, terminal disease; suppose they were there because of an accident. A building collapsed and they were all buried beneath the rubble.

Who, then, is responsible for their deaths?" he asked with a shrewd glint in his eye. "The contractor who, to save money, did not build it right? The inspector who was bribed to look the other way? Or the gifted physician who eased the suffering of people who would not have been in that position- dying in agony- had it not been for their criminal negligence?

That's what the testimony of Samantha Wilcox taught me: the question about creation, the question about the beginning. How did this terrible thing begin? Who created the situation in which Marlowe and the others found themselves? Why were they out there, forced to do what they did? None of this would have happened if the Evangeline had not sunk. And why did the Evangeline sink? Who is responsible for that?"

"But the Evangeline went down in a storm! You're not going to try to blame it on God?"

Darnell stroked his chin. He looked at her from under lowered eyelids. "No. That was something else Samantha Wilcox taught me. She doesn't believe that God controls everything; she believes in free will. It was not God's decision that they start sacrificing one another so that some of them could survive. God came into it only when they drew lots. In that sense, it doesn't matter who or what created the situation in which they found themselves: it was their decision- a decision Marlowe carried out- to take the lives of those whose names were drawn."

"Just as it would not matter who was responsible for sending those people to the hospital; I did not have to kill them."

"Which gets us back to what makes this trial different, what sets it apart from all the so-called mercy killings we read about: if Marlowe had not done what he did, none of them would be alive."

A question had been building in her mind almost from the day Darnell had told her that he had taken the case. She asked it now because of a feeling that it went to the heart of what was really at issue, and what he had been struggling with all along. "Do you think it's better that he did? Do you think it's better that he killed those people so the others could live?"

"No, I don't; but then, neither does he. Nor do any of them, I suspect; except perhaps Trevelyn, and I'm not absolutely sure about him. The only thing worse than what they did- what they had to do- is that Marlowe should now be punished because of it. That's why I have to give the jury a reason to believe that Marlowe had no choice, that he was put in a situation where it was the only thing he could do. But I have to do more than that: I have to give them a reason to believe that someone did something wrong, that the Evangeline went down because of something someone did or didn't do, and not because of the storm or any other act of God. I have to give them someone else they can blame."

CHAPTER SEVENTEEN

"The defense calls the defendant, Vincent Marlowe." This was unorthodox, a break with convention. The defendant, if he was called to testify at all, was usually called last. The other witnesses called by the defense would give evidence that should, in one way or another, help demonstrate his innocence. Only then would the defendant take the stand. With no one to follow him, no one to contradict what he said, he could give his own account of what happened and swear by whatever he held sacred that whoever had committed the murder, it had not been him.

Roberts darted a glance at Darnell. He could read nothing in the older man's eyes. Reaching for his ballpoint pen, he wrote Marlowe's name on the top line of a blank sheet of paper in a small hand. Then he waited, ready to take what could sometimes be verbatim notes as he listened to a witness called by the other side.

Though the jury had seen Marlowe every day, sitting there with that same stern expression on his face, they watched him now as he took the oath with intense curiosity. Their eyes were all over him, trying to find in the way he looked the difference, the thing that set him apart, that made him peculiar, unique- the thing that made him a man capable of things they themselves could never do. There was a kind of shock, a sense of puzzlement and almost disappointment, when he settled into the witness chair and began to answer questions in a manner and a voice that, to all appearances, seemed quite normal.

For those who had never seen him outside this courtroom, who had never known him before this trial, he was what you might expect of a man who had lived his life among the other strangers who spend their days and nights at sea. There was the quiet confidence, the unhurried look, and the sense of inevitability that seemed to accompany even the smallest thing he did. If the eyes of other men were in constant motion- measuring, comparing, appraising; taking their bearings by the customs, the habits, the expectations they saw all around them- Marlowe looked straight ahead, oblivious, or indifferent, to what other people thought they wanted.

"I want to begin at the beginning, Mr. Marlowe." Darnell paused and, with his hand resting on the front corner of the counsel table, briefly lowered his eyes and smiled. "You understand that the reason I don't call you by your first name- Vincent- is because the rules require a certain formality?" he asked, raising his eyes, not to the witness, but to the jury.

"Yes, of course," said Marlowe in a voice that could be heard as clearly at the back of the courtroom as at the front. He was used to making himself heard in the open air; he had none of the lifeless whisper of an indoor voice.

"Where were you raised, Mr. Marlowe?"

Seattle. We did not always live there, in the city, but always somewhere on the Sound. Everett for a few years, Port Townsend for a year or so after that."

"And was it because of your father's work that you always lived in the Seattle area?"

"My father worked on ships. He was a boilermaker by trade."

"How long did you live there- in Seattle?"

Marlowe spread his knees apart and hunched forward. He held his large hands together and squinted into the dull glare of the courtroom light. "Until my father died. Then I left."

Darnell waited, expecting more, but Marlowe had the habit of economy in speech as well as in other things. "Would you explain for the jury," said Darnell in a gentle, soothing voice, "what happened- how your father died and what, because of his death, you had to do?"

"He died when I was twelve. It was an accident; happened while he was working on a freighter come in for repairs. There was not any money- all my mother had was a small widow's pension- and there was my sister to raise."

This time Darnell did not wait quite so long. "Your sister- how old was she?"

"Just a baby- a year...a year and a half. With my father gone, I had to do my part. I didn't mind; I had grown up with ships and I was waiting for the chance. I wanted to go to sea. I wasn't all that good in school."

"You had grown up with ships? You mean, listening to your father?"

"That, and going with him when he had one to work on. It was great fun for me- a boy of eight or nine- having the run of a ship, free to explore every nook and cranny. The men who worked in them, holed up in port with nothing pressing they had to do, would tell you stories of things they had seen from all the different places in the world. My head was always filled with thoughts of adventures, of mysterious places I would one day explore, a seaman on one of those freighters taking cargo from one side of the ocean to the other."

"You went to work with your father? You mean on those days you weren't in school?"

"Saturdays, mainly; and most days in the summer- including the one when it happened."

Darnell had begun to move from the counsel table across the front of the courtroom to the jury box. He stopped in mid-stride and abruptly turned his head. He had not known. "You were there? You were on the ship the day your father died?"

Marlowe sat back in the chair and slowly nodded. "I was out on deck, near the stern, watching a couple of hands mending rope. The explosion almost tore the ship in two. I knew my father was gone the moment it happened. He knew the risk. He always had me in another part of the ship, away from where he did the work."

The fretted lines on Darnell's forehead spread and deepened as he studied Marlowe a moment longer. Was it, he wondered, as a witness of his father's death that Marlowe had learned the double lesson that every life was settled in advance and that every fate was unknowable?

A wave of fatigue came over Darnell. He rested his hand on the jury box railing, staring down at the floor as if he were watching in his mind what young Marlowe had been through. When he raised his eyes to the witness, the sense of weakness had passed. "You shipped out- went to sea on a freighter- when you were how old again?"

"Twelve. I knew the captain of a ship from Singapore. He had known my father. I was a cabin boy."

"And how long has it been now? How many years have you lived your life at sea?"

"More than forty."

"And are you married? Do you have children of your own?"

"No, I never married. I suppose I never felt the need. My home was always where I happened to be- on a ship, or in whatever port I found myself when one voyage ended and I was waiting for another."

Darnell was in no hurry. He wanted the jury to get to know Marlowe in a way that went beyond the narrow facts of his biography; he wanted those twelve people, all of whom had led their lives in the sheltered comfort of urban congregations, to get some feel for the harsh imperatives and the distant solitude of the sea; he wanted them, so far as they were able, to enter into Marlowe's strange, exotic and solitary life.

Darnell stood near the jury box, drawing Marlowe out, asking him to explain- to men and women whose only adventures away from land had been on some short commercial cruise- a life spent in constant motion, in which each destination was only the next point of departure. Darnell wanted desperately to convey the sense that because nothing around Marlowe ever stayed the same, the only firm ground was to be found in the man himself. The scene was always shifting, the world became a child's kaleidoscope, but the eyes that saw it were always those of Marlowe and Marlowe never changed, Marlowe endured.

That was the difference Darnell wanted to show, that

the whole panoply of modern life- the passing fads, the latest advanced opinion all right thinking people had to share- had no meaning once you stepped off the apparent solidity of the shore. Whatever else you might think of him, Marlowe was real. It took all morning, and lasted until sometime after lunch.

Finally, in mid afternoon, Darnell brought the questioning up to events that were closer to hand. "You had spent much of your life on cargo ships, on freighters. The Evangeline was a sailing vessel. It did not carry a cargo; it was a pleasure craft that carried passengers. What happened to make you go from the one to the other?"

"When I started, years ago, the ships I sailed carried cargoes in the hold: sacks of grain, bales of wire, timber, iron ore. The ships were not that large and the crews that sailed them were, for the most part, small. The ports we went to might be miles up a river. Then they started building container ships that could carry hundreds of freight cars on deck, ships ten times larger than the ones I had sailed, ships so large there were harbors you could not enter because there was not room enough to turn around. The ships were larger, and because of that, had not so much life in them…"

"I'm sorry," interjected Darnell with a puzzled smile. "'Not so much life in them'?"

"The action of the sea, the closeness of it. If you were in the navy, it's the difference between being on a battleship or a carrier as against living life on a destroyer. The bigger they are the more like being on shore. Do you see my meaning?"

"Yes, I do. Thank you. Please, go on. You went from freighters to sailing vessels?"

"Yes, but like everything else, it was all a matter of chance. I had been injured- hurt my leg in an accident on board the freighter I had been on- was laid up in the hospital for a while, out in Sumatra. The captain of a British schooner was in the bed next to me, suffering from a siege of malaria. He offered me a berth, and once I had been out on a ship like that- the quiet way they run, the wind whistling by you- I never much wanted to go back to the other. It was a relief, really. The freighters were all too big, the engines too large and powerful, the routes they sail too safe and predictable: the sea isn't just some straight-lined road you take from point to point."

"So from that time on, you made your living on board sailing vessels?"

"Yes. I still had some work on freighters, but less of it all the time until, finally, all I did was hire out on sailing ships."

"Does this mean that you had earned a reputation as a man who knew his way around ships, or boats, of this kind?"

"I learned my way well enough."

Darnell gave the jury a look which said that, for men of Marlowe's type, understatement was even more a fact than a habit. "And is that how you happened to become the captain of the Evangeline? Because Benjamin Whitfield had heard of you by reputation?"

"No, it wasn't that at all. That was also chance. We met here- in San Francisco- a couple years back. I was working for a Mr. Elgin, and Mr. Elgin was a friend, a business associate, of Mr. Whitfield. He- Mr. Whitfield- had an interest in sailing ships. He had become an avid racer, and went all over the world to do it."

"He designed, or helped design, the Evangeline, did he not?"

"Mr. Whitfield always wanted the best. What had been built by others did not measure up."

"The Evangeline was built here, in the United States?"

"Yes, in Seattle."

"Where you were raised?"

"Yes."

"And were you involved in any way with the construction?"

"Mr. Whitfield had me oversee it," said Marlowe, then immediately shook his head. "No, that's putting too much importance on what I did. The design followed Mr. Whitfield's conception- the look he wanted, what he wanted

143

her to do- but he employed a naval architect to do it. My job was just to be there, to be his ears and eyes; but, more than that, to learn everything I could about her by seeing the way she was built."

"Would it be fair to say, then, that you were comfortable with the way she was built? That you were confident in the ability of the Evangeline to sail anywhere in the world?" There was nothing in Marlowe's eyes to suggest that, even now, after everything that had happened, he had any doubt that the ship was everything she was supposed to have been and more.

"She was the finest ship of her kind ever built."

Up to this point, Darnell had been the soul of geniality, asking questions the way a curious friend might inquire into the recent travels of a man he had known intimately for years. Now, suddenly, he looked at Marlowe with hard, skeptical eyes. "You can say that? After she sank like a rock in the south Atlantic? After all those lives were lost? After what those of you who survived had to do? How can you possibly tell me now that she was the 'finest ship of her kind ever built'?"

"There is nothing made that is ever perfect," Marlowe answered right back. "Yes, she sank; sank in the worst storm that in more than forty years I ever saw."

Darnell moved away from the jury box railing and took a step closer to the witness stand. "But worst storm or not, she sank in a way you could not have expected; sank in a way she would not have sank had she been built to the specifications of the original design. Isn't that what happened, Mr. Marlowe? The Evangeline sank quickly because her hull broke in two?"

A look of distress, of grim disillusion, stretched across Marlowe's strong, broad mouth. Nodding slowly, he peered deep into Darnell's watching eyes. "Exactly right; just as you describe it, Mr. Darnell. We were in the middle of that storm, the wind howling like a banshee- a terrible, piercing scream- the waves crashing down on her, turning us high up on one side, then the other.

"Then it all went quiet, and the sea, suddenly all calm, and then this strange whisper, like the distant roll of a drum, as if an army had started marching towards us but was still miles away; and then that awful God-forsaken roar, as if the whole ocean had been drawn up from the bottom- lifted right off the earth- and then hurled back with all the force of God Almighty, thrown down like some prehistoric avalanche that took all the mountains with it.

"It was like being hit by a locomotive: there was a sickening, sharp cracking noise; the ship seemed to cave in on itself. The passengers, the crew- the ones who were hanging on in their cabins, trying to ride it out- must have all been dead, drowned or beaten on the head, almost right away. The ones who were either already out there, or some- how got out on deck- some of them made it to the lifeboats, some of them survived."

Darnell held Marlowe's gaze tight. "Why did the Evangeline break in half? Why did it "cave in on itself "?"

"Because the metal plating of the hull was not strong enough- the center could not hold."

"But the crack in the hull had been repaired." Darnell reminded him as he turned towards the watching eyes of the jury. "You remember the testimony of Benjamin Whitfield. He was asked about the defective weld; he was asked about the report- this report that has been offered into evidence," he said, waving it in the air. "He testified that the repair had been made."

"Yes, I heard," said Marlowe with a baleful look. "And I also heard that they could have checked the hull in its entirety, seen if any of the other seams had not been welded properly."

Darnell shook his head. "You heard Benjamin Whitfield testify that after the repair the ship was perfect."

Marlowe rubbed his large hands together. There was an anguished look in his eyes. "She was not perfect that night she sank! She might have lasted years in normal weather, but strains put on the hull in a storm like that ...It is like putting your foot on a glass; you can put some pressure on it and nothing happens- but then, just a little more, and it shatters."

"But if that is the case- if the risk was so great- why did you not insist that Benjamin Whitfield have the hull examined? Why didn't you insist that this be done before you took the Evangeline on a long voyage around Africa?"

"There was no occasion."

Darnell stared at him. "No occasion? Lives were at stake!"

"No occasion, because Mr. Whitfield never told me about the report; he never told me about the repair."

"He did not tell you that there had been a crack below the waterline?" asked Darnell with a cold, determined look.

"No, sir- never. He told me the Evangeline had passed her sea trials with flying colors."

"He told you that? There's no mistake?"

"I wouldn't have taken her out if he had told me what I heard him say in court. When he told me how well she had done in her sea trials, I was more convinced than ever that she was exactly what I thought: the finest ship of her kind ever built."

"So you were sent to sea, sent to sail around Africa with a crew of eight and nineteen passengers, having been told the ship was safe and sound- when she was not?"

"It appears so, yes."

CHAPTER EIGHTEEN

If Marlowe was telling the truth, if Benjamin Whitfield had not told him about the problem with the aluminum hull and what had, and what had not, been done about it, then Whitfield had not only lied to him, but by his failure to mention this all important detail had misled the court. But while this deepened the mystery of why the Evangeline had been allowed to set off around Africa in the first place, it intensified, and in a way clarified, the sense that everyone on board, whatever they may have done to survive, had been as much a victim as anyone killed.

The author of a newspaper column written at the end of Marlowe's first day of testimony spoke for a great many people when he remarked that to blame the survivors for what they did was a little like blaming the gladiators who had been forced to kill or die for the amusement of the Romans who had left them only that choice. It was what Darnell had hoped to show the jury: that Marlowe had not put everyone in danger, Whitfield had.

Whether through a negligence he was now trying to hide, or through deliberate and inexcusable indifference, Whitfield had placed all those lives at risk. Marlowe had tried to save them, or as many of them as he could. That was the point that Darnell tried to make the second day he had Marlowe on the stand- that he could not save them all, and that to save anyone, others had to die. He knew before he started that it was the last thing anyone wanted to believe.

"Yesterday you testified that when the Evangeline went down some of the passengers and crew were killed instantly, but others got away. Did all of those who managed to get off the Evangeline make it to one of the lifeboats?"

Wearing the same suit and tie he had the day before-the same suit and tie, the only ones he had, he wore every day to trial- Marlowe shook his head. "No."

"We have heard testimony," said Darnell, moving towards his favorite position at the far end of the jury box, directly in front of the witness stand, "that one lifeboat- one of the inflatable rafts- got away but was never seen again. Was that the lifeboat for which Aaron Trevelyn had responsibility?"

"Yes, but you can't blame him for that. He was right when he said that there was not any time."

"But you managed to reach the boat that was your responsibility?"

"I was on deck, at the wheel. I didn't have far to go."

Darnell placed his hand on the jury box railing. He knew that Marlowe could not help himself- that he believed, and always would, that everything that happened had been his responsibility and his alone.

"I'm not asking you what you think of Aaron Trevelyn and whether he acted honorably. I'm simply asking you to describe what happened. Two lifeboats got away, the one for which you had responsibility and the one for which- had he been able to get to it- Mr. Trevelyn would have had responsibility. Is this correct?"

"Yes."

"The other boat- do you know how many people were in it?"

"No, I barely had a glimpse of it. If I had to guess, I'd say maybe four or five."

"Would you say, then- though you just had a glimpse of it- that it had fewer people in it than it was capable of holding?"

"It seemed to me it was at least half empty."

"And the one you were in...? Do you agree with the testimony already given, including that of Mr. Trevelyn himself, that it held more people than it should have?"

Marlowe's look was grave, distant, as if he could not only see it in his mind, but also feel again what it was like, the howling desperation of that fatal storm. "We had as many as it could handle."

Darnell peered intently at him from under lowered

eyelids. "And there were others, still in the water, trying to get in?"

Marlowe clenched his teeth; his neck and head became rigid. He opened his mouth to answer, but not a word came out.

Darnell took one quick step forward and asked, or rather insisted, "Which means that there would have been room for everyone if that other boat had taken as many as it should have- isn't that correct?"

Marlowe's head jerked up. "If there had been time!"

"Or if Trevelyn had done his job," Darnell fired back. He turned on his heel to face the twelve men and women in the jury box. "Tell us what happened then- what you had to do- with a boat already filled to the point of swamping and others trying to get in, to save their own lives. Isn't this when Trevelyn started swinging an oar at them, beating them away? How did he get into your boat anyway?"

"He might have jumped; a lot of them did. What else could they do? The Evangeline was going down, everything was dark, the wind, the waves...None of them had any choice but to get off any way they could."

"He jumped. That's when he broke his wrist. But he still had the strength to keep others out?"

"He did what he had to; he did what he was told."

Darnell gave him a sharp look. He was not certain he had heard him right. "Did what he was told?"

"It was worse than you think, Mr. Darnell, worse than anyone can imagine. It was not just that the boat would sink, that everyone would drown if even one more person got into it- the boat already was sinking with those we had!"

Darnell was frozen to the spot. "You mean you...?"

"Some had to go; someone had to decide. I did that, Mr. Darnell. I was the captain- it had to be my decision. I put two men over, members of the crew, both of them men I had hired. I told them they had to take their chances, that there was another lifeboat, that it could not be too far away. I told them to try to save the others, the ones still alive in the water, the ones we would not let on board, the ones we had done whatever we had to- including, yes, hitting them with oars- to keep them out. I had to do it. There was not any choice. The only way to save some of them was to sacrifice the rest."

Darnell tried to hide his surprise behind a look of stern sympathy, the kind reserved for those forced by necessity to commit cruelties otherwise inexcusable. "When you were finally away- the survivors in the lifeboat- safe from the storm, how did you...?"

Darnell suddenly remembered what Marlowe's admission had made him forget. "Trevelyn jumped, and so did some of the others apparently, but what about Hugo Offenbach? He did not get there on his own, did he? He had a heart attack. You got him into the boat; you saved his life- why? Here's a man who was dying anyway- you could have left him behind. Instead, you risked your own life to get him- and not only your life, you risked the lives of other people, the ones who depended on you to handle the lifeboat.

"You kept other people out of the boat so it wouldn't sink; you put two men into the sea in order to keep it afloat- but Hugo Offenbach was probably closer to death than any of them. Why didn't you just let him go?"

"It wasn't a question of calculation; there wasn't time to decide whether what you did made sense in terms of what it would do to the chances of others. Mr. Offenbach was starting across the deck when I first caught sight of him, hanging on to that case, the one that held his violin. That's what did it, I think- what made up my mind.

"Strange, the things that go through your mind at a time like that. I saw him, this frail old man, clutching that violin of his as if it were more important than his life, that it was- what he could do with it- the whole meaning of his life, and I knew I had to help him. It was just when I got to him- he looked at me, tried to say something- but you could hear nothing in that awful wind- when he grabbed his chest and doubled over. I got him into the boat- he wasn't much to carry- and then, with everything that was going on- all the commotion, all the terrible things that happened, all the terrible things I did- I didn't think about him again until we were out of the storm and we could start to take stock of what had happened and what we had to do."

"You could have just carried him and left the violin."

"That would not have been saving his life; that would have been more like killing him. Besides, it wasn't heavy."

"It took up room."

"He held it on his lap, when he wasn't playing it. And if he hadn't played it, none of us would be here to tell about it. That's a fact."

For the rest of the morning, until court recessed for lunch, Darnell had Marlowe describe the way they had rigged a sail and set a course for South America, and what they had done at the beginning for water and for food. It was only in the afternoon that Darnell finally asked the question that everyone had been waiting for.

Despite the fact that it was expected, the question was greeted with a sense of disbelief, as if even now there was still the hope that it might not be true, that what the witnesses for the prosecution had said had been the product of minds unbalanced by the trauma of what they had gone through. Darnell stood now, not at the end of the jury box, but at the side of the counsel table near the two empty chairs. The jury's eyes would have to move from him to Marlowe and back again with each exchange.

"There was a point at which you were out of food and water. What did you do then?"

It seemed to Darnell that Marlowe began to age before his eyes. The lines in his haggard face cut deeper into his heavy skin; the corners of his mouth bent under the burden of what he knew. His eyes, never cheerful, became somber and withdrawn, as if they had pronounced a judgment of harsh unforgiveness on everything they had seen.

"We elected to do whatever was necessary to survive."

In normal conversation it might have passed unnoticed, but Darnell was in that heightened state of sensibility that comes with total concentration. "'We elected,'" he repeated, searching Marlowe's eyes for a meaning Marlowe himself was not aware of. "You decided that the only way any of you could go on living was from the blood, the flesh, of one of the others?" asked Darnell.

His voice was firm, unyielding, as if the events they were about to explore were unfit for the normal range of human sympathy and understanding. "And when I say you, I mean all of you, everyone who was still alive. But it was not a thought that came to all of you at once, was it? Someone thought of it first- someone suggested it to the others. Was it you? Or was it Trevelyn?"

Marlowe bent his head; his brooding lower lip trembled. "Trevelyn may have been the first to suggest it; I don't say he was the first to think it. The possibility we would have to face that alternative was in my mind almost from the beginning, when I realized how many of us were left and how little there was to eat. When that ship- the one Trevelyn described- would not stop to pick us up, then I knew it was only a matter of time before there wouldn't be any other choice."

"But it was Trevelyn's idea?" insisted Darnell.

"He was the one who started it, pushed for it, said it was the only way- that someone had to die if any of the others were to live?"

Marlowe was being offered a way to absolve himself of at least some of the responsibility, but that would be an act of moral cowardice, and Marlowe would not accept it.

"Trevelyn spoke his mind, said what he thought needed to be said. We were all nearly dead, but he was worse off than most, with a wrist that was broken and a foot black with frostbite, the toes nearly gone. Sure, he spoke from fear, but I wouldn't fault him too much for that. He could still speak, still make sense; some of the others were already half out of their minds, seeing things that weren't there and saying things that were plain crazy."

"But he was the first to speak of it openly," repeated Darnell in a quieter voice. "The first actually to suggest that someone be killed...?"

Marlowe's mind appeared to be elsewhere. He did not

hear the question. "I knew what we were going to do- what we had to do- when that ship passed by, when they ignored us. I knew it when Mr. Wilson jumped in after them."

Marlowe bent forward. "No one tried to stop him. Stop him? They were glad he was gone, glad there was a little more room, glad there would be one less man with whom to share whatever food we could get. That's when I knew how far gone we were, how starved and demented we had become. I knew before Trevelyn had said a word about it that we were at the point where we had to choose the way we were going to die."

"You mean, choose the way at least some of you could live, don't you?"

There was something stern and implacable in the look that Marlowe gave Darnell, something secret and remote in his dark, impenetrable eyes.

"None of us were going to live; we were all going to die. And I think most of us knew it, whatever we might have said to encourage each other. I knew we weren't going to be rescued. I thought there was a chance of it until that ship that could have saved us sailed out of sight. We were doomed, and I knew it. We were all going to die; we were never going to be rescued."

"But you didn't tell the others that, did you? You didn't tell them there was no chance of rescue. You stayed on a course for South America. If you were convinced you were all going to die anyway, why not just give up? Why start taking the lives of one another if you were going to die anyway?"

"That was just it, you see. That was the one thing we couldn't do, the one thing I couldn't let us do. We couldn't just give up. Tell someone he's dying of cancer, that he doesn't have more than a month, would you have him take a pistol and put it to his head? Wouldn't you tell him that he might still have a chance, that miracles sometimes happen, that he has an obligation- not just to himself, but to others- to set the right example and keep fighting to the end?

"No, Mr. Darnell, you have to go on! We were going

to die, I believed that. No, I knew it! And once I knew that,
I knew something else as well- that it was just us out there
and that none of the normal rules applied. We had to have
rules of our own, both about how we were going to live and
how we were going to die. All us were going to die, but
every death was going to count, every death was going to be
a sacrifice, a way to save another life. It was the only way to
give any meaning to what was going to happen to us.

"Some died so others could live. It did not matter how
much longer any one would live; it mattered that we did
not give up and all die at once. And so we died one by one,
instead of all at once; and we lived off their bodies because
it was not yet our turn." Marlowe gazed out at the courtroom
crowd, more concerned, it seemed, for the shock he knew he
must have caused them, than for how they felt about him.

"Whatever the reason it was done, this was something
agreed to by all of them?" asked Darnell. "There weren't
any who objected to having someone sacrificed so the others
could live?"

"There were some who did, some who argued against
it; but they were bound like all the others. We agreed among
ourselves that whatever the majority decided, all of us would
follow that decision."

"You mean the decision on the question of whether
someone would be chosen to be killed so the others could
use him to keep on living?"

"Yes."

"And once that was decided, lots were drawn to see
who the first victim would be?"

"Lots were drawn."

"Why that method and not another? Why not decide
the same way the first question had been resolved: by vote of
the majority?"

"That would have been an obscenity, to have us decide
who was going to live and who was going to die. What we
had decided- all we could decide- is that we were willing to
die for one another; but who should do it, and in what order,
that was something which could only be left to chance- left

to God, if you would rather."

Darnell turned to the jury. He looked at each of the jurors in turn, drawing their attention to the importance of the question he was about to ask. "But you did decide who was going to live and who was going to die, didn't you, when you decided that neither you nor Hugo Offenbach would be included, that the two of you would continue to live?"

Marlowe nodded grimly. "We were all going to die," was his only answer.

"But you did not, did you?" asked Darnell, staring right at him. "You thought you were all going to die, you thought that with the passing of that ship you had lost your last, your only, chance at rescue, but you and Hugo Offenbach and four others survived. If you had known that, if you had known that some of you were going to be rescued, wouldn't you have had to do the same thing: sacrifice some so at least a few could survive?"

"Yes."

"And you had to be one of the survivors, because you were the only one who could handle the boat?"

"No," said Marlowe vehemently. "Trevelyn could have done that."

"Trevelyn? He was too weak, too injured."

Marlowe was not listening. He was angry, enraged. His eyes were wild; he looked half-demented. "If I had thought there was any chance, any chance at all, that we would ever be rescued, do you think- does anyone think- that I would have allowed it? Do you think I would have let anyone die before I did? Good God, do you believe- does anyone believe- that I would not have killed myself before I let anything happen to that boy?"

CHAPTER NINETEEN

Darnell felt the ground crumbling beneath his feet. His whole defense- the only defense he had- had been based on the proposition that there had not been any choice, that if Marlowe and the others had not decided that someone had to die, no one would have survived. But now Marlowe had told the jury that before the first victim was chosen, before that first grim lottery was played, he knew that none of them would ever see the shore, that every last one of them would die at sea.

What was it one of the survivors, one of the witnesses for the prosecution, had said? Better they all should perish of hunger and thirst than start a slaughter that would go on until there was only one of them left alive and no one left to kill? Now Darnell had to argue that it did not matter what Marlowe had thought about their chances of survival- the simple fact was that they had survived, and that all of them would have died if they had not done what they did.

"Forget for the moment what you thought were the chances that anyone would ever find you. There was a point at which you knew that death- not just for you, but for all of you- was imminent. Isn't that when the decision was made to sacrifice one to save the rest?"

"Yes," replied Marlowe.

"You were out there forty days before you were rescued?"

"Yes."

"The ship that saw you but did not stop, the one that Arnold Wilson jumped in after, this happened somewhere around the tenth day after the Evangeline went down in the storm?"

"Yes, about then."

"And by this time, many of those people whose safety and well being you felt to be your responsibility were already sick and dying, and some of them, like Arnold Wilson, nearly out of their minds from exposure and the lack of food?" Marlowe bit hard on his lip and nodded.

"You could not have lasted- any of you- more than another day or two, if that?"

"It's hard to say how long any of us might have lived."

Darnell dismissed the answer as being of no account. There was a more important point he was trying to make. "Could any of you have lasted another two weeks?"

"No, we would all have been dead by then."

Darnell gave him a look that demanded more precision. "Some of us might have lived a few more days."

"So even if you had known- if, for example, the ship that had passed by told you that they couldn't stop, but that they would send help which would arrive in two weeks- it would have done no good?"

Marlowe seemed not to understand the question. It was just the reaction Darnell wanted.

"It would have done no good to know that you would be rescued forty days after the Evangeline sank, because you would all have been dead by then. It would have done no good, unless you did exactly what you did- take the lives of some to save the others. Isn't that true, Mr. Marlowe? No matter what you knew or thought you knew, no matter what you thought your chances were, the only choice you had was to do what you did, or let all those people whose lives were in your care perish!"

Before Marlowe could answer, Darnell turned quickly to the bench. "No further questions, your Honor."

Roberts was on his feet, moving around the counsel table. The question of personal sympathy, of what he felt for the terrible moral dilemma in which Marlowe, and not just Marlowe, had been placed had been pushed aside. However easy it might be to understand what had made them do it, what the survivors had done was in some ways worse than murder. Men and women killed each other out of love and hatred, greed, jealousy and obsession- all the range of violent emotions- but they never, or almost never, argued that it was the better thing to do. If you accepted what the defense was arguing, that it was permissible to kill some to save others, where would it stop?

"Mr. Marlowe, let me begin where Mr. Darnell ended. You did not know that you and the others would be out there in that lifeboat for forty days before you were rescued, did you?"

"No."

"You had no way of knowing that?"

"No."

"Instead of forty days, it could have been sixty?"

"Yes."

"You testified that you were certain- after that ship refused to stop- that you would never be rescued. Isn't that what you said?"

"Yes."

"And you were wrong, weren't you?"

"Wrong that we would not be rescued? Yes."

"The plain fact is that you didn't know whether you would be rescued or, if you were, when it might happen- correct?" Roberts stood straight in front of the witness stand, ten feet away. He looked at Marlowe with a cold, determined expression. "For all you knew, for all you could have known, you might have been rescued not forty days after the Evangeline sank, but the day after the ship that passed you sailed out of view. Isn't that true, Mr. Marlowe? For all you knew, or could have known, another ship might at that very moment have been coming straight towards you?"

"For all I knew, for all I could have known, that might have happened- but it did not. No ship came, and I-"

"My point, Mr. Marlowe, is that because you could not know whether a ship might not appear the next day or even the next hour, there was no necessity to do what you did!"

Marlowe's only reply was a stoic glance. All he knew was what had happened.

"Do you disagree, Mr. Marlowe?" asked Roberts, insistent on an answer.

"No ship came-"

"You could not know that it wouldn't!"

"No ship came, and it was not likely one would at that time of year in that part of the south Atlantic. It was not something you could count on. That was how we found ourselves, Mr. Roberts- shipwrecked and out of food, all of us sick and dying. I won't quarrel with you if you say we should not have done what we did to stay alive. I wouldn't quarrel with that at all. But we elected not to do that, not to die before we had to. Let there be no mistake about one thing: if it was wrong for us to have done that, I'm the one who has to bear the burden. Trevelyn was right: I made the decision, the decision to allow it, and I'm the one- no one else- who did it. You have the right man, Mr. Roberts. I'm the one who did it; I'm the one who killed those poor souls; I'm the one responsible- no one else."

"Because you had to? Because it was necessary?" asked Roberts, anticipating the defense. "That is the question, isn't it? Whether you had to. And if you had to, or thought you had to, why you were in that situation in the first place."

Roberts poured a glass of water from a pitcher on the counsel table and took a drink. "Mr. Trevelyn testified that he went to a lifeboat, but it was filled with boxes of champagne and caviar. You were the captain of the Evangeline. Why was a lifeboat used for this? Why was it not ready?"

Marlowe did not blink. "It was my fault. There was no place left to store it."

"But you did not have to take boxes there was no room for."

"It wasn't my decision. But you're right, I didn't have to take them and I shouldn't have. There would have been time to get rid of them, throw them out in any normal emergency. There would have been time if the Evangeline had not started sinking so fast, if the boat had not taken so much water, if there had been any stability."

Roberts held the glass of water next to his chest, staring down at the water's surface as he moved the glass back and forth. "But the storm had been growing gradually, becoming more intense. You could have emptied the lifeboat and made it ready before the storm got worse."

"It happened too quickly. The storm had been getting worse, but I didn't think there was any danger. I thought the Evangeline could sail through anything. There isn't any question but that I was negligent. I should never have allowed anything to be stored in that lifeboat."

Roberts put down the glass. "So only two lifeboats got away, and one of them was never seen again, correct?"

"Yes."

Roberts started to move towards the jury box but then, as if he had made a conscious decision against it, he came back to the counsel table. With a solemn, almost mournful expression, he raised his eyes and looked at Marlowe. "You killed the boy first, plunged a knife into his heart, and then gave directions to the others to drink his still-warm blood- is that correct?"

Marlowe held himself stiff and alert, a rigid discipline that could not hide the anguish in his eyes.

"Is that correct?" repeated Roberts in the face of Marlowe's determined silence.

"Yes, that's correct. I killed him; I told the others what to do."

Everything Roberts did now was pure calculation, each question a ruthless attack on what Marlowe had done. "Describe how you did it- how you held that fourteen-year-old boy so he could not move and stabbed him in the heart!"

"Objection!" cried Darnell as he sprang to his feet. "The witness does not have to do any such thing and the prosecution knows it! Let him ask his questions- Mr. Marlowe will answer. The prosecution doesn't have the right to demand that he provide some macabre description, the only purpose of which is to induce a sense of revulsion!"

Homer Maitland agreed. "This is cross-examination, Mr. Roberts. Ask a question."

Roberts's gaze, which had not left the witness, became more intense. "You held your hand over his face?"

"Yes."

"Did you stab him through his shirt, or did you make him open it first?"

"I told him he should open it," said Marlowe in a bleak, whispered voice.

Roberts's eyes flashed with recognition. "Because it was easier to drive the knife in and because, if he had been wearing the shirt, it would have soaked up the blood instead of letting it gush out- wasn't that the reason, Mr. Marlowe? Isn't that the reason you made him open it?"

"Yes," said Marlowe with downcast eyes. "And because that way death would be just a little quicker."

"You were concerned about that, were you? Concerned about sparing him any unnecessary suffering?"

Marlowe's eyes came up. There was a look of warning in them, as if Roberts had threatened something Marlowe could not allow. "Yes," he said, his voice slowly rising. "Killing him was the hardest thing I've ever had to do."

"But you did it, didn't you?" Before Marlowe could answer, he asked, "And you drank his blood, too, didn't you?"

"I did."

"To stay alive?"

"To stay alive."

"And after the blood, there was still the body. We've heard testimony that the head was cut off and, besides that, the hands and feet. Is that true? Is that what you did?"

"Yes, sir, I did."

"Because you couldn't stand to look at the face of the boy you murdered?"

Marlowe's gaze grew distant. In the midst of all the taunting questions and all the prying glances, a part of him had left. He gave the answers the way a man might repeat the lessons learned in his youth, without a conscious thought as to what any of it meant.

"No, it wasn't that. He was dead; the body had to be prepared."

"And so you...?"

"Removed the head, the appendages, gutted it- what

you do with anything you have killed for food."

Marlowe's eyes suddenly came back to life, raging with self-hatred that quickly turned to anger at the audacity of the question. He gripped the arm of the chair and bent forward. "Do you want me to tell you more? Would you like me to tell you how I carved him up? Would you like to know what it was like to eat human flesh? He's dead! I killed him! Isn't that enough?" he cried as the courtroom erupted in noise.

"Not another word! Not another sound!" ordered Homer Maitland. He beat his gavel hard and kept doing it until he had silenced the boisterous crowd. "One more word from anyone- I'll clear the room!"

Roberts had heard the noise, felt it vibrate up through the floor and go straight to his bones. It drove him forward, made him even more relentless. His eyes cut into Marlowe with all the force he had. "And then, a few days later, when you had done with him, when there was nothing left, you chose another; a woman this time, Helena Green. You killed her next, yes?"

"We drew lots a second time. Yes, it's true."

"Killed her and drank her blood?"

"Yes."

"Killed her, drank her blood, then removed her head, her hands, her feet, and then gutted her body. Is that what you did?" asked Roberts in a fury. Marlowe nodded, and then waited, silent.

"And then you ate her?"

"Yes, to stay alive."

"Yes, to stay alive," repeated Roberts in a scornful voice as his eyes moved towards the jury. "And then, after Helena Green was used, you had another drawing, and another victim was chosen. Isn't that- ? Wait," he said, suddenly remembering something. His head bent at a puzzled angle, he looked at Marlowe.

"The boy- he was stabbed in the heart. Why did you stab her in the throat?"

Marlowe looked down at his hands. "She asked me to,"

he said in a barely audible voice.

"What did you say?" asked Roberts, incredulous. "She asked you to?"

"I think she thought it would be immodest to expose her chest. She didn't want to be that naked."

Roberts started to attack the answer, to insist that it could not have happened that way, but he stopped himself- staring hard at Marlowe, he realized that it was true. He began to pace slowly in front of the jury box. A few seconds later- which, in the tense heated atmosphere of the court- room, seemed much longer- he placed one hand on the railing and with the other stroked his chin.

"You killed the boy first, then the woman, and then a third person, and then another. And you kept doing this because it was the only way to keep the rest of you alive?"

"Yes."

"But you did not think there was any chance that any of you would be rescued? Isn't that what you testified in response to a question from Mr. Darnell?"

"No, I didn't think any of us would survive. I was sure we would not."

"But then nothing that you did was necessary, was it?" asked Roberts in a voice that struck a solemn chord. "Forget for the moment that you were found, that six of you were saved- you didn't believe that would happen, so that was never the reason why you killed the others, was it? It was not because you thought it was necessary so that at least some of you could survive the shipwreck, it was because you were willing to do anything- even murder- just to live a few more days. Isn't that what happened, Mr. Marlowe? Isn't that why you killed six people? Because you would rather murder someone than give up even just a few days of what, by your own admission, was a painful, tortured existence that some might think worse than death itself?"

"That wasn't why I did it. That wasn't the choice I had. It wasn't die without killing, or kill and die a little later. We were all going to die- that's what I was so certain of. We were going to die. That was never a question. The question was how we were going to die- by just giving up, or by letting each one believe that with his death, someone else would live? Each of those who died thought he had made himself a willing sacrifice to save the others. That was why I did it, why I agreed to that terrible lottery- so the death of each of them could be heroic, so there was some meaning in their lives. There was nothing wrong with what we did. What was wrong is that we lived."

CHAPTER TWENTY

There was something missing, something not quite logical, in Marlowe's explanation of the lottery they had played to put one another to death. It had been based on an illusion, a myth that, if Marlowe did not invent it, he had done nothing to dispel: the belief that some could live, if only others were willing to die. But had not Marlowe as good as admitted that no one had really thought there was any chance they would ever see land again? Had he not admitted that, whatever they might have said to encourage one another, they knew they were all going to die?

Roberts tried to drive home the point. "You were in the middle of the south Atlantic, the only ship that had seen you had sailed off. You just testified that you did not think there was any chance of rescue, and you told us earlier that, deep down, the others must have known it too. But if they did not believe there was any chance of rescue, they could not possibly have believed that their deaths would make a difference, that their deaths would be heroic, could they?"

"It did not matter what they thought. I told them that there was still a chance, that we could not give up hope, that we had to keep trying. What else could we do? I was the one in charge. The Evangeline and everyone on her was my responsibility. I had failed in that- she sank- I could not fail in this! I told them that every day we stayed alive we were a day closer; I told them that another ship would come.

"Another day! Do you know what that means, when death is hovering over you, waiting to take you away? Yes, we were all going to die, and maybe all of us knew it, but the heart and mind don't always stick with what we know. We aren't made like that; we have to have something we can cling to, some faith that makes sense out of what we can't avoid. Death was coming, Mr. Roberts- what else could we believe in if not that life would go on?"

Marlowe's large deep-set eyes drew back in on themselves. He was about to add something, to explain his thought, but he changed his mind and just shook his head. Then he changed his mind again. "That's why each time it happened, each time someone was about to be killed so the others could live, we said a prayer."

Roberts looked at him sharply. "A prayer? You said a prayer when someone was 'about to be killed'? What are you saying? That you tried to turn murder into some kind of ritual, some twisted idea of a religious service?"

Marlowe raised his chin. "No, just a prayer that this would be the last time we would have to do it, and that we would be forgiven for what we had been forced to do."

"And then you killed him- or her- and used the blood, the body, to stay alive?"

"Yes."

"Though you knew- or thought you knew- it was only a matter of time before you would all be dead?"

"Yes."

"And you would have gone on like this, killing each of them in turn- and saying that same prayer each time you did it- until there was no one left? Was that your plan, Mr. Marlowe- to kill them all?"

"Yes, it was."

Angry, disturbed, Roberts stalked back to the counsel table where he threw open a file folder that lay on top and, while he studied something in it, caught his breath. "You would have killed them all," he muttered as he closed the file and looked at Marlowe in the dim light that filtered through the courtroom windows.

He tapped his fingers on the table and then, as if it were the only way to stop the habit, moved two steps away, too far to reach it. "You were very careful about the way you answered Mr. Darnell's questions about how this decision was made in the first place. You say you are willing to take responsibility for what happened, but you want us to believe that it was, in a manner of speaking, only after the fact: that there was something like a consensus- yes, I know, there were a few dissenters- that something had to be done, that someone had to be sacrificed or everyone would die.

"But even if that is true, why didn't you convince them to do what Aaron Trevelyn claims he suggested? If you could not wait until someone died of natural causes, why didn't you choose the person who was already closest to death? Would that not have been more reasonable, more humane, than to leave it all to chance?"

Occupied for most of his life with thoughts of his own, without interest in the things that drove the ambitions of other men, Marlowe did not see the question that lay just beyond his answer. "It would not have been right to single out the sick. We could not let calculation enter into it. We had to leave it to chance, and, at least in that sense, let God decide."

"God and you, don't you mean? Or was it God who told you to decide who would have to enter your lottery of death and who would not? Or was it you who told God whom he could pick from and whom he could not?

"That's what happened, isn't it?" asked Roberts in a caustic voice. "You decided that two of you would be immune. You decided that neither you nor Hugo Offenbach would have to take your chances with the others, didn't you?"

The look on Marlowe's face was the look of blasted hopes and broken dreams; the look of a man with nothing left who goes on living only because he still has one more duty to perform. "I tried...I wanted to take his place. I would have, if he had not made me promise to try to save the others," he mumbled, as he looked around the courtroom in a half-mad search to find the face of someone who might understand.

"You killed him, killed that fourteen-year-old boy. You left his life to chance, but you would not allow Hugo Offenbach to run the same risk. Just how was that a question of necessity, Mr. Marlowe? How was that something about which you did not have any choice?...Well, Mr. Marlowe, what is your answer? Why wasn't Hugo Offenbach subject to the same risk as the rest?"

"Because he was better than the rest of us, because he has the kind of gift that only God can give!"

"But you would not let God decide!" Roberts shouted back. "Better than the rest of you? You're saying he had a better right to live?"

"Better right to live? Yes, I wouldn't doubt it. Look what he can do for others, what he brings to the world. If you had to choose, Mr. Roberts- if you had to choose between him and me...If any of you," he said, twisting his shoulders until he squarely faced the jury, "had to choose between us, choose whether I was going to die or Mr. Offenbach, why would anyone choose me?

"It's all well and good to say we both should live, and to say that we're both equal in the sight of God, but leave all that for God and eternity. Someone has to die- not tomorrow, not someday, but now! Of course you choose him to live. It would be immoral if you didn't."

"That doesn't answer the question. You said you knew there was no chance of rescue," Roberts insisted, his voice harsh and strident. "No one was going to survive, so why didn't he have to take his chances the same as all the others? Where was the necessity, Mr. Marlowe? Where was the necessity? That's what I'm trying- what we're all trying- to understand!"

"It was what the woman said- Mrs. Wilcox. He gave us a reason to go on living. It was the music. Don't you see? We were huddled together in that boat, living off the flesh and blood of each other. We weren't human, except for the hope we had and the music, his music, the music he made. We were living in the filth of our own excrement, diseased and dying, some of us in the grip of hallucinations- and, despite all that, we still had the knowledge, each time he played, that we were human after all, and that maybe we could somehow get through yet another day.

"The others- the ones who died- they kept the rest of us alive and breathing; but he was the one who made us want to live, he was the one who made it seem worth doing what we had to, for as long as we could."

"The choice was to let everyone die a peaceful death, a death from natural causes, or to engage in violent acts of slaughter so you could live like cannibals for just a few days longer- and you chose murder! Was it really that important to listen to Hugo Offenbach play the violin?" asked Roberts with contempt as he wheeled away from the witness. "I have no more questions of this…"

The look of open hostility faded from his eyes. He looked at Marlowe without emotion. "Mr. Marlowe, let me ask you point blank: do you think what you did was excusable? Do you believe that the killing of these people should be forgiven because it was the only way to save the others who had survived the shipwreck of the Evangeline?"

"No, sir, I do not. I did what I thought I had to, but that doesn't make it right. It was the least evil thing I could do, but that doesn't make it good." A murmur ran through the crowd, a silent tribute to Marlowe's unflinching honesty.

"No further questions, your Honor."

Judge Maitland peered over his glasses at William Darnell, who sat slumped in his chair, staring into the middle distance. "Mr. Darnell, is there anything you wish to ask on redirect?"

Darnell was aware, as he sat thinking about what he wanted to do next, that every eye was on him, waiting to see what surprises he had in store. He let them wait.

"Mr. Darnell?" Maitland prodded gently.

With a grave expression, Darnell rose slowly from the chair. He stood right there; he did not move a step. Placing his hand on his hip, he bent slightly forward at the waist. "In answer to one of Mr. Roberts's questions, you admitted that you could not really know whether a ship might appear. I believe what Mr. Roberts said was: 'For all you knew, for all you could have known, you might have been rescued not forty days after the Evangeline sank, but the day after the ship that passed you sailed out of view.' And then he added- and it is a point that struck me so forcibly that, if I wanted to, I could not forget his words- 'For all you knew, or could have

known, another ship might at that very moment have been
coming straight towards you.'

"Do you remember that, Mr. Marlowe? And do you
remember what you said- that for all you knew, or could
have known, that might have happened? My question, Mr.
Marlowe, is whether it is still your testimony that, as Mr.
Roberts insisted, you could not have known- not with any
kind of certainty- whether rescue might not be just hours or
days away?" Darnell barely waited for Marlowe to say that
he had no reason to change what he had said.

"So we now have the rather unusual situation in
which, on a point crucial to the case, both the defense and
the prosecution agree: you did not know when or whether a
ship might suddenly appear. Mr. Roberts takes that fact to
mean- what was it he said?- 'because you could not know
whether a ship might not appear the next day or even the
next hour, there was no necessity to do what you did.' I take
that fact- and I believe any reasonable person would take that
fact- to mean that there was indeed a necessity to do what
you did."

Roberts was on his feet, insisting that Darnell should
make his argument during his summation.

"I will," said Darnell. "But right now I'm trying to
ask a question, if counsel will allow it!" He turned back
to Marlowe. "It's true, isn't it, that whatever you may have
believed, whatever you may have feared, Mr. Roberts is
right, you could not have known whether a ship might
suddenly appear?"

"Yes, I suppose that's true."

"And if you had just waited, as Mr. Roberts seems to
suggest you should have, and let- how did he put it?- 'let
everyone die a peaceful death', there would have been no
survivors. Isn't that true, Mr. Marlowe?"

"Yes, none of us could have lived."

"So there was a necessity for what was done, wasn't
there? The choice that Mr. Roberts put to you was false,
wasn't it? It was not a choice between a peaceable death
and a violent one, it was the choice between the death of

everyone and the life of as many as you could save. Because, again, whatever you may have thought about the chances of rescue, Mr. Roberts is right- you could never really know. Isn't that correct?"

"Yes, I suppose."

"No, not suppose, Mr. Marlowe. It is a fact. Now, Mr. Roberts was at some pains to insist that, once again, the choice was between a peaceful and a violent death. My question is: was the death you inflicted violent in the way that word is normally understood? Let me explain. You testified- and others have as well- that these deaths, these necessary deaths, were of people who had agreed in advance that this was the thing that should be done. Is that correct?"

"Yes, they had agreed."

"And they agreed that the one chosen each time would be chosen by chance- correct?"

"Yes."

"Did any of them, after they were chosen, try to resist?"

Marlowe shook his head. "No, they all died bravely."

"You testified that the second person chosen, the actress Helena Green, did not want to die like the boy, that she asked you to end her life another way?"

"She had seen what happened when the knife went into the boy's heart. The thought of it was more than she could bear. She didn't want to half-undress, and she did not want to see the knife going in. I told her the fastest way would be the throat, and that she wouldn't feel any pain. She had as much courage as any man I ever knew."

"She did not resist? She did not try to get away?"

"No, she placed herself in front of me and lifted up her chin. She told me not to blame myself for what I had to do."

"And was that true of the others as well? They accepted, without complaint and without objection, that it was their turn to die?"

"We were all so tired, all of us in so much pain, that for some of them- they seemed almost glad of it."

"In part, I take it, because they knew there was a

purpose in their death; that because of them, the others would live?"

"Yes, there is no mistake that they believed that, that they had that hope."

"And because they knew that the way each of them had been chosen- drawing lots- had left the decision in the hands of fate, or God?"

Marlowe nodded. "And that was true for all of them, all except the boy," he said with a weary look in his eye.

Marlowe had made a mistake. Darnell gave him the chance to correct it. "Except the boy? But he was the first one chosen after you had all agreed to draw lots to decide."

"Yes," said Marlowe, "but I made sure he was the first one taken, the first one to die."

Darnell was staggered. His face turned ashen.

"You mean you fixed the result? But why?" he asked, then was struck by a thought. "Because he was dying anyway; because he was the closest one to death; because you hoped that his would be the only death- that before another life would be taken, you would all be saved. Was not that the reason?"

"No, it was not because I thought he would be the only one who had to die. It was because I did not want him to be the last. I did not want him to have to live through the horror of what we were going to do. The others- they were all old enough to understand what we had to do and the reasons for it; but he was just a boy, barely fourteen...I could not allow it. It was too obscene. He was too young, too decent, for that."

"But other witnesses testified that when the boy's name was drawn, you tried to take his place!"

"When I was faced with it, having to end his life, I could not do it. I wouldn't have, either, if he had not begged me, told me it was his part to help save the others. All of you can make what you want to out of the fact that, despite what I believed, we were rescued, the six of us who were left.

"You can argue that it made what we did excusable under the law because the only choice was that or death, but the day the White Rose came, the day they pulled us out of the sea, I knew that I could have saved him, saved the boy- but that I had murdered him instead. It doesn't matter what the law says, I'm as guilty of murder as any murderer who ever lived. Worse, because I had the responsibility to keep him safe, and now he's dead when he should be back home with a long full life ahead of him. I should not have listened to him- I should have trusted my first instinct and killed myself instead!"

CHAPTER TWENTY-ONE

Darnell had promised Summer Blaine that on Saturday he would neither talk nor think about the trial. He needed to clear his mind, to stop brooding on what, in any event, he could not control. It was, she insisted in that firm, friendly way she had, essential for his health. They would spend the day just being themselves.

"But that is being myself," he protested with an amiable grin as she drove north across the Golden Gate Bridge. "It's what I've spent my life doing. That's all there is to me; there isn't anything else."

"That isn't true and you know it."

"Isn't it? I wonder. It's certainly all I know."

She glanced across at him, a look of pleasure in her eyes. "You know me- and I think I know you."

"You ought to know me, the way you poke and prod me and run all those tests. Of course, you don't think I'm just a lawyer; in your eyes I'm a patient, a guinea pig on which to test your latest theory, an entry in your book of failed experiments, the subject of the next ground breaking article in the New England Journal of Medicine!"

"We can control that now," she said with a mocking smile. "I can give you a prescription to keep you from getting quite so manic!"

The laughter in Darnell's voice subsided; his smile became subdued. He looked across the bay to the rolling hills on the other side. "I doubt it would be so easy to cure the sickness in Marlowe's soul. In all my years, I've never had a client anything like him." Darnell remembered his promise, and with a silent glance told Summer that he had not meant to break it.

"Where are we going for lunch?" he asked, patting her gently on the knee. "Sausalito?"

Summer drove into the village and made her way

along the narrow, crowded street to a restaurant at the far end of a jetty that formed a breakwater for the marina. From a table in the corner with a view of San Francisco, they watched the sailboats race across the bay.

"Do you mind if I ask you something about the trial?" asked Summer rather tentatively halfway through lunch.

It was as if Darnell had been waiting for it, the chance to make the reply he had filed away for future use. A smile of cheerful triumph crossed his mouth. "I wouldn't mind at all, but my doctor won't allow it."

Summer rolled her eyes. "You've never listened to her before."

"Are you sure you haven't been sitting in court, watching Roberts?" he asked with a wounded look. "That's the kind of quick, lethal response he's so good at giving. Of course you can ask me about the trial. You want to know what happened yesterday, when Marlowe said that the choice of the boy as the first victim had not been a matter of chance."

"Did you know?" asked Summer in a quiet, thoughtful voice.

Slanting through the broken clouds, the sunlight caught the side of Darnell's pale cheek and made him seem younger, and more rigorously healthy, than his years.

"Did I know?" he mused. "No, but I should have. I was stunned when he said it; astonished, I suppose. It had never occurred to me that Marlowe would arrange it so that the boy would be the first to die. It's what makes him different from anyone else I've defended, maybe anyone else I've known- the way that everything you find out about him is so much in keeping with his character.

"Whether or not you agree with something he's done, it was never because there was any advantage in it for him; it was always because, as best he could understand his duty, it was what he had to do. He's a kind of force of nature, everything about him is elemental; the way we all were, I imagine, before we became so civilized that we felt this constant need to question and analyze everything we do."

Darnell looked out the window at the sailboats leaning hard against the wind. A faint smile flickered across his mouth. He shook his head and turned back to Summer.

"Everyone who heard him, everyone who was there in that courtroom- none of them would tell you that what Marlowe did was right. And yet, if they had to choose someone to be in charge when they were in trouble- if a ship they were on went down in a storm- every last one of them would choose him and not think twice about it."

Summer shoved her plate aside and put her hands on the table. She studied them with a careful, experienced eye, like someone searching for the first sign of something wrong, the slight failure to function perfectly that announces the beginning of the end, the slow descent into incapacity when you can no longer do the work you were made to do.

"Do you think that's really true, that no one who was there in the courtroom believed what Marlowe did was right? Or only that none of them would ever say so? Because I get the feeling that it is one of those situations where we think we're supposed to say one thing while what we feel is something quite different. If I had been in his situation, knowing what he knew about their chances, I could not say that I wouldn't have done what he did: made certain that the boy died first."

"You may have been right," said Darnell with a rueful smile. "This case may kill me. Marlowe is right- Marlowe meant it- when he said there was nothing wrong with what they did, nothing wrong except that they lived. If they had all died and an empty boat had been found, and inside it was a journal Marlowe or one of the others had left giving an account of everything they had done- how they decided to die, each one in his turn, so the others could live a little longer- then we would all be paying tribute to Marlowe's courage and the essential decency of making certain that at least the boy would not have to go through it. But instead, we look at Marlowe with almost as much contempt as he feels for himself. The boy did not have to die at all- he could be alive today! It might have all been different if Marlowe had not been so damnably well-educated."

"Well-educated? I thought he had barely gone to school. Didn't he leave home to become a cabin boy when he was only twelve?"

"I said well-educated, not well-schooled. Take all the years you and I went to school-grade school, high school, college, law school, medical school- add them all up and what have we got? You're a fine doctor and I'm a passable attorney, but what in all those years were we really taught about the meaning of anything, including the things we were trained to do? We simply assumed that what we did was important. Everyone told us that, and we believed it.

"But Marlowe? Marlowe was on his own, alone in the world, seeing everything with his own eyes; seeing things as they were, instead of seeing things the way that years of other people's teaching told him he should. He listened to what he heard, to the stories he was told on the ships he sailed; he heard the stories, some of them no doubt embellished and distorted, about the ships that were wrecked and the things that had happened, the things that men were driven to do, in order to survive.

"But Marlowe was born with a mind more curious than most. He read everything he could about the sea. Everyone read Moby-Dick; but Marlowe read everything he could find about the Essex. Remember when I told you that the survivors lived on human flesh? In the days of sailing ships, before the telegraph, when the first anyone knew a ship had gone down was when it did not return to port, it was the unwritten custom of the sea. It was understood that the lives of some would have to be sacrificed so that the others could live.

"There was a rule, however; a rule that had to be followed, the only way to make it fair. No one could decide that someone else had to die- it had to be left to chance; they had to draw lots. Marlowe knew that, understood it, believed it was right. If he had not known that, he might have done what I know for certain Trevelyn, and not just Trevelyn, wanted. He would have decided who was closest to dying anyway and killed him first. But then none of those who died- including, perhaps more than any of them, the boy himself- would have been given the chance to die an honorable death. That is the question, really- whether I can make anyone see that. We don't believe much in honor anymore."

Summer Blaine placed her hand on top of Darnell's. He smiled gently at her, acknowledging the comfort it gave him. There were times now when the memory of his wife seemed to merge with what he saw in Summer's face, as if what he had felt for the one had continued on in the other. Instead of betraying the memory of the woman he had loved and buried, it seemed in some strange and unexpected way to enhance it.

"This is no way to spend a Saturday afternoon, dwelling on something as grim as death. Why don't you tell me what you did this week? How many children did you bring into the world- none of whom, we'll hope, ever has to face Marlowe's cruel dilemma?"

She wanted to know more about the trial, more about what he thought about Marlowe and what he had done, but she had the feeling that he was desperate for some distraction from what had become the almost intolerable burden of the trial. She knew he seldom slept during the week and that the weekends were not much different.

That morning, when he got up, he seemed to show not just his age but something more alarming. Each movement betrayed a conscious effort, as if he were afraid he might lose his balance and fall. He claimed that he had not slept well, and that after a shower and a cup of coffee he would be as good as new. And he was, at least to all appearances- but she knew that what she had seen was not just fatigue. He had, in his own indirect way, admitted as much when he joked that she may have been right and that the trial might kill him.

She knew it would not do any good to tell him that he had to take better care of himself, but she had to do something. "You haven't been back to Napa since the trial started," she said lightly.

He started to explain, but she stopped him with a look. "You won't have time to, until the trial is over. I have a couple of weeks of vacation owing, and I thought it might be good to get away. I thought-"

"You thought you might like to spend your vacation- which you haven't taken, by the way, in years- here in the city? And as long as you are going to be here anyway, you could keep an eye on me, make sure I take my medicine and get some proper rest like the good, docile patient you know I want to be?"

It made her angry with herself that he could see right through her. Feeling frustrated and inept, she tossed her napkin at him and shrugged helplessly. "If you want to kill yourself, I suppose you have that right; but you might at least wait until the trial is over before you do it. You may not owe it to me to take decent care of yourself, but don't you owe something to your client? Do you think he should have to go through a second trial, live through everything all over again, because his lawyer wouldn't bother with stupid things like getting enough sleep, much less taking the medication his doctor prescribed, and died the day before the case was supposed to go to the jury?"

Darnell had never seen her angry and only seldom seen her upset.

"I promise that won't happen," he said, devastated by the tears she was fighting to hold back. "I promise I won't die."

"You promise you won't die!" she exclaimed, laughing through the tears she tried to rub away with the back of her hand. "I really think you believe that, that all you have to do is promise and it won't happen.

"You're just like Marlowe: you think the only thing that matters is what people believe. If they believe their death will allow someone else to live, they can die know- ing their death has a meaning! If you believe you can't die because the trial isn't over, then you don't have to do anything to prevent it! I wish I could share your belief, but You've got a heart condition, William Darnell, and that isn't

179

a question of what you believe or what you promise. If you don't take care of yourself, you're not going to live long enough to see what that jury decides!"

"I'm all right- really!" he said with all the assurance he could. "And I do take all those pills you give me, and in the order in which I am supposed to. I have the names of all of them memorized. Would you like me to recite them?"

Wiping away the last fugitive tear, she fixed him with a physician's skeptical stare. "Tell me the truth. Has anything happened? Have you felt any dizziness? Any loss of breath? Have you had any chest pains? Anything?"

He had already made the mistake of dismissing her offer to stay with him as not just unnecessary but as a kind of intrusion. His pride, his stupid insistence on his own independence, had hurt her. He had to tell her the truth. "The other day in court, I suddenly felt weak. Everything started to go black. But within a minute I was fine, and it hasn't happened again. Just that one time," he said with a confident smile.

Summer reached across the table. He started to take her hand. She shook her head and held his wrist, counting to herself as she listened to his pulse. "Let's go for a walk," she said as he signaled to the waiter for the check. "We'll watch the sailboats out on the bay and look across at the city. I've always thought it's the best view there is of San Francisco. And then we'll find a bench and you can tell me what you're going to do this week at trial and I'll tell you how much you're going to like having me there, waiting for you when you come home each day from court, making certain you get all the right things to eat and plenty of sleep."

"In other words," said Darnell as he paid the waiter, "I should now consider myself under house arrest?"

Summer smiled. "I'll try not to make it seem too much like prison."

Outside the restaurant, Darnell took Summer by the hand. For a long time they walked in silence, listening to the wind snap the canvas sails of the boats that were close to shore and to the sounds of cheerful voices that echoed, dreamlike, from the shiny decks half hidden in the waves.

"Everything else changes," he said as they stopped at a bench and watched the ferry pull out from the dock, heading back to the city on another thirty-minute run, "but this never does, the sight of boats on the bay. Maybe that's why people love the sea, why they're always drawn back to it.

"There was something Marlowe said, almost the first time I met him: that you begin to understand how simple it all is out there, how the rest of it is all a fiction, the made-up story of other men's dreams and ambitions- that the only thing that matters is life and death, and how you live them. Not just how you live your life, mind you, but how you live your death.

"I can't honestly tell you that I didn't quite understand it, but when he said it, I believed it. Marlowe does that, you know- he gives you the sense that he knows things you don't, and that he won't tell you all of it because you might not be ready to hear the whole, unvarnished truth."

CHAPTER TWENTY-TWO

If William Darnell had never had anyone like Vincent Marlowe as a defendant, neither had he ever had a witness like Hugo Offenbach. There had been a few trials he could remember, most of them in the early years of his career, in which someone of remarkable intelligence had been called by either the prosecution or the defense. They had usually been mathematicians or involved in one of the more theoretical sciences, like physics or genetics- disciplines that, because most of us had studied some part of them in school, were not entirely beyond the average comprehension.

Hugo Offenbach was another kind of genius, less understood and more mysterious. It did not matter which of two people followed the same mathematical formula to the correct conclusion; it mattered a great deal which of two musicians played a violin concerto. Genius in science was known by its method; genius in music and the arts was known by its result, a feeling that you were in the presence of something great and inimitable, something you might never experience again.

Offenbach was a genius, but that did not mean that the major critics thought he knew anything about music. His views on certain matters were considered hopelessly out of date, the uninformed opinions of a musician so well trained in the classical tradition of his instrument that he failed to grasp the important changes made by modernity. In a long-forgotten essay, published in a periodical with a circulation so limited that issues were hand-addressed to each subscriber, Offenbach had first given expression to a point of view from which he had never departed. Speaking of the end of the nineteenth and the beginning of the twentieth centuries, he wrote:

'While everyone spoke of progress, measuring the vast improvement in the material conditions of existence and the spread of democratic institutions and the rights of individuals, music and art began a long descent into madness.'

Lacking all talent for evasion, Offenbach, to the lasting mortification of friend and foe alike, offered as examples of the 'new barbarism' Bartok's violin sonatas, numbers 1 and 2, and Webern's 'Four Pieces for Violin and Piano', works which he resolutely refused to play, because 'it would be like writing an obscenity on the wall of a church.'

If he had not been the greatest violinist of his age, he would have been dismissed as a harmless crank. If he had not been the greatest violinist of his age, the crowd that watched him enter the courtroom on Monday morning, the next witness for the defense, would not have felt the same sense of wonder. Even to people who had no interest in classical music, Offenbach's face was famous because of the distinction of his accomplishment.

He appeared not to have changed, at least in any obvious way. His thin lips were pressed together in a straight line the way they usually were; his eyes, intelligent and alert, looked straight ahead. The eager crowd, turning towards him with its unremitting gaze, had no effect. He was used to being on stage, all attention centered on him. The gate in the railing swung shut behind him. The clerk was waiting, ready to administer the oath. But first Offenbach stopped, turned to his left and quickly walked the few short steps to the counsel table.

"It's good to see you again, Mr. Marlowe," he said in a firm, even voice. Marlowe had risen from his chair as Offenbach approached. They looked at each other like old war comrades, men whose memories are secrets no one who had not been there could understand.

"Thank you, Mr. Offenbach," whispered Marlowe. He lowered his eyes and, with what seemed like reluctance, let go of the older man's hand. Offenbach settled into the witness chair, turned to the jury and, without any change of expression, gave the kind of formal nod with which he might have acknowledged a concert audience.

He looked across at Darnell, who was standing just in

front of the counsel table, and nodded again, signaling this
time that he was ready to begin. Darnell could not quite help
himself. He stared down at the floor, smiling to himself at
how Offenbach had managed with just two small gestures to
make the usual formalities of the courtroom seem somehow
lax and undisciplined.

"Mr. Offenbach, let me ask you first why you were
aboard the Evangeline. As a concert violinist, was it not
difficult for you to take that much time away from your
schedule?"

Hugo Offenbach was short- five foot six, perhaps five
foot seven- and of less-than-average weight, but he held
himself with an almost military bearing, his thin shoulders
square, his small, round head moving only when his shoulders did. Every movement was quick, sharp and precise, the
way his fingers worked when he played. His sat motionless
while Darnell asked his question, then turned his head and
shoulders to the jury.

"I was invited by an old friend of mine, Basil
Hawthorne, who was a friend, or at least a business acquain-
tance, of Mr. Whitfield. I had never met Mr. Whitfield
myself. I had just finished a fairly lengthy concert tour in
Europe. I was tired. I thought it would be good to get away,
to be out on the ocean with no one else around. I've spent so
much of my life indoors."

He paused and looked at Marlowe. "I did not know it
would end like this. No one did."

"Basil Hawthorne was what I think is called an impre-
sario, someone who arranges concert tours for musicians?"

"And my dear friend."

"He was lost at sea?"

"The night of the storm. I don't know what happened
to him. He may have been in the other lifeboat. All I know is
that he did not survive."

"On that night, the night the Evangeline sank, what
happened to you? How much do you remember?"

"Captain Marlowe did not want to alarm anyone,
but I could tell that something was wrong and that he was

worried. The sea had been rough for days, but- and it's the strangest thing- the worse it got, the better we sailed. Perhaps Marlowe can explain it, or someone else who has spent his life at sea- I'm ignorant about such things but I can try to tell you what it was like

"The Evangeline seemed to come to life, to breathe, as if the storm had shocked her into the conscious knowledge of what she could do. It affected all of us. We were like children set to gallop on a horse that did not need a hand on the reins to tell her what to do. For those few days, the days before that night, I don't think I've ever been quite so aware of my own existence, or felt quite so connected with the world around me.

"And then the storm changed- not in degree, but in kind. And the Evangeline changed, too. She was not running over the sea anymore; the sea was running over her, crushing her to death. The equipment- all the electronics- had failed. Marlowe was holding on to the wheel with all the strength he had. He saw me come on deck and told me to grab a coat, something warm, and to brace myself because he did not know how much longer he could keep her headed into the storm.

"That's when it happened, just seconds after that. The boat seemed to lift right out of the water as if it were being tossed end over end, and then there was this ghastly shudder as if it had been ripped apart." Offenbach stared down at his hands as he slowly shook his head. The silence in the courtroom was heavy.

"I don't know what happened next, except that Marlowe saved me. I had a heart attack, not strong enough to kill me, but I lost consciousness. Marlowe somehow got me into the lifeboat."

"And your violin?"

"Yes, and my violin."

Darnell moved across the front of the counsel table, close to the jury box. "Who first suggested that it might be necessary to kill someone to save the others?"

"Trevelyn," replied Offenbach immediately.

"You're sure? There isn't some possibility that others were talking about it and you simply remember his voice more than the others?"

"Trevelyn," he repeated so quickly that their two voices echoed together. "No one else had said anything like it. As far as I know, no one else had even thought it."

"The defendant, Vincent Marlowe, testified that not only had he thought it, he had known it was something that would have to be done when that ship that could have picked you up sailed by without stopping. Does that surprise you?"

"That Marlowe would say it? No. He would say it whether he ever actually had that thought or not. In his mind, it would not make any difference who said it first or who thought about it first, because he allowed it. He's wrong about that, of course. Trevelyn- and not just Trevelyn- would have killed someone to get what they needed. But I agree with Marlowe that it would be wrong to blame Trevelyn, or anyone else. We were not civilized people living in comfortable homes, debating after dinner about where we wanted to spend our next holiday. The choice was stark, simple: kill or die.

"If it hadn't been for Marlowe, some of us, I'm afraid, would have ripped the others apart, driven mad by hunger and our own repellent taste for blood. Marlowe put an order on things. He changed us from a pack of dying animals to something at least a little more human."

Darnell looked him squarely in the eye. "Is it your testimony that, whatever he may have thought about this himself, Marlowe was driven to it by the force of circumstances in which he found himself? That if he had not stopped them, men like Trevelyn would have taken matters into their own hands and killed whoever they wanted?"

"I'm afraid that is exactly what would have happened."

"But Marlowe made sure that did not happen," said Darnell, glancing at the jury to reinforce the full significance of this. "Instead of the rule of the jungle, everyone for himself, he established a kind of government, a set of rules by which all of you could live. And everyone agreed to this?"

"Yes. There were some- and who could blame them?- who did not want to be part of any killing, who thought it better to let death come when it would; but even they agreed that we should all be bound by what the majority decided."

"And everyone whose life was taken, everyone who died so the others could live, was chosen by chance?"

"Yes- or so I thought before I read what Mr. Marlowe said about the death of the boy. At first, I must tell you, I did not think it was true; I did not think he could have done that. But then I realized that it was exactly what he would have done- tried to spare the boy from having to live, even if only for a little while, with what we were about to do.

"The boy worshipped him and Marlowe knew it. When we were on the Evangeline, the boy followed him everywhere. Marlowe was harsh with him, barking at him when he was not doing what he should, giving him one of those stern looks when he told him he had work to do. The boy would just stare at him, waiting for the change that always happened, the sudden sparkle in Marlowe's eye, the reluctant laugh as he sent him on his way.

"Marlowe did not believe there was any chance of rescue- he told me that, when we made our agreement- but I wonder whether he would not have done the same thing anyway to spare the boy from learning about the awful things human beings can be made to do. Marlowe was strong enough for that...The look on his face when he had to kill the boy- it must have been what Abraham looked like when he was told by the Lord that he had to sacrifice Isaac."

"The agreement?" asked Darnell. "You said 'when we made our agreement'. Do you mean the agreement that all of you made to decide by lot who would die?"

A troubled smile crossed Offenbach's lips. "Marlowe told me that I had to play the violin; I said I would not. He said I had to help the others forget for a while what they were suffering and how they had no hope. I told him I was barely alive, that my hands hurt so much I did know if I could even hold the bow. I told him that there was no point to it, that it was a fool's game he was playing to pretend that we had any chance of being saved. That's when he told me that I was right, that it was as good as certain that we were all going to die."

Hugo Offenbach stared into the silence, fascinated by what he was watching in his mind. "Marlowe said that was the reason we had to do it, why we had to stay alive; we had to make the others think that there was a reason to live, because it was the only way to make them believe that there was a reason to die.

"I told him I wanted to die myself. He asked me what good God had done to give me this talent if He had made me too much of a coward to use it when it was most needed."

Offenbach looked around the courtroom at the sea of uplifted faces. "As you might imagine, I had no answer for this. So I agreed to what he wanted; but he was right about me, you see. I was a coward, and so I said I would do it, play as often and as well as I could, but on one condition."

"One condition?" asked Darnell, almost mesmerized by Offenbach's bright, piercing eyes. "What condition was that?"

"That when it was all over, when we were the only two left, that he would kill me first; that he would not kill himself and make me live alone."

"And did he agree to that condition?" asked Darnell, his voice a whisper. "Did he make you that promise?"

"He promised he would kill us both."

A death-like stillness descended on the courtroom, the only sound the slow creaking of the chair as Darnell pulled it back from the counsel table and sat down.

"Do you have any questions, Mr. Roberts?" asked Homer Maitland in a voice that sounded tired and distracted.

"Just a few, your Honor." Roberts stood at the end of the table, his hands shoved deep into his pockets. He glanced down at the tablet on which he had scribbled half a page of notes. With his head still bent to the side, he raised his eyes and studied Offenbach for a puzzled moment.

"This agreement you had with the defendant, Vincent

Marlowe- this was a systematic plan for murder, was it not?"

"No, I reject that categorically!" was Offenbach's immediate reply. "It was just the opposite. It was the only way to stop them killing each other."

"It's a strange logic, is it not, to argue that the only way to keep people from killing each other is to kill them yourself?"

"It was the only way to keep us from becoming even worse than we were. And, as you might remember, it is only because of Marlowe that any of us are still alive!"

"But by your own testimony, that wasn't the way you planned it. By your own testimony, you agreed- you and Marlowe- that there was no chance of survival and after all the others had been killed, Marlowe would kill the both of you. Isn't that what you just said?"

"Yes, but is that really so different from how we live anyway?"

Roberts was stunned, confused. He stared at Offenbach with a look of utter incomprehension.

"I mean, all of us- you, me, everyone sitting out there. We live for a short while, a few years- sixty, seventy- and at the end, always death. Why do we do it? What drives us?- Isn't it for most of us the thought that we're leaving something behind? And what is that for most of us but the use we made of our bodies- children, their existence, the extension of ourselves. We were all going to die. What meaning could we give our death if it wasn't so that others could live?"

"And so you think that cannibalism was permissible? And not just permissible," said Roberts, giving vent to his growing irritation, "but- what was it you said?- made you 'a little more human'?"

"That's not what I meant!" cried Offenbach. "Not what we did- never that- but the way we did it. What Marlowe did was to bring what would have been pure barbarism under the kind of rule that left us at least a little of our dignity and self-respect.

"Do you imagine, Mr. Roberts," said Offenbach, his

eyes burning with such brilliant clarity that it was impossible to underestimate the power of the intelligence behind them, "do you imagine that it was any different in the beginning, when our ancestors first raised themselves out of the swamp, before they first began to sense there might be some difference between what they were and the other living things around them, when their first impulse when they saw each other was to kill? It took millions of years to become what we are now, beings who understand something about what we are supposed to be; but do you think that even now we're really that far from where we started? Do you really believe that, if it weren't for people like Marlowe, we would be any better than we were?"

"You believe, then, that what Marlowe did was right, that it was not murder?" asked Roberts sharply.

"Marlowe did what he had to do. That's the tragedy of it, don't you see? He did what he had to do and He'll never tell you that what he did was right. Why are you charging him with murder? Don't you know he's already convicted himself of that? Do you think you can punish him for what he did? That you can make him feel remorse? Don't you understand that to his dying breath he's going to wish that he had died out there instead, that he had died and not the boy or any of the others who died so we could live? Don't you understand that, worse than any of it, is the knowledge that if he had to do it all over again, he would, because it was the only thing he could have done- there was no other way?"

"No other way? You're alive; all those others are dead. The other way would have been to let each of you die in turn, not murder anyone. But this way, because of your agreement, you and Marlowe are still alive!" cried Roberts with one last withering glance. "No more questions, your Honor!"

Darnell jumped to his feet, his own face red with anger at what Roberts had done. "You haven't given a concert, you haven't performed anywhere in public, since your rescue, have you?"

"And I never will," said Hugo Offenbach, staring

down at the hands that had lifted the spirits of millions and, if Marlowe were to be believed, saved the lives of the other five survivors of the Evangeline.

"I have too much respect for the music," he explained, raising his eyes to Darnell's waiting glance. "I won't become a sideshow, nor will I tolerate pity."

"The violin you had, the one that Marlowe saved, the one you played during your long ordeal- there was no mention of it in Captain Balfour's list of contents of the lifeboat. Do you know what happened to it?"

A sigh, and then a shudder, passed through the witness. A sad, distant look clouded his eyes."I let it go, buried it at sea, when the White Rose came; buried it at sea with the people buried there; buried it at sea and wished I had been buried there as well."

CHAPTER TWENTY-THREE

Roberts knew that Darnell never did anything without a reason, but he still was not sure why the defense would call as a witness the man who designed and built the Evangeline. John Mulholland was by all accounts one of the most respected naval architects in the world, but there was no dispute about why the Evangeline had sunk and he could not know anything about what had happened to those who had survived it.

Darnell appeared to offer an explanation when he began to ask his questions, but Roberts suspected that the old man had something more in mind than simply giving the jury a better sense of what the Evangeline had been like to sail.

"Mr. Mulholland, you designed and built the Evangeline?"

John Mulholland was of middle height, with clear brown eyes and short blondish hair graying at the temples. He had the crisp, clean look of a man in his early fifties who enjoyed perfect health, the only sign of age a pair of glasses he slipped on with a certain self-consciousness when he was asked to look at a document.

"I was the chief designer, but there were dozens of people involved in building her."

"Yes, I understand," said Darnell in an easy, amiable manner as he fiddled with the pages in an open file that lay on the table in front of him. "That would be at the Wiegand Shipyard in Seattle?" he asked, glancing at the page on which his fingers had stopped.

"Yes, it would."

Darnell flashed an embarrassed grin. "Before we go any further, perhaps you could help me with a difficulty. I've never been quite certain what to call her- the Evangeline. It doesn't sound right to call her a ship; but on the other hand, a boat doesn't sound right either."

"The Evangeline was a yacht, the finest one we ever built- and, I would venture to say, one of the finest in the world."

Darnell lifted his eyebrows, a look of sober admiration in his eyes. "Most of us think of a yacht as a pleasure craft, something slow and stable, perhaps fifty or sixty feet in length. The Evangeline was not like that, though, was she?"

"She was certainly made for pleasure; but no, she wasn't like that. She was something different altogether. She was not fifty or sixty feet in length; she was more like three and a half times that- one hundred and ninety- eight feet, ten inches, to be precise. I said she was a yacht, and she was, but the actual category is 'cruising sailboat'."

"Put this in some kind of perspective for us, Mr. Mulholland, if you would. I read somewhere recently that back in the 1830s or 1840s the United States sent out a six- ship expedition to map the islands of the South Pacific, and that the largest ship- a frigate of the United States Navy- was one hundred and twenty feet in length. Does that sound right?"

"Yes, I'm familiar with the accounts of that expedi- tion. You're right, that was the length of the frigate on which the commander sailed. If I remember correctly, it carried a crew of nearly two hundred."

Darnell appeared incredulous. "Two hundred? On a ship not even two-thirds the size of the Evangeline?"

"In length, yes; but a frigate like that was broader at the beam and had several decks below. Also, you must remember, in those days the crew slept in canvas hammocks with barely any room between them."

"Nor, I suspect, was that the only difference, Mr. Mulholland," said Darnell with a shrewd glance at the jury. "The Evangeline had every kind of modern advantage, didn't she? State-of-the-art technology, electronic navigational equipment rather different from the compass and sextant used by the sailing ships of the nineteenth century. I have here a list of devices that were used on board; would you mind reading off just a few of the most important ones so we can get a sense of just how extraordinarily sophisticated the Evangeline was?"

The clerk took the two-page document from Darnell and walked to the witness stand. Mulholland put on his glasses, glanced down the list and then went back to the beginning.

"An Anschutz Nautopilot D and Gyrostar Gyrocompass." He looked up. "The Evangeline had direct cable steering that was perfectly balanced. You could control her with the tips of your fingers. When the autopilot was engaged she could be steered hydraulically. The gyrocompass told you your exact position anywhere at sea." His eyes ran further down the list.

"B & G Hydra 2000 depth, wind, navigation tec., Furuno depth sounder, 2 x Furuno radar FR8100, Satcom A ABB Nera Saturn 3s 90."

He turned the page, about to continue, then shrugged. "She had the most advanced navigational system in the world. If you want, I can go through each item and explain what it did, but they were all to the same purpose: the certain acquisition of perfect knowledge. That is, everything about where she was, where she was heading, and what- wind, water current, depth- she was going to encounter. We built her so she would be ready for anything; there would be no surprises."

"No surprises?" asked Darnell, with a quick sidelong glance. "You mean no surprises while everything- all this wonderful, sophisticated equipment- was working?"

"Yes, of course. I didn't mean..." replied Mulholland, biting his lip at the thoughtless imprudence of what he had said. It was the kind of honest mistake that made him believable in a jury's eyes.

"No one suggested that you did," said Darnell. "The equipment failed. We know that. But that isn't the reason the Evangeline sank. I want to ask you something about the yacht's construction. I've read through the plans and the other materials, and, while I'm the first to admit my almost total ignorance about such matters, one thing caught my eye."

Darnell reached inside the file folder and pulled out a thick document with a black cover. "You say- I believe this was something you wrote...," he said as he turned to the page he wanted. "Yes, here it is. 'A unique feature of the sail handling controls is the self-tailing captive winches. Powered on 24v DC current, the winches take full advantage of the yacht's enormous generators and battery capacity. They provide for more efficiency and reliability than their hydraulic predecessors and permit extended periods of "quiet-ship operations'.

Darnell let the document dangle from his hand. "What does 'quiet-ship operations' mean, exactly? Does that mean when the only source of power is the wind in its sails, when it is not using the diesel engine- an engine, which if I recall correctly, was capable of producing a thousand horse power?"

"Yes, but it means more than that. 'Quiet-ship operations' means that no engines or motors are running anywhere. The electrical power required for the winches, among other things, is supplied entirely by battery. 'Quiet-ship operations' means that the yacht is sailing without any more noise than a ship would have in the days of sail, before steam and electricity. It is the closest you can come to what it would have been like to sail on that voyage you mentioned earlier, the expedition that charted part of the South Pacific."

"Except, of course, that with a ship like the Evangeline you could always turn the engine on," said Darnell immediately. "Except, of course, that even when she was running 'quiet' she was still using electricity, battery powered electricity, to operate not just the winches, but all that electronic equipment- when that equipment was still working."

"Yes, I didn't mean..." said Mulholland, doubly chastened.

"I know you didn't. I apologize. I'm a little too caught up in the case, in what happened. Let me get us back to the point at issue. Everything you did in the way you designed and built the Evangeline was to give it speed, to give it- and I think you used this phrase somewhere- a 'feeling of closeness to the sea'. And that is part of the importance of this 'quiet operation' we were just talking about. Or have I not properly understood what you were trying to do?"

"No, that's what we were after. Mr. Whitfield wanted the Evangeline to combine modern technology with the classic feel of sailing ships. He wanted something that could go anywhere in the world, something that was safe, dependable, streamlined and fast."

"In other words, he wanted all the old sense of adventure with none of the old fact of risk?"

"Mr. Whitfield was quite emphatic. He wanted to know what it was like to sail the ocean before the age of steam. That was the way he once described it."

Darnell's eyes narrowed into a strange, wistful look. "But he really didn't want that, did he? The Evangeline had more than just the most advanced navigational systems- she had all the modern comforts of home: television, stereo, dishwashers, washing machines, refrigerators...If I'm not mistaken, one of the master suites even had a treadmill that folded into the floor. The Evangeline was not a sailing ship- the Evangeline was a yacht with marble floors and marble bathrooms!" Darnell's eyes lit up. He nodded twice vigorously. "In fact, on this ship that was supposed to have a nineteenth-century feel, weren't all the staterooms air conditioned?"

"Yes, as I've said, no expense was spared; everything was state of the art."

Roberts had heard enough. "Your Honor, while this is all quite fascinating, it isn't entirely clear what it has to do with the issue in the case. The prosecution is perfectly willing to stipulate that the Evangeline was everything the witness says she was- if that will help to move things along."

"But it is relevant to the case, your Honor," interjected Darnell before Judge Maitland had a chance to respond. "The construction and capabilities of the Evangeline go directly to the issue of how she sank. It goes, your Honor, to the ultimate question of responsibility."

Maitland gave him a stern look. "Then make the connection, and do it quickly."

Darnell turned back to the witness. "The Evangeline was, again, how many feet in length?"

"Close to two hundred."

"And that frigate we talked about earlier- the one that led the expedition- how long again?"

"A hundred-twenty, or something close to that."

"And it had a crew of- what did you say?- nearly two hundred?"

"Yes."

"It took a crew that large to sail her?"

"Everything had to be done by hand. You needed men to let out the sails and roll them up, men to cook, men to scrub the decks- everything."

"The crew of the Evangeline- how large was it?"

"Eight."

"Eight. And is that because nearly everything could be done by machine? Like those electric-powered winches you described earlier, and that steering system that allowed fingertip control?"

"Yes. The Evangeline could almost sail herself."

"And the marvelous electronic systems that allowed all this to happen- did you design redundancy into them? In other words, were there backup systems that would take over if any part of the system failed?"

"Yes, of course."

"But all of them were dependent on an electric power supply?"

"Yes, that's true."

"And if that failed, then all the systems shut down, leaving everything in the hands of the men who sailed her?"

"Yes."

Darnell raised his gray eyebrows and, turning to the jury, searched their eyes. "Just like in the days of sail," he said in a quiet, thoughtful voice. "When you designed the Evangeline," he went on, looking back at the witness, "when you design any ship, I assume you plan for every contingency, including the worst?"

"Of course."

"Then you must have planned for the possibility of a storm, even a storm of unusual force?"

Mulholland had no doubt: the Evangeline should have been able to survive anything.

"Even if her masts had been torn loose, shattered by the enormous power and weight of the water that hit her?"

"She would not have been able to sail, obviously; but the engine was powered by diesel, so that even if the electrical system could not be restarted, the engine would have been operable and the Evangeline would have been able to get back to shore."

Darnell bore in on him, his eyes cold and unforgiving, his voice hard and insistent. "If the hull had held, you mean. But it did not hold, did it? From the testimony we've heard, the Evangeline did not just sink, she broke in half. Does that surprise you?"

"Of course it surprises me."

"But you had a warning that might happen, during the sea trials, when a crack appeared below the waterline."

"And that crack was repaired. One of the workmen had used the wrong welding rod and-"

"Yes, we know that," said Darnell impatiently. "We know that he made a mistake, that he used the wrong welding rod, the one that was supposed to be used on stainless steel and not aluminum But we also know that you did not bother to check all the other welding seams to see if any of them also had problems."

"We had identified the problem; we knew which workman had made the mistake; and we knew where he had made it."

"Are you still going to insist, after everything that has happened, that there was no reason to check any further than you did? Are you going to tell this jury, Mr. Mulholland, that the hull of the Evangeline was exactly the way you had designed it, that all those seams in the metal plating had been welded properly, that she was perfectly safe on the day she sailed out of the Mediterranean?"

With a bleak expression, Mulholland slowly shook his head. "No, of course not. I only meant that, as far as anyone knew-"

"But there was a way to know for sure, wasn't there? In fact, in that report of yours, you said it was something you were prepared to do. You said- do you want me to read that part of the report to you?- that you could X-ray all the seams."

"Yes, that's correct. It was up to the owner."

"Up to the owner?" asked Darnell with a skeptical smile. "But your report seemed to tell him that there wasn't any compelling reason to do it. Your report said that the problem had been taken care of. Your report said that you were convinced that everything was fine. Why would the owner want to...?"

Darnell suddenly realized what had happened. He looked at Mulholland with something close to anger. "Money! That was the reason, wasn't it? You were shifting responsibility. If you had said that the only way to be sure that all the seams were properly welded was to X-ray every one of them, the cost would have been on the builder. But by telling Benjamin Whitfield that it wasn't necessary, that everything was fine, you were shifting the responsibility and expense to him. If he wanted all the seams checked, he would have to pay for it himself. That's a very expensive procedure, isn't it, Mr. Mulholland, checking each of the welded seams like that?"

The color had drained from Mulholland's face. For what seemed an eternity, he stared glumly at the floor. "We did everything we were supposed to do," he said finally in a ghostly, shattered voice.

"We were convinced that the rest of the aluminum plates had been welded properly. We had no reason to think otherwise. We were already a little behind schedule. To check every one of those welds would have delayed delivery by several more weeks. It was our honest opinion that the

Evangeline was safe. But, yes, you're right; the only way to have known for sure would have been to X-ray every seam. And that is exactly what I told Mr. Whitfield the last time we talked."

"You had a conversation with Mr. Whitfield about this? After you had sent him the report?"

"We weren't trying to hide anything. I told him that we had not found anything to warrant further investigation, but that there was only one way to be absolutely certain. I told him it was time-consuming and that it would add to the expense, but that if he wanted us to do it, we would."

Darnell studied Mulholland intently. "Did you also tell him that if any of the welded seams were defective, the consequences could be catastrophic?"

"Yes. He said that with all the technology on board the last thing anyone had to worry about was safety."

CHAPTER TWENTY-FOUR

"Hubris- pride," said Darnell, scoffing at the apparent ease with which Benjamin Whitfield had dismissed any suggestion that there might be something that could not be conquered by science and technology. He shoved aside the plate that held his half-eaten dinner. He was too preoccupied for food. Staring at the thickening fog outside the window of the small neighborhood restaurant where he and Summer Blaine liked to come, he wondered if the jury had the same reaction, or whether- because they were, on average, so much younger than he- they had failed to grasp the strange irony of what Whitfield had tried to do.

"That is what I wanted to show them: that the same two things are completely different."

Summer Blaine started to laugh at the seeming paradox, but Darnell had a point to make. "Two sailing ships set out on voyages that will take them around a continent. But imagine a member of the crew on that first one- sleeping in hammocks, climbing the rigging, setting sail; out there for months, with the only sound that of the sea and the noise of other men- imagine him on the Evangeline! What would he think? After he had marveled at all the changes, all this incredible mechanical power, I wonder whether he might not decide that something had been lost? That the older way was better, because it was closer to the sea?

"Maybe that is just my own ignorance speaking, the romantic version of things I've never done; it's just the feeling I get from Marlowe, the sense that the closer you are to the sea, the closer you are to finding out the truth of things. He's like someone who traveled to a different country so he could better understand the one he left; only he went off to the middle of the ocean, and instead of passing judgment on a single country, passed judgment on the whole of civilized existence.

"But those people on the jury, they've never known anything except the safety of a comfortable existence. I wanted them to see how much we take for granted and how quickly it can collapse. I wanted them to hear from the architect who designed her how big she was; how she had all the most advanced technology in the world; how every contingency had been considered and planned for; how nothing could harm her; how fast, how sleek- how safe- she was!

"Everyone thought the Evangeline was like the sailboats we see floating out there on the bay; a little larger, a little more advanced, a lot more expensive- a rich man's toy, something on which Whitfield could entertain his friends on breezy, blue-sky days. They could understand how a sailboat could get into trouble in a storm. But a boat bigger than the biggest navy frigate in a famous expedition? Almost two hundred feet in length? That is another story. That isn't a boat; that is a ship- and the kind of storm that could take her down, broke her right in half- that's a nightmare.

"I watched the jury when Mulholland was finished, when he left the stand after the few questions Roberts asked. They were looking at Marlowe in a different light, as someone who must have done something extraordinary to save anyone from the Evangeline in the middle of a storm that could sink a ship like that." Darnell ordered coffee. Summer worried aloud that he had scarcely slept all week.

"I never get much sleep during a trial. Even when I do, I dream about it. Doesn't matter, really. I'm not that tired; and besides, it's almost over. One more witness; maybe two, depending on what I learn tonight."

Summer regretted her overcautious tone. She was there because she wanted them to have as much time together as they could, not because she was his doctor. She wanted him to enjoy her company, not worry about whether she approved of what he did. Knowing full well that it would keep her up half the night, she ordered coffee as well.

"What you learn tonight? She's here, then? Cynthia Grimes, the other woman who survived, the one who had been having the affair with Benjamin Whitfield?"

"It was all I could do to convince her to come. It was hard enough to find her. She left the country just days after she walked out of the hospital. She went back to Nice, where this whole dreadful business started. At first she would not even talk to me on the telephone; then, when she did, she made it plain that she would not come back, ever. I couldn't force her. She's out of the jurisdiction; I could not put her under subpoena. The only thing I could think to do was call her every few days and tell her what was going on at the trial, tell her what each of the witnesses had said."

Summer looked surprised. "Did she really want to hear about that? I would have thought- after everything she had been through- that the last thing she would want is to have to remember any part of it."

"That was her first reaction. She started to waver when I told her what Samantha Wilcox had said- that she believes there is a reason for everything that happens, and that she has no right to feel anything but gratitude for being saved. But it was only when I told her what Marlowe had said that she decided to come back."

"Marlowe...?"

"What he had done to make sure the boy died first. It shocked her- that's the only way I can describe it. There was a long silence- I thought the line had gone dead, that for some reason she had hung up- and then I heard her start to cry. I don't know why. She would not tell me. I assume it's because, like Marlowe, she knows now that the boy could have lived. In any event, that changed everything. She flew in last night and is staying at a hotel on Sutter Street, registered under a different name. No one knows she's here."

"Not even the prosecution?"

"She made me promise I would not tell anyone. When she walks into court tomorrow morning, everyone is going to be surprised. And, depending on what she says, I may be more surprised than anyone."

"You don't have any idea?"

"None. I've done most of the talking in our conversations, trying to draw her interest, trying to get her to trust me. She knows something; I can feel it. And it's not just what happened between her and Whitfield. They were having an affair; she was upset, angry, when he left her to take the trip without him. But it's more than that. It was the way she reacted, the way she listened, the way she dissolved into tears. Something happened, something about what Marlowe did, something that no one else knows. I'm going to put her on the stand and I don't know whether her testimony is going to help Marlowe or bury him."

Summer Blaine did not believe it. She had heard too much about Marlowe to credit the possibility that a woman would come all this way, give up the anonymity she obviously prized to cause him harm.

"It's the boy," she said with earnest conviction. "That's why she's willing to put herself through this; willing to let everyone gawk at her in court; willing to have her picture taken when she walks out of there knowing it will be flashed on television screens and shown in newspapers around the world. It's the fact of what he did- what he thought he had to do- to save a child.

"Maybe it's just what she saw on Marlowe's face, that awful anguish that some of the others have talked about. Maybe she knows something more about it, maybe it was something Marlowe said- but it has to be that, or something like it, something she knows will explain what Marlowe did, make it more...I was going to say necessary, because I've heard you speak of necessity so often; but no, not necessary-more like forgivable."

"I hope you're right," said Darnell, glancing at his watch. "I should know in another hour."

"You said two witnesses," Summer reminded him. "Depending on what you learn tonight."

Darnell slowly sipped his coffee. He was thinking about the way he had to fit all the pieces together. Everything had to unfold with the rigorous logic of a fate foretold, all the gruesome violence of desperate people living off each other's blood and flesh nothing short of unavoidable once the Evangeline went down. But that had to be the beginning, and not the end, of the search for the first link in the chain, the moving cause of what they had been forced to do.

He had to show the jury, he had to make them believe, that the Evangeline was not sunk by a storm or by any other act of God; that what happened was the consequence of human pride and negligence- if not, indeed, something worse. His best chance of saving Marlowe was to show the jury that they had someone else to blame. Darnell had almost convinced himself.

"I've sometimes wondered," he said, as his eyes came back to Summer, "whether Whitfield did not do it on purpose. He had a motive, and maybe more than one."

She searched his eyes to see if he was serious. "Do you mean he sent the Evangeline out to sea, knowing that if he did not check those seams she might sink? But why would anyone do that, put all those lives at risk?"

"Money. That's why- the oldest motive of them all."

"But Whitfield is a rich man."

"Whitfield is overextended. The Evangeline was insured for nearly thirty million." With a pensive expression, Darnell tapped his middle finger three times on the table-cloth, paused, then tapped it three times more.

"Of course, if that had been his intention, there was almost no chance it would work. The Evangeline sailed all the way across the Atlantic to the Mediterranean in that first shakedown cruise and had not sunk, and the crack below the waterline had been repaired. What were the chances she would ever run into a storm like that? My point isn't that he planned it, that he did something to make certain that the Evangeline would be lost at sea. It was not so much a conscious, as a fugitive, thought; that evil wish we so often disguise from ourselves; that fleeting, immediately denied, calculation of how we might benefit if something bad happened to someone else.

They tell him that the hull is fine, that there isn't any danger, but he knows there is only one way to be sure. That will cost more money, though, take more time; and then what if it needs more repairs? Why does he need to bother with this now? There isn't any real danger of something happening to the Evangeline. If she starts to leak again, they can head back to port and fix her the way they did the last time. A danger that she might sink? He tells himself with a kind of secret pleasure that he could only hope to be so lucky. It is a risk he does not mind taking. What does he have to lose?"

"The lives of a lot of other people," replied Summer, shocked at the possibility of a calculation that cunning.

"With all that electronic equipment? With all that modern communications technology? I'm not saying that he thought it all the way through, that he planned what happened. He never grasped the danger; he never believed anything like that could happen- not in this day and age. Even now- you could see it when he testified in court- he can't quite believe it really did happen; even though, as I say, there was a part of him that almost hoped it would. There is not always such a clear distinction between the intentions of good and evil people. The lines grow blurred when emotions like greed and love enter into it."

"Love? Do you mean the affair with your witness, Cynthia Grimes?"

"We know they had had some kind of falling out. We know she was angry. When he told Marlowe that the Evangeline had passed her sea trials with flying colors., when he thought about the money and how much he needed it, when he had all those thoughts and feelings jumbling around in his head- what do you think he must have thought about her? Do you think he might have thought, if only for a brief, fleeting moment, how good it would be if she were not in his life anymore, ridding him of another complication he regretted and did not need?"

Summer finally understood. "Whitfield is your second witness? He was a witness for the prosecution, and now you're going to call him as a witness for the defense? And this is what you're going to do with him- ask him questions about his need for money and the insurance, his involvement with Cynthia Grimes and why he wanted out of it? You want everyone to think that he had something to do with what happened to the Evangeline? That he wanted her to sink? Is that right? Is it fair?"

Darnell sat straight up and swung his legs away from the table. He held his arms folded across his chest and lowered his eyes, brooding on her final question and all its implications.

"Is it fair? All I know is that it is necessary. Is it fair? If Whitfield had done what he should have, the Evangeline might have stayed afloat and none of those lives would have been lost.

"Is it fair? If he had not lied to Marlowe, if he had told him the truth, Marlowe would not have taken her beyond the Straits of Gibraltar and neither he nor anyone else would have been condemned to live their lives ashamed of what the world thinks of them and of what they think of themselves.

"Is it fair? He did not do what he should have, then lied about what he did, and because of that Hugo Offenbach will never play again. What isn't fair is that the famous and respected Benjamin Whitfield never had to draw lots with the others!"

An apologetic smile dashed across his mouth. He did not need to give instruction on life's unfairness to Summer Blaine. She could have taught that lesson a dozen times better than he ever could.

"We need to go," he said, checking his watch. "I didn't realize it was so late." He dropped Summer at the apartment and drove downtown to the hotel on Sutter Street where Cynthia Grimes waited with a story that would change everything he thought of Vincent Marlowe and what Marlowe had done. He spent hours talking to her, and when he finally got home, Summer was asleep in a chair, the book she had been reading lying open in her lap. He had not taken two steps inside the door before she woke up.

"What happened?" she asked, alarmed at the pallor of his cheek and the strange, almost haunted, look in his eyes. She jumped out of the chair and took him by the arm. "What happened?" she repeated as she led him to the sofa.

"Is it your heart? Don't lie to me, Bill. Are you having chest pains?"

He shook his head. "No, it isn't that. It's what I've just been told. You were right about Cynthia Grimes. The reason she agreed to come, the reason she agreed to testify, is because of what Marlowe said about the boy."

"What about the boy? What has you so upset?"

Darnell slowly shook his head. "It's the saddest story I've ever heard."

CHAPTER TWENTY-FIVE

Darnell sat at his desk in the study, staring out the window at the fog twisting through the city lights. There were important decisions to be made, and he did not know how to make them. Should he call Cynthia Grimes as a witness or would her testimony be too disturbing for the jury? But the truth, however harsh and painful, was the promise he had made at the beginning. Could he turn his back on it now?

When the pink-fingered dawn finally stretched across the sky, Darnell realized that there was no choice to be made. This was not a trial in which the verdict was the only thing that mattered; this was a trial that was, or would become, a catharsis, a way to reconcile what we wanted to believe about ourselves and what we feared we could still too easily become.

He had to call Cynthia Grimes, but he did not have to call her first. He could call Benjamin Whitfield back to the stand. Whitfield had lied, and Darnell could prove it. Call Whitfield, then call her; concentrate the jury's attention so much on the importance of what had happened before the Evangeline set sail that perhaps what Cynthia Grimes had to say about what had happened after the Evangeline sank might not be quite so shocking.

In the final gray light of morning that 'perhaps' began to take on a hollow, artificial ring, the forced attempt to imagine what could never happen.

"You didn't sleep at all, did you?" asked Summer Blaine as she came up behind him and placed her hands softly on his shoulders. "How are you going to get through the day? There is a limit to how long even you can keep running on adrenalin."

"I'm indestructible. I thought you knew that." While he showered and dressed, she made them a small breakfast of bacon and eggs. After he was finished, she handed him two pills.

"Take these: one now, one at lunch. Tonight- whatever happens at trial, whatever you think you have to do for tomorrow- you are going straight to bed. And if you have any trouble sleeping, you're going to take a sleeping pill. You can't go on like this. Your heart won't take it. You're not young anymore, William Darnell, and you'd better remember it. You can live ten or fifteen years longer or you can die tomorrow. You promised me before this trial started that you wouldn't do that; you promised that you would take care of yourself."

"Nothing is going to happen to me. It is an old rule of the Common Law: a lawyer has to stay alive until the trial is finished. Death is considered malpractice!" he insisted, his eyes shining at her failed attempt to keep from smiling. She had put him in the proper mood, though that had not been her main intention.

Tomorrow would take care of itself; he could not worry about the consequences of what he did, or did not do, this morning. This was a trial- unusual, even unique, but still a trial. There were always witnesses who created situations you had not quite anticipated; that was what kept things interesting, what made him feel so alive.

What he had told Summer Blaine was very nearly the truth: he was indestructible, at least while he was still in court. And that, after all, was what really mattered: that he could still work, still function, still do what he did as well as, or better than, anyone else.

The courtroom was filled to overflowing when Darnell arrived. Marlowe was sitting at the counsel table, his back to the crowd. Each day he seemed to draw further inside himself, seldom saying anything unless Darnell spoke first. He had become something ghost-like, unreal, the shadow left behind when the spirit that had dwelled within him had disappeared. There were times when, catching the distant look in Marlowe's eyes, Darnell wondered if he even remembered where he was. Darnell had seen that look before, on the faces of men who knew their lives were over, men who knew that there was nothing for it but to play out the hand that fate had dealt them and wait with quiet courage for death's deliverance.

"The next witness I am calling is Cynthia Grimes," Darnell told Marlowe quietly. Marlowe stared straight ahead. Darnell knew he had heard him, but there was no reaction. In the looming silence, he put his hand on Marlowe's shoulder and bent closer.

"I don't have to call her; and I won't, if you prefer. I don't know whether what she'll say will help or hurt us, but it will certainly raise some questions about what was done out there. On the other hand, we've said from the beginning that we did not have anything to hide."

Marlowe turned, the lines across his forehead cut deep by concentration. "More like everything to hide, but no way to do it," he said with a strange, enigmatic smile. "I'd hide it from myself, if I knew the way," he added, as the smile became painful and twisted. "But it's better if she doesn't-try to hide, I mean. Better she tell the truth, or what she knows of it; better she put as much of this behind her as she can. She was the one of all of us who was never thinking of herself."

"But not the only one," Darnell tried to remind him, though he knew his words would have no effect. Others might forgive Marlowe what he had done, but Marlowe never would.

The bailiff stood erect; the courtroom crowd, by a crowd's instinct, fell silent. The side door opened and Homer Maitland marched quickly to the bench. "Mr. Darnell," he said after the jury had returned to the jury box, "please call your next witness."

Darnell was on his feet. He curled his lower lip and scratched the back of his neck, like someone not yet certain what he was going to do. With a slightly puzzled expression he looked at Maitland and then, shifting his balance to the other leg, at Roberts, as if one or the other might help him decide. He placed his hands behind his back and studied the floor as if the answer might be found there. There was not a lawyer alive who knew better how to create a response from a moment's thoughtful pause. Suddenly, his head snapped up, his shoulders spun around.

"Your Honor, the defense calls Cynthia Grimes!"

Everyone knew she was missing; no one knew he had found her. Since the day Darnell revealed the fact of her affair with Benjamin Whitfield and her quick and inexplicable disappearance from the hospital, she had become first a mystery and then a legend, a woman about whom anything could be imagined because so little was actually known. She was young and beautiful- that much was certain; she was less than half the age of Whitfield and younger, much younger, than Whitfield's wife. But this was not the reason for the gasps that came from the crowd when the door at the back of the courtroom opened and she appeared: Cynthia Grimes was pregnant.

With one hand on her stomach, she raised the other and took the oath. Everyone there knew immediately that she had become pregnant before the Evangeline had sailed. Darnell confirmed it. "You were pregnant, I take it, before you left with the others to sail around Africa?"

She spoke with a kind of shy reserve; unwilling, it seemed, to look at the jury, or anyone but Darnell.

"Not quite two months."

"You're not married, are you?" he asked in a warm, sympathetic voice.

"No, I'm not."

"You understand there is a reason why I ask these questions? That no one wants to embarrass you or to intrude on your privacy, but that-"

"Benjamin Whitfield is the father," she said, shaking off any suggestion that she might be reluctant to discuss it. "That is the reason why he left Nice, why he didn't go on that voyage- he wanted to get away from me."

Darnell moved from behind the table to the railing of the jury box. He looked straight at her. "You left San Francisco immediately after you were flown here from

Brazil with the other survivors, and you've been out of the country until just the day before yesterday, if I understand correctly. Are you aware that Mr. Whitfield testified earlier in the trial, and that he gave an entirely different reason for why he did not join the rest of you on the Evangeline?"

"Yes, I'm aware of that."

"And would you please tell the jury how you happen to know this?"

"Because you sent me transcripts of the trial so I would know exactly what was said."

"Yes, and the reason I did that- can you tell the jury what I said?"

For the first time, she turned to the jury. She smiled, or started to, but then, as if that were the limit of her bravery, dropped her gaze and fled back to the waiting eyes of William Darnell. "You said you wanted me to know everything that was said because you hoped I would change my mind and come back to testify."

"And because of what you read, because of some of the things that have been said in the course of this trial, you decided that was something you wanted to do?"

"Yes."

"You're not here under subpoena?"

"No."

"You're here of your own free will?"

"Yes."

"Tell us then, what makes you think that Benjamin Whitfield was not telling the truth when he said that he had to return to the United States because his father was in the hospital dying? The fact that you were pregnant, the fact that he was the father- neither of those things proves that what he said was false. It would be quite natural, would it not, for him to want to be with his father when his father's death was imminent?"

"It would be, in any normal situation, but most men don't hate their fathers the way Benjamin hated his. Return to be with him when he died? Benjamin could not wait to spit on the old man's grave! When he first heard that his father was dying- not from anyone in his family, but from the family's lawyer- he said he wished he felt more religious so he could believe in Hell. He did not return because of his father; he returned because of me."

"I still don't understand. You were lovers; you had just learned you were pregnant with his child- was he angry with you because of that?"

"Angry doesn't quite describe it! He had been planning this trip for months. It was our chance to spend a few weeks together. At least that is what he said when he asked me to come along. He was still married, but that was over, or so he told me when we began our affair. They were getting a divorce, but there were certain financial considerations to be resolved first- things about the way the stock would have to be handled if he was going to keep the controlling interest in that company of his.

He told me he wanted to marry me; he told me that he wanted children. He told me a lot of things, and I suppose he may have meant them when they were still only promises and the time to keep them seemed a long way off. He had a gift for making you believe the future would be everything you wanted and that it was already as good as here. When I found out I was pregnant, I felt like we were already married; but when I told him, I discovered that it had all been lies."

Darnell dragged his hand along the railing as he moved a step closer. His eyes, full of encouragement, never left her. "He was angry- more than angry- you said?"

"He told me that I was an idiot, a fool! He could not understand how I could let it happen, why I had not taken precautions. He told me that it was my fault and that I would have to fix it."

"Fix it?"

"Yes. Have an abortion and do it right away. I said I would not. I did not know what I wanted to do, but I was not going to let him decide. I suppose I also thought that he was upset because of all the other things going on in his life- the financial problems he was having, the trouble he was in- and that he did not really mean the things he had said. I suppose I thought that when we were finally out at sea, when he had had time to think things through ..." Her voice drifted off; a rueful smile came slowly to her lips. "He was right. I was an idiot, a fool. When I said we could decide all that when we got back, he started screaming, telling me that I had to do something about the baby, that it could not wait. I told him I was not going to do anything until the Evangeline came back.

"That's when he said it, when he said he was not going, and that I could go alone. He said he had too many things he had to take care of, too many problems at home; that if he had not invited all those other people on the trip he would get rid of the Evangeline, sell her for whatever he could get. That was the last thing he ever said to me- that if he did not have either the Evangeline or me to worry about, his life would be a whole lot better, that both of us had 'already cost him far too much!'"

Darnell gave her a moment to compose herself. "So you went on that voyage alone. And while you were sailing on the Evangeline did you come to any conclusions about whether or not to keep the child? I mean before the storm and what happened after?"

"I knew that it was over with Benjamin, that there had never been anything there to begin with. It was one of those illusions we believe because we want so much for it to be true. There was no Benjamin for me to marry; no father for my child. When we got back to Nice, when we had finished the trip around Africa, I was going to do what he had suggested- not because he wanted me to, but because I did not want to be a single mother."

"But something made you change your mind? Was it something that happened after the Evangeline broke apart, when you were out there in that lifeboat with the others who had managed to get away?"

Her eyes moved with tender caution to where Marlowe sat alone. "It was because of the child that he saved my life."

"The defendant, Vincent Marlowe? Tell us what you

mean, what he did."

"I was scared. No, terrified. I was a coward, pure and simple. I did not want to die. I wasn't brave like Helena Green or the others who died with so much courage; I wasn't as brave as that fourteen-year-old boy. I told Marlowe- I begged him. I said I was pregnant, that I did not want to lose the baby. And I was not lying when I said it. At least I don't think I was. I was so weak, so exhausted- we had not had anything to eat or drink for days, and the conditions… you've heard about them from other witnesses, but you really can't imagine how awful things were. I used to close my eyes and hope that I would never open them.

"But then, when it was decided what we had to do, I felt an instinct I had not known I had. I could let myself die, but I could not let that happen to my child. I thought we were all going to die out there, but I knew that as long as there was any chance, any chance at all, I had to do whatever I could to save the life inside me."

"You told Marlowe you were pregnant so that you would not have to draw lots with the others?"

"Yes. I thought he would see that he could not do it, that there was this life inside me that could not be taken."

"Did you tell anyone else you were pregnant? Did you try to convince the others to leave you out?"

"No, only Marlowe. The others, some of them, were mad with hunger. If he had not got everyone to agree that it was only right and fair to choose by lot, if the ones chosen- and especially that boy- had not been so willing, if they had not shown such courage- if they had not shamed Trevelyn and those who thought like him- the stronger would have killed the weaker and then started murdering among themselves."

"So Marlowe decided by himself that, because you were pregnant, you would not be included?"

She looked again at Marlowe, this time in a way that suggested that she had finally grasped something she had not understood before. "Marlowe said he could not do it; that he was sorry. It was only when I learned from the transcripts that the boy was not chosen by chance, that I knew that he had done the same thing for me: made certain that I would not be chosen, at least not until the end, when there was no chance left for anyone.

"Marlowe saved me- I know it now, because I knew it then. It was the way he looked at me each time we had to draw again, as if he were telling me that I and the child I had inside me would be safe a little longer. That's why I'm having the child, why I did not abort it- too many people died so I could give it life!"

CHAPTER TWENTY-SIX

Finally Roberts understood. Darnell was even better than he had thought. Other lawyers tried to shift the blame from the defendant to someone else, to make it seem that the defendant was as much a victim as the actual victim of the crime, but he had seldom seen it done with such subtlety and craft.

First the naval architect to show with how little effort the Evangeline could have been made completely safe; then the young woman, pregnant and beautiful, to show how little Benjamin Whitfield had cared about anything but himself. There was only one conclusion the jury could reach: if it had not been for Marlowe, none of those whom Whitfield had sent with such blind indifference to an almost certain death would have come through their horrifying ordeal alive; if it had not been for Marlowe, Whitfield's child would never see the light of day. Darnell was making a hero of a man who had admitted to murder.

Roberts had to stop it. "Tell us, if you would, Ms Grimes," said Roberts as he began his cross-examination, "did Mr. Whitfield ever say, even in anger, that he hoped that the Evangeline would sink?"

"No, of course not."

"Of course not? Because whatever difficulties in which he may have found himself, whatever financial obligations he may have had, he would never have wanted anyone on the Evangeline to be harmed- correct?"

Cynthia Grimes was no ordinary witness, and no ordinary woman. She had a rather different sense of human motivation than she had had before. The Evangeline had made her quicker to see beyond the surface into the darkened heart of things. "Are you asking what he might have wanted, or what he might have done about it? No, I don't think he would have deliberately done anything to cause us harm. But do I think he would have minded? Why don't you ask him what he thought, when he first heard that the Evangeline might be missing?"

"You agree that he would not have done anything to harm those aboard the Evangeline. Good. As far as you know, then, the decision he made with respect to the time-consuming and, according to the builder, unnecessary check of the welding seams in the hull was made in perfect good faith? He never said to you, 'I'm not going to check them because if it sinks I can collect the insurance money', did he?"

She seemed almost to enjoy it, this effort to protect the innocence and good name of the man who had betrayed her. It provided certain possibilities for revenge. "Benjamin Whitfield did not get where he is by saying such stupid things. But no, in answer to your question, he never said that," she said with a bitter smile. "Of course, neither did he bother to tell me- or any of the others he waved goodbye to- that there had even been a question about whether the Evangeline might break apart in a storm!

"Nor has he offered to use any of that insurance money- the millions that he collected because the Evangeline sank- to compensate any of us who suffered because of his selfish negligence!" she cried.

The courtroom erupted into a bedlam of noise. Maitland slammed his gavel hard against the wooden bench until the crowd fell silent.

"I know this is difficult, Ms. Grimes," said Maitland, bending towards her, "but you must restrict your answer to the specific question you are asked. If there is anything you later wish to add, I'm sure that Mr. Darnell will give you the opportunity to do it on redirect."

Roberts had made a mistake and he knew it. He moved to a different line of questioning, one that would not involve her feelings towards Benjamin Whitfield.

"There are just a few questions I want to ask you about what happened after the Evangeline sank. You told Mr. Darnell that you asked Mr. Marlowe to spare you because you were carrying a child. I understand that you now believe that he did that, that he made sure you were not chosen to be one of those who had to die; but he told you at the time that he could not do it because it would not be fair. Did I understand you correctly?"

"He said he could not do it, that except for himself and Mr. Offenbach, everyone had to be in it. But it was not true, of course, because he made sure the boy was chosen first and made sure I was not chosen at all. The important thing was that everyone believe that we were being treated the same, that we all had the same chance."

"Even though, as we now know, you did not?"

"We had to believe that, believe that we were all doing what we had to so that there was at least the chance that some of us would survive."

"Because it was important, wasn't it- Marlowe has said it was important- that everyone have the sense that there was something to be accomplished by their death; that death would have a meaning if it meant that others could live? Is that how you understood it?" asked Roberts, an expression of the utmost certainty on his face.

"Yes, that is exactly what I thought, what we all thought."

"And those who were chosen, whether chosen by chance or, like the boy, chosen on purpose- all of them met their deaths bravely, without resistance?"

"Yes, all of them."

"My question, then, is why, if everyone was willing to sacrifice themselves for the others, no one thought to ask for volunteers? Instead of this lottery, instead of supposedly leaving it all to chance, why didn't Marlowe call for volunteers? Why didn't he just ask if someone wanted to die so that the others could live?"

She had no answer, but an answer was not what he wanted. He had another question that would make his point even more dramatic.

"Marlowe was in charge, wasn't he?"

"Yes."

"Because Marlowe was the captain of the Evangeline, and the passengers were under his care?"

"Yes."

"Then why, if it was his duty to take care of all the rest, did not Marlowe volunteer- can you tell us that? Why did not Marlowe volunteer to be the first to die?"

Cynthia Grimes looked at Roberts with open contempt. "He did! You heard him! You heard what he said- that he could not go through with it, that he could not kill the boy, that he would have taken his place!"

"Yes, but he did not do that, did he?" said Roberts with a scornful look of his own. "And whatever he may have said before he killed the boy, I don't recall that he volunteered to take the place of any of the others he killed- do you?"

Darnell resisted the temptation to stop Roberts with a well-timed objection. He let him go on, working himself to a fever pitch, while he, Darnell, stared idly at the ceiling, like someone who has heard it all before and is not in the least impressed. He kept staring at the ceiling, as if he had fallen asleep with his eyes wide open, when Roberts finally finished. He was still staring at it when Homer Maitland peered down from the bench and asked if he had anything he wished to ask on redirect.

Slowly, Darnell looked around, as if he had thought that Roberts was still at work, shouting invective at a young, pregnant witness. He stood up, smiled across at Cynthia Grimes and apologized, not for himself, but for what his 'good friend, Mr. Roberts, had been forced to do'.

"It is one of the necessities of what we sometimes do as lawyers: try to beat an answer out of a witness who cannot possibly know what was going through another person's mind. Mr. Roberts wants to know why Mr. Marlowe did not ask for volunteers. Isn't it true, Ms. Grimes, that that is exactly what Mr. Marlowe did?"

She wanted to be helpful, but the question did not seem to let her. "I'm not sure I...?"

"What I mean is that, at the very beginning, when there were the first discussions of what you might have to do, everyone agreed to be bound by whatever the majority decided. This is another way of saying, if I'm not mistaken, that every one of you entered into that agreement voluntarily. Isn't that true, Ms. Grimes? Didn't you, along with the others, agree that this had to be done, that someone had to sacrifice his or her life to save the lives of the others and, in that sense, volunteer as one of those who might be chosen?

"The point I am trying to make is quite simple," said Darnell with a modest, disarming smile. "No one was forced to die; everyone died of their own free will; everyone who met their death at Marlowe's trembling and unwilling hand was in fact a volunteer. Is that the way you saw it?"

"Yes, exactly."

"No further questions, your Honor."

Maitland glanced at the clock, and then at Darnell. "You have another witness, if I'm not mistaken." He turned to the jury. "We'll take our noon recess a little early. Instead of starting again at two o'clock, we'll start at one-thirty."

There was too much to do to bother with lunch. Darnell shut himself inside a small windowless room where lawyers could confer privately with their clients. For the next hour and a half he pored over the transcript of Benjamin Whitfield's prior testimony and the copious and meticulous notes he had taken of the testimony of certain other witnesses as well. He did not need to read more than the first few words of a paragraph, or sometimes of a whole page, to refresh his memory of what had been said. The pages turned one after the other under an intense concentration whose only physical manifestation was an almost catatonic stare. Someone could have fired a gun just outside the door and he would not have heard it.

The clock inside his head, the clock that never worked when he had to be anywhere but court, told him when it was time to stop. At twenty-five minutes after the hour, Darnell shut his briefcase and headed back down the hall. The pills that Summer Blaine had given him that morning, the pills that he had promised to take at lunch, lay forgotten in his pocket.

It did not matter; he had not felt this well in ages. There was a bounce to his step when he entered the courtroom, the place he always felt at home. He sat down next to Marlowe, but did not speak to him. He smiled to himself with anticipation. With one final witness, he would bring the trial full circle and show that the only crimes that counted had been committed not on the high seas, after the Evangeline had sunk, but before the Evangeline had ever left port.

Homer Maitland burst through the door at the side. The courtroom crowd rose as one. Maitland nodded to the jury and, with a motion of his hand, told the crowd to sit. "Mr. Darnell," he said in a firm, rough-edged voice, "are you ready with your next witness?"

Darnell was on his feet. "Your Honor, the defense calls Benjamin Whitfield."

Maitland reminded Whitfield that because he had not been formally excused, he was still under oath. "Even though, this time, you're here as a witness not for the prosecution, but for the defense."

Benjamin Whitfield looked more worried, and more cautious, than he had before. He had read the newspaper accounts of what other witnesses had said at the trial. He had been besieged with requests for interviews after what Marlowe had said. He had read about what the naval architect had said about the hull. Someone had no doubt told him what Cynthia Grimes had said that morning. He knew that, whatever other reason Darnell might have had to put him under subpoena, he was going to be asked to explain why, as a witness for the prosecution, he had lied. Darnell was surprisingly pleasant.

"It's good to see you again, Mr. Whitfield," he said as he moved across the front of the courtroom to the table where the clerk kept the various exhibits that had been marked and introduced into evidence. "May I have the photographs, please, the ones introduced by the prosecution when Mr. Whitfield testified before?"

Darnell handed Whitfield the pictures that he had

earlier identified as being of the Evangeline before she started her last, ill-fated voyage. "You remember these photographs, don't you? Two taken when she was christened, three of them while she was on her sea trials, and the last- that one," he said, pointing to the one Whitfield had just turned over, "- taken the day she left, the day she sailed out of Nice for that trip around Africa she never completed."

"Yes, of course," said Whitfield warily, holding the photographs in his hand.

"I was struck at the time- and I'm sure the jury was struck as well- by how beautiful she was."

Whitfield nodded, and waited.

"But despite that old saying about a picture being worth a thousand words, in this case the pictures perhaps hid more than they told- wouldn't you agree?"

"I don't think I quite understand what you mean."

"Oh, I think you do, Mr. Whitfield," replied Darnell with a sidelong glance at the jurors. They were watching the witness with new eyes, seeing him now through the lens of what they had been told since his first appearance, no longer willing to accept what he said at face value. He was aware of their suspicion, bothered by it to the point that he would not look back at them.

Darnell stood at the far end of the jury box, so that Whitfield would have to look right past them.

"I think you do, Mr. Whitfield. But there is also something else about those pictures that may not be immediately apparent. It certainly was not apparent to me when I first saw them. The size, Mr. Whitfield, the size.

"Here, look at them, each one of them. The Evangeline is all alone; there are no other boats, no other 'sailing yachts' around her. It was not until Mr. Mulholland, the architect you commissioned to design and build her, testified that any of us first understood how large she really was- almost two hundred feet in length! No wonder you thought she could go anywhere in the world; no wonder you told him, the man who designed and built her, that no one who sailed her would ever have to worry about safety."

Darnell paused, as if he wanted to make sure he had not been misunderstood. "That is what you told him, isn't it? That with all the technology she had on board, safety- well, I don't want to be imprecise. I think your exact words, at least as Mr. Mulholland remembered them, were: 'the last thing anyone had to worry about was safety'." Darnell lifted his eyebrows with an air of expectancy. "Isn't that what you said?"

"Perhaps I said something like that; I'm not sure." Whitfield bent forward, rubbing his hands together. "She should have been safe; she would have been safe if-"

"If some of the equipment had not failed; if she had not encountered a storm of such unexpected ferocity; if a lot of different things had not happened. We have heard all about that, Mr. Whitfield. But all of it, I must tell you, comes down to this: she would have been safe if you had not lied!"

"I didn't lie! Not about anything that mattered!"

"Not about anything that mattered? You lied to Marlowe: you told him the Evangeline had gone through her sea trials without a problem!"

"I didn't lie to him on purpose. Don't you understand? Everything was falling apart. Everyone wanted something; there were questions about everything. When Marlowe asked about the sea trials- I had so many things going on, I don't even remember that he did- I must have told him what-ever I thought he wanted to hear. The Evangeline had just sailed across the Atlantic. She was fine. A little crack needed fixing, that was all. She was what I said she was before, what Mulholland said as well- the finest vessel of her kind ever built!"

Darnell threw it right back at him. "The finest vessel of its kind in the world- and you did not want to make abso-lutely certain that she was safe to sail on? All you had to do was make one phone call!"

"What do you mean?"

"All you had to do was call the shipyard where the Evangeline was built. They would have examined her for you; or you could have had it done right there in Nice. Any major shipyard would have had the right equipment. Just one phone call, Mr. Whitfield. Isn't that all you had to do?"

"Yes, I suppose; but as I said, it didn't seem that important. Mulholland said he didn't think there was a problem. And again, there were so many other things going on that-"

Darnell was incredulous. "You were too busy, you had too many problems to be able to make any clear decision- is that what you are saying?"

"It did not seem that major, not with all the other things I was dealing with."

"The news that Cynthia Grimes was pregnant with your child, for example? The news that, for some reason, she thought you wanted a child and that you wanted to marry her- other things like that?"

"I was not thinking that clearly. I said some things I probably should not have said." Whitfield stared down between his hands to the floor below.

"You did not go back to the United States because your father was dying, did you? You went back because of her, because of Cynthia Grimes, because of what she had told you. Isn't that true, Mr. Whitfield?"

Whitfield raised his eyes, a look of desolation on his face. "There were a lot of things going on, none of them good. But, I swear to you, I would not have let the Evangeline sail if I had thought for one moment that there was any chance that-"

"If you had thought for one moment! But you weren't thinking, were you? Isn't that what you just said- that there were too many things going on, too many questions, too many people wanting too many things? You did not have time to think about the Evangeline and what might happen to the people aboard her! You did not have time to think about the woman who was pregnant with your child! The only thought you had, Mr. Whitfield, was about yourself! You did not…"

The words died in midair as he felt the pain. It hit him like an electric shock, starting deep inside his chest, then shooting quick and lethal down his left arm. He staggered, stumbled forward, wondering how he could have been so stupid as to think that it could never happen to him, that he could never die of a heart attack while he was still in the middle of a trial. He fell to the floor and lay there helpless, staring up at the crowd of people gathering around him. For an instant, he saw, or thought he saw, Summer Blaine. He thought it odd that it might mean either that he was still alive or that there was something after death. Then everything turned black and he could not see or feel anything at all.

CHAPTER TWENTY-SEVEN

He was dead, yet her face, the face of Summer Blaine, hovered in front of him, floating disembodied in the air. He wanted to say something, to let her know that he could see her, but he had forgotten how to speak. He wanted to lift his hand, make some gesture to let her know what he had forgotten how to say, but he could not remember how to move. Was this what it meant to leave the light for eternal darkness: that you would always be aware, if dimly, of what you had left behind?

"Clear the courtroom!" ordered Homer Maitland, waving frantically to the bailiff. "Is there a doctor anywhere?"

Kneeling next to Darnell, Summer Blaine looked up. "Would someone please call an ambulance?" she said in a voice that sounded much calmer than she felt. Darnell was in serious trouble, but she refused to let it show; there was too much she had to do. With the siren wailing, the ambulance raced through the city streets. Darnell's vital signs were weak and getting worse.

"You promised me you wouldn't die," whispered Summer. "You gave me your word."

An oxygen mask was fastened over his mouth; his breathing was shallow, labored and faint. She held his hand between her own, offering words of love and encouragement as the ambulance sped on its way.

While Summer Blaine waited helpless and impatient, a team of cardiologists went to work. Three hours later she was told that the surgery had been successful and that William Darnell would live.

"It was a very close call," said the surgeon with a weary smile. "If you had not been a physician and known what to do, he would have died before the ambulance ever got here. It's still something of a miracle that he pulled through."

Summer stayed at the hospital as long as they would let her and was back again in the morning. She sat next to him on the bed, where he lay unconscious with tubes running everywhere, telling him he was going to be all right. After a while, tense and exhausted, she went outside and, where no one could see her, lit a cigarette. She held it between two trembling fingers, took one drag, then another-then, shaking her head at how weak she could become, she stamped the cigarette out.

That night she went to bed early and slept straight through. Darnell would be awake in the morning and perhaps even able to sit up a little. She put on a cheerful blue dress, one she knew he liked, and tried to think about the best way to tell him that someone else would have to worry about Marlowe and the trial. He could never go back to court again.

He was not going to have to live his life as an invalid. It was important that she tell him that right at the beginning. He was not to think that his life was over. He could still do pretty much anything he wanted. But trial work was too demanding; there was too much stress. He could lead a normal life, as long as he paid strict attention to the need for rest and a decent diet. He could even practice law. There was no reason he could not continue with the firm, advising clients and giving direction to the other, younger lawyers who could learn so much from him.

It was all so reasonable and intelligent, any sensible person would find it completely logical and persuasive. It would, of course, have no effect on him. Darnell did not care what was good for other people; he did not care what anyone else would do. As far as he was concerned, the best argument for not doing something was that other people did. But it was different this time. She had to make him understand that. He should have been dead already, and now he was out of chances.

"Have you seen this?" he demanded when she opened the door to his hospital room. He was sitting up, two days' worth of newspapers scattered over the bed. "These idiots are saying that the trial will have to start all over; that 'the famous defense lawyer, William Darnell, is in the hospital and no one knows how long He'll be there or even whether he'll recover'! I have to put a stop to this!

"I've already called Homer Maitland and told him I'm perfectly fine, that I'll be back in court on Monday. I told him he could check with my personal physician if he needed confirmation."

Darnell paused, put down the newspaper he had been waving, and looked at her with grateful eyes. "I saw your face; I thought I was dying, and I saw your face. Of all the things in the world, all the memories I have in my life, when I thought I was dying, the only thought I had was seeing you. They tell me you saved my life; that if you had not been there, had not changed your mind and decided to come to watch a little of the trial, that I would not have made it. Thank you for that- and for making sure that, just like I promised, I won't die, I'll finish the trial."

Summer started to protest, to tell him all the things she had carefully rehearsed in her mind; but she saw in his eyes that none of it would do any good. He was going to finish the trial, and there was nothing she could do to stop him. And even if she could stop him, what would be the use? So he could live out the few years he might have left, broken by the knowledge that a great career had come to such a useless close? There was all the difference in the world between living as long as possible and having a reason to live.

"What do you want me to do?" she asked as she sat on the edge of the bed and placed her hand on his.

"Don't let anyone here make any statements about what happened. Don't let anyone say anything about a heart attack. Tell anyone who asks...no, don't do that. I won't have you become a liar on my account. No, we'll let the facts speak for themselves- or, rather, we'll let the facts tell lies on our behalf," he said with a shrewd glint in his eye.

"Tell them that I've been sent home already; that I'll

be back in court on Monday morning, ready to call my next witness."

"Sent home? They'll want you here at least until the middle of next week. You've just been through...When? When were you planning to go home? Tomorrow?"

"No, not tomorrow; today. I don't need all this," he said, growling at the various monitors that measured his vital functions. "Get me out of here; take me home."

She seemed to hesitate. He took her by the wrist, squeezing it to show his strength. "If I stay here, a nurse will check on me every so often; if I'm home, you're there all the time. Aren't I better off with a full-time doctor than a part-time nurse?"

The grip on Summer's wrist grew tighter. "If I wasn't meant to finish the trial, don't you think I would have died the other day in court? I have to see it through to the end; I'm the only one who can save Marlowe. This isn't just vanity talking. Cynthia Grimes told me something, something Marlowe told her. I have to do this, and you have to help me."

Darnell did not want Summer Blaine to lie, but she did it anyway. With the kind of duplicitous precision any lawyer would have envied, William Darnell's physician issued a short statement that was in all its parts truthful, and as a whole misleading.

'William Darnell was released from the hospital today after a routine medical procedure alleviated a slight arterial blockage. He is expected to make a full and complete recovery and resume his normal schedule by the beginning of the week.'

"Or kill himself trying," she muttered under her breath after she read the brief statement to the reporters gathered outside the hospital. The day after Darnell returned home, Homer Maitland and Michael Roberts came to see him. Summer greeted them at the door. "He's expecting you," she said with a cheerful smile. "He's been looking forward to it all morning."

Darnell was sitting in an easy chair next to a window

in the living room. With his hand on the arm, he braced himself as he got to his feet. "I should have warned you," he said to Roberts as he took his hand. "There is no limit to what I will do to win the sympathy of a jury."

The look of self-assurance, the eager gleam with which he said it, made Roberts wonder for an instant if it was not something close to the truth- not that Darnell would have collapsed on purpose, but that his first thought after-wards would be how to take advantage of it.

"Then I'm afraid it was a useless gesture. If I'm any judge of juries, you have had their sympathy almost from the beginning," said Roberts with quiet candor. They sat on the blue sofa across from Darnell's chair, in the clumsy posture of visitors who do not know how long they should stay. They made the usual polite inquiries about Darnell's health, the normal superficial conversation that carefully avoids any suggestion that someone may have come close to death.

Finally, Maitland flashed a broad, practiced smile. "I know you want to finish the trial, and of course we want that as well. I've talked to Michael about this already, and he agrees that we could work an abbreviated schedule, stretch it out a little so we would not have to do quite so much every day. That would be easier on us all. We'll do whatever we can."

"That's an extremely thoughtful offer," said Darnell, "but it really isn't necessary. What happened looked much worse than it was; I was never in any real danger."

He looked at Roberts. "I have a heart condition- nothing too serious; I've had it for years. Every once in a while it acts up a little. More annoying than anything, and damned inconvenient."

Turning back to Maitland, he explained that, in any event, he had only one more witness to call.

"Maybe two, but not more than that. Monday is the only day I need. If Michael doesn't call any witnesses on rebuttal, we can make our closing arguments on Tuesday and the case can go to the jury. There is no reason to abbreviate the sessions. Two more days and we're through. And I can promise you," he said as he got to his feet, this time without bracing himself, "I won't have any trouble doing that."

Darnell looked Roberts right in the eye as he shook his hand with all his former strength. He turned to say goodbye to Maitland, but the judge put his hand on Roberts's sleeve and told him that he was going to stay behind for a few more minutes.

"We have at least two things in common," said Maitland when they were alone. "We're both too damned old to be working, and we both lie about our health. I've had a heart attack; I know what it's like. I know something else, too- I know you should be in the hospital, that you have no business being home. But you did it, got yourself out of there so you could convince everyone that you were all right to finish the trial."

Maitland looked past Darnell to the gray sunlit bay and the bright-colored Golden Gate and the thick, white clouds moving across the azure sky. It was one of those postcard days when everything is the way you have always remembered it, when you have the sense that San Francisco is the one place that never really changes, the one place that always stays the same.

"Makes you want to live forever, doesn't it?" said Maitland in a voice filled with quiet nostalgia. He patted Darnell on the shoulder and looked straight at him. "I don't want to try this case over from the beginning, especially if I have to do it with someone else handling the defense. But I'd rather do that than have you fall down dead in the middle of your summation. So don't lie to me. How bad is it, and what kind of chance am I taking if I let you go on with this?"

"Blockage of the artery, but now it's clear. If I was going to die-" he began.

Maitland cut him short. "Don't try that one with me. I've used it too often myself. That witness of yours, Samantha Wilcox- even if she is right, even if there is a reason for everything that happens, who knows what that reason is? Do you really believe that you were saved so that you could finish the trial? For all you know you were given one last chance to quit the trial before it killed you."

The sunlight through the window slanted across Maitland's face, shading and deepening the lines that creased his skin, the lines that helped make him seem a man of experience whose word you could trust. "You see the effect this trial has had? Nothing seems quite normal anymore. I've started to see everything in terms of the terrible, stark choices those wretched people had. Tell me the truth- this is just between you and me. If this were any other trial, if it were just a man on trial for the kind of murder we get every day, you would still be in the hospital doing every-thing the doctors said, wouldn't you?"

"I have to finish this; there isn't any choice."

"Which is my point exactly. We have been sitting there, day after day, listening to what they all went through; to what Marlowe, rightly or wrongly, thought he had to do. And we start to measure ourselves by a standard so diffi-cult that we are not even sure anyone should try to meet it. Marlowe was right; Marlowe was wrong...Whatever we may think about what he did, he has made cowards of us all- because we know, don't we, if we are honest with ourselves, that faced with the same awful choices, we probably would not have had his courage. And so you are going back into court on Monday, even if it kills you, because if you don't, you will think that instead of doing what you should have done, you thought only of yourself. And because I would like to think that I would do the same thing myself, I don't seem to have much choice but to let you."

As soon as Maitland left, Darnell sank into his chair, exhausted from the effort of disguising how weak he felt. Two more days in court and the trial would be over. He wondered if he could do it, and then, with a grim smile as Summer helped him to his feet, wondered if he could even make it into the next room and bed.

Darnell slept the rest of the afternoon and then, after a light dinner, slept until morning. For much of the day, he sat in the living room chair, watching with a listless eye the changing light outside. Caught by the simple truth of Homer

Maitland's words, he kept running them over in his mind. The sight of it- the sun on the Pacific, the light on the bridge- did make you want to live forever and, what Maitland had not said, made you think you could.

"I have someone coming over tomorrow afternoon," he told Summer. "It won't take but an hour, and I need to see her before the trial starts again."

"Her?"

"Vincent Marlowe's sister. She hired me to represent him, but she has not even once attended the trial. There are things I need to talk with her about, things which may decide the fate of her brother."

Darnell looked worried and, more than worried, distressed.

"You told me early on," said Summer, "when the trial had just started, that you did not think what Marlowe had done was right, however necessary it may have been. Have you changed your mind about that? Not that you think what he did was right, but that- how shall I say this?- that it was not quite as wrong?"

Darnell turned back to the window. The voice of Homer Maitland was still a whisper in his ear. "Days like this make you think you'll never die," he said to Summer, staring at the bay. "What Marlowe said about needing to have something worth dying for or there is no meaning to your life- that's a brave thing to say, maybe braver than I believe."

Darnell's eyes gave up the light. He turned to Summer with a tired, bleak expression. "I don't know how wrong or right he was. All I know is that he's been punished enough."

Summer was not sure she understood. Darnell's expression grew bleaker still. "Everyone will understand soon enough. The only way I can save him will destroy him. Which may be what he has wanted all along."

CHAPTER TWENTY-EIGHT

Darnell looked at the empty chairs in the jury box, at the empty bench where the judge would sit, at the bailiff standing idly in the corner, at the quiet way the courtroom crowds were filling up the benches. The court reporter, a woman he might have walked right past on the sidewalk outside without remembering her face, a woman whose name he had not bothered to learn, was putting a thick roll of tape into the stenotype machine.

He had spent most of his life in a courtroom, but seldom noticed the other people who spent most of their lives there as well. He was like an actor who had played the same role for so many years and in so many cities that, at the end, he had forgotten all the theatres and could remember only the play.

And now, at the end of his career, he was looking at the courtroom the way he had the first time he had appeared as counsel for the defense, with the awestruck eyes of a young lawyer who wonders, as he tries to clear his throat, if he has not made a terrible mistake. He does not know the first thing about trying cases and he is sure that, five minutes into his opening statement, there won't be a person on the jury who does not know him for the fraud he is.

Darnell had not thought about that first trial in years, but suddenly he remembered it as if nearly a half a century had vanished in a week. It did not seem possible that the beginning was really so long ago and that the end was now so close. Today and tomorrow, that was all the time he had left. And after that- what? A brief retirement, a gradual and irrevocable decline, a slow enfeeblement under death's laughing eye?

Two more days …He began to think it might have been better if Summer had not been there, and he had died in court. It was a moment's self-pity- and, worse, it gave him credit for bravery he did not have. He did not want to die, that was the truth of it; the real reason he wanted no part of retirement was what would follow after it. When he was in a trial there was work to be done, he had a reason to live- there was no time to think about death.

Was that what Marlowe had understood? Is that what those poor desperate souls had grasped? That the only way death could win was if you thought the mere fact of your own existence more important than what you did with it?

Homer Maitland came into court and took his accustomed place on the bench. Darnell remembered what he had said about both of them being too old to keep working and knew it had been a lie, one of those civilized, polite half-truths we believe might be good advice for others but would never think to follow ourselves. Maitland on the bench looked indestructible; Maitland without a black judicial robe looked just like other tired men his age.

With a quick, cursory nod of his head, Maitland ordered the bailiff to bring in the jury. While he waited, he concentrated on a written motion submitted in one of the dozens of other cases he would be hearing over the next few weeks. With the ordered steps of a practiced choreography, the twelve jurors filed into the jury box, careful not to bump into each other, smiling when they did. Six men and six women, twelve common, ordinary people- but nothing like a representative cross-section of the community in which they lived; nothing like that jury of one's peers of which the civics books speak so glowingly and no defendant ever sees.

Darnell watched them as they settled into their chairs and prepared to listen to another day of testimony. They did not dress the way jurors did in that first case he tried, when the men wore coats and ties and the women all wore dresses. Now everyone wore what they wanted, and what they wanted was, for the most part, neither very fashionable nor very interesting. It also seemed to Darnell that that first jury had been more keen-witted and alert.

Darnell shook his head at his own stupidity. If he had learned anything, it was that you could never tell much about a jury from the way it looked. They would sit there, day after day, twelve blank, impenetrable faces; incapable, to all appearances, of registering an emotion. Then, at the end of it, after you had given up all hope that they had understood a word of what was said, they would come back with a verdict as good as, or better than, you could have done yourself.

But there was something else that had begun to intrigue Darnell, something that every jury had in common, but which in this trial bore an eerie correspondence to what the jury was there to decide.

No one thought much about it when Darnell had occasion to point it out, but the jury, for all its flaws and imperfections, was the only truly democratic institution. No one was elected to a jury; the names were drawn at random. The same method by which the survivors of the Evangeline had decided who among them would be the next to die was used to choose the twelve people who would decide whether murder, even if required by necessity, should have been left to chance.

Darnell looked around the courtroom, wondering if he would ever see another one. For a brief, fleeting moment, he thought he knew what it must have been like, out there in that lifeboat, with a storm raging all around, or sitting stiff and crowded, the sea becalmed, drawing lots and then waiting to hear whether Marlowe might call your name.

"Mr. Darnell," said Maitland with a smile that welcomed him back, "are you ready to call your next witness?"

Quickly, and with energy, Darnell was on his feet, dispelling any doubts that he might not be back in form. His eyes darted from Maitland to the jury to let them know that what they were about to hear would be important, and perhaps decisive, for the case.

"Your Honor, the defense recalls the defendant, Vincent Marlowe." He had not told Marlowe that he was going to bring him back as a witness. He wanted Marlowe to be surprised, and he wanted the jury to know it. He began with an apology.

"Because of what happened in court last week, because the doctors, always overcautious, wanted me to rest, I was not able to tell you that I would need to ask more questions."

Darnell stood at the front corner of the counsel table, smiling confidently as he looked Marlowe in the eye. Marlowe held himself with the same stoic reserve he had shown throughout the trial.

"I want to ask you first about the testimony of some of the other witnesses. And though I think the answer is implicit from what you said on the stand before, to avoid any possible ambiguity on this point, let me ask you the question directly.

"Would you have sailed the Evangeline into the south Atlantic if Benjamin Whitfield had told you the truth? Would you have attempted to sail the Evangeline around Africa if he had told you that a crack had been found below the water-line, and that, though it had been repaired, the other welding seams had not been checked?"

"No," replied Marlowe without a moment's hesitation. "Not that I would have thought there was any great danger; more because it is always better, especially at sea, not to take half measures."

"Because, I take it, there is always some chance of the unexpected?"

"Always," said Marlowe, with a defeated look. "Always."

"My next question has to do with what Cynthia Grimes told the court. Was her assumption correct? Did you, after telling her that the fact she was pregnant would not excuse her from taking her chances with the rest, do exactly that, make sure she was never chosen? Did you, deliberately and without telling any of the others, make sure that she never drew the fatal lot?" Marlowe shook his head.

"No, not exactly all of what you said is true. I talked to Mr. Offenbach about it. I wanted to know what he thought we should do. We both knew that it was only a matter of time; we knew that we were all going to die out there. We decided that she, and the child she carried, should stay alive until the end. We had no reason for doing this; it was not because we thought there was still a chance a ship might come. It was a feeling- a feeling that we might as well all die at once and be done with it, than take the life of a child its mother wanted to save. That's what it really was, I suppose: the belief that the rest of us could make our own decisions about dying so that someone else could live, but that we could not do that for a child who was not yet born; that the only one who could do that was the unborn child's mother."

"Why didn't you explain that to the others? Why didn't you at least tell Ms. Grimes?"

Marlowe rubbed his fingers back and forth across his lower jaw. His eyes narrowed as he turned his head to the side. "There weren't that many who might have agreed with me." The glance he gave Darnell spoke the hope that he would not have to go any further to make his meaning clear.

"One other question about the method that was used. You heard Mr. Roberts ask why you did not ask for volunteers instead of leaving things to chance. Was it because this whole arrangement was actually based on voluntary consent? Because everyone agreed to do what the majority decided, and the majority decided that the fairest method was to have everyone draw lots?" asked Darnell, so certain of the answer that he was thinking ahead to the next question.

"No."

Darnell was sure he had not heard him right. He swung his head from the jury box to the witness stand. "No? I don't think I understand. Are you saying that the lottery was not based on the consent of all the others?"

"No, I'm not saying that either," said Marlowe as he looked away from Darnell's inquiring gaze.

"Then what are you saying?" insisted Darnell, certain that Marlowe was hiding something. "You have to answer: you're under oath."

"You asked why I did not ask for volunteers."

"Yes, it's the same question Mr. Roberts put to Ms.

Grimes. I don't quite see...?"

"Ms. Grimes doesn't remember. She may not even have known. I did not ask any of the women."

"You mean...?"

"I asked for volunteers. I asked if anyone was willing to die."

"And no one would?"

"One only- Mr. Offenbach. But I could not let him do it. I could not let Mr. Offenbach- you know the reasons already. So I asked again. I asked Trevelyn if he would do it, if he would volunteer, but Trevelyn refused."

"It was only then- after no one else would volunteer- that the other method was chosen?" asked Darnell as he paced slowly in front of the counsel table, staring intently at the floor.

"Yes."

Darnell stood still. He twisted his head just far enough to catch Marlowe's eye. "But you made sure that the first person to die was not chosen by chance at all. You made certain that a fourteen-year-old boy would be the first one you had to kill. And you did that because you wanted to spare him from having to live through the awful things you knew were going to happen- is that correct?"

Marlowe's eyes became bleak, remote. Darnell did not press him.

"Yes, that was your testimony, as I'm sure the jury will remember. There are only a few more points I want to clarify. You said, if I remember correctly, that you first went to sea when you were only twelve- is that right?"

Marlowe seemed, if not to relax, to become less rigid. He looked at Darnell and nodded.

"Yes, I was twelve when I first went to sea."

"On a ship from Singapore, the captain someone who knew your father?"

"Yes, that's right."

Grasping the edge of the counsel table behind him, Darnell stared down at the floor, wrestling with an inner dilemma. Finally, he looked up. "Your father died in an

241

explosion, on a ship he was working on in Seattle. Your mother was left with only a small widow's pension and there was your sister- a younger sister, if I remember right- still to raise. You went off to sea, willing and, I dare say, eager, to help in any way you could!"

Darnell's gray eyebrows arched high above his eyes, a gesture of admiration for what the boy had done to become a man. He stood straight up. "Your mother passed away some years ago, didn't she?"

"Yes, she's been gone almost ten years now."

"Which left your sister; but of course she's all grown up now with a family of her own. No, I'm sorry- how thoughtless of me. Her husband died a year or so after they were married, didn't he?"

With a baffled look on his face, Roberts rose slowly from his chair. "Your Honor, I'm not at all clear what relevance any of this has and-"

"Which made it almost as difficult for her as it had been for your mother, didn't it?" asked Darnell in a voice that made Roberts turn. "Your mother was left with a daughter to raise while you went off to sea; your sister was left with a son to raise and, once again, you did everything you could to help. Isn't that right, Mr. Marlowe? To all intents and purposes, you became a second father to the boy, didn't you?"

All the life had gone from Marlowe's eyes. He was staring into the abyss, greeted by his own reflection.

"You did everything you could for the boy, even promising that one day you would take him on one of those voyages he used to love to hear you talk about. And you kept that promise, didn't you, Mr. Marlowe? You kept your promise because you loved him more than life itself, didn't you?

"And that is the great tragedy of the Evangeline, isn't it? The boy you killed to save from suffering, the boy who- had you only known there was still a chance of rescue- would be at home today, safe with his mother, was your mother's only grandson, your sister's only child!"

CHAPTER TWENTY-NINE

Homer Maitland did not try to hide his ignorance. With a casual shrug, he informed the two attorneys that he had looked everywhere and there was simply no law- at least none that was, as the lawyers like to say, directly on point. "It isn't all that surprising, when you think about it. Why would you expect to find any law to cover a situation that no one has ever faced?

"Yes, I know," he added before Darnell could interrupt. "There were a few cases, but those were in the nineteenth century, and no matter how far back you go, you won't find a single case in this jurisdiction where the defense of necessity has been raised against a charge of murder. This is the first, and that means it's up to me to fashion an instruction on that defense for the jury."

Maitland glanced at a yellow legal pad on which he had written out a draft. "After I give the standard instruction on murder, I will instruct them that, 'It is a defense to the crime of murder if a reasonable person would have believed that both the death of the person killed and the death of others would have taken place if that person had not been killed, and if the method by which that person was chosen did not unfairly single him out."

"That leaves out the important question of time," objected Roberts. "It is one thing if you have to act within hours or minutes to save the lives of others- the situation of the mountain climber hanging on the rope, which will bring down all the others if it is not cut right away- it is something else again to decide that you should kill someone because you might face that situation at some indeterminate point in the future."

"I thought of that. I agree with the importance of the distinction. The difficulty is to know exactly where to draw the line. It seemed to me better to leave it to the jury to decide on the particular facts how long it would be reasonable to wait. It is, after all, part of what defining necessity is all about. "After the jury retires, you can both put whatever objections you have, to this or any of the other instructions, on the record."

"I wonder what instruction would make it clear to Marlowe what he did," said Darnell, his eyes opened wide and not a speck of hope within them.

"His own nephew, his sister's only child," said Roberts, repeating the phrase that kept echoing in his mind. He looked at Darnell, sitting next to him, and acknowledged the truth of what Darnell had told him at the beginning. "This trial has ruined a lot of lives, hasn't it?" Roberts paused.

He was aware of the irony in the fact that he had prosecuted Marlowe for murder because, sworn to uphold the law, he thought he did not have a choice. "Or were their lives ruined already, and the trial has given at least a few of them a kind of release which, if not redemption, is something still worth having?"

"I think that may be true; though, curiously, not for the men involved, only for the women," said Darnell. "I'm too old to believe that women were ever equal to men; they're better, far better, than men could ever be. They have a strength, an endurance, men can seldom match. Samantha Wilcox and Cynthia Grimes: those are two people anyone would be proud to know. But Trevelyn? DeSantos? A couple of sniveling cowards!"

"You say the trial might be good, but "only for the women"," said Homer Maitland, sitting back, his ankle on his knee. "Leave aside Marlowe- I can understand that he's a special case- but what about Hugo Offenbach? Did he get nothing out of this? You wouldn't put him in the same category as those other two?"

"He and Marlowe are both outside the common run. They care nothing, or next to nothing, about the judgments of the world. They both, I think, thought this trial was part of the punishment each of them deserved, the price they had to pay because they lived. Offenbach at least had the satisfaction of letting everyone know the truth of what happened and what Marlowe did; all that Marlowe got was the chance to add another measure of punishment to what must already be unendurable."

No one said a word. The silence deepened. Finally, and as quietly as he could, Maitland reached for the court file and the instructions he had prepared for the jury. "If this had been tried to the court without a jury, if I had to decide what to do- if things were what they were years ago, when the sentence was entirely within my own discretion- shall I tell you what I think I would do, the way I would try to cut this Gordian knot?" Maitland searched their eyes, telling them with a piercing glance that despite his placid, affable demeanor, the trial had taken a toll on his emotions as well as theirs.

"Just between the three of us, and just within these walls, I would find him guilty of murder and then, as a sentence, set him free- on the ground that living with what he had done, what in his own honest good judgment he had been forced to do, was all the punishment anyone should have to suffer."

Darnell pushed himself up from the chair. "And how would you decide it now, when, if you found him guilty, you would have no choice but to send him away for life?"

Maitland held his hand over his mouth, pondering the harsh stupidities of the law, the absence of all intelligence and understanding, the drive for retribution and revenge that had removed all proportion between the sentence and the crime. "All I can do is give the coward's answer and tell you I'm glad the case is going to a jury."

He looked at his watch. "We'd better get started if we're going to be finished by this afternoon."

When the jury was brought back into the courtroom, Homer Maitland greeted them with a solemn instruction on the limits of what they were about to hear.

"At the beginning of the trial each of the attorneys-

Mr. Roberts for the prosecution and Mr. Darnell for the defense- made an opening statement in which they gave you a preview of what they expected the evidence to show. Now, after you have heard all the evidence that is going to be offered in this case, after you have listened to the witnesses called by each side, the attorneys are going to give their closing arguments. These summations, as they are sometimes called, give the prosecution and the defense an opportunity to argue what the evidence means. I cannot emphasize too strongly that, while you should listen and consider carefully what the two attorneys say, the judgment as to whether the evidence you have heard is sufficient to support a conviction is yours and yours alone. Mr. Roberts, if you're ready."

Roberts was on his feet, moving directly to the jury box. He wasted no time. "Everyone who has listened to the evidence in this case must have asked themselves what they would have done had they had the misfortune to find themselves in Vincent Marlowe's position- alive, but barely, out there in the middle of the ocean with a dozen other people in a lifeboat that was not made for anything like that number, with no more food or water.

"Everyone must have wondered at the courage, the bravery, with which the people who were Marlowe's victims- the people he killed- faced their deaths without resistance. Some of us- and let me admit that I include myself in this- must have marveled at the almost unnatural determination with which Marlowe forced himself to plunge that knife of his into each victim, and the way he then set about the grim business of first sharing out their blood and then turning the bodies of the people he murdered into food for those still left alive.

"But the question, the only question, you are here to decide is whether he had to do this- not did he kill six people, for you have his own sworn testimony that he did, but did he have to? Was that the only choice he had? Was there really no other way?"

For nearly an hour, Roberts reviewed the testimony of the witnesses for both the prosecution and the defense. He seemed to go out of his way to balance what one said against the other. There was a point to this, but it was not fairness.

"Trevelyn seems to have been the first to talk about it, the need to kill someone, and Trevelyn did not hesitate to insist that it should be someone else. Trevelyn wanted to live. Whatever else you might think about him, he was brutally honest- no matter how much he might lie about it now. Someone has to die so that I can live, that is what Trevelyn wanted, and I have no doubt that he would have killed someone if Marlowe had not stopped him. Yes, I mean that. Marlowe stopped him; he would not allow Trevelyn to choose his own victim.

"But what did Marlowe do instead? Did he stop any murder from being committed? Did he insist that, if they were going to try to stay alive a little longer- and remember he said that he did not think there was any chance of rescue; remember that he killed his own nephew so that the boy would not have to suffer!- did he insist that, if they were going to live like cannibals, devouring human flesh, they really leave it in the hands of chance or God and wait until the first among them died of natural causes?

"They could not do that, he tells us, because when the body is dead the blood becomes unusable! They could not do that because, if they had, those deaths would not have been so heroic!

"Whatever merit there might have been in a defense of necessity, it falls apart on this one irrefutable fact: Marlowe, by his own admission, as well as by the testimony of Hugo Offenbach, did not believe that there was any chance of rescue. He did not believe that anyone would survive. Then why was it necessary that anyone be killed? So that others could live? For what? So that, as Samantha Wilcox put it, they could keep killing each other until there was no one left?

"No, it was necessary, according to Vincent Marlowe, so that their deaths would have some meaning, so that they could each die with the illusion- an illusion Marlowe did not share- that they were sacrificing themselves so that others could live!"

Roberts looked back across the courtroom to where Marlowe sat, staring straight ahead, giving no sign that he had heard a word, or that it would have mattered if he had.

"It is impossible not to feel a profound sympathy for Vincent Marlowe- I know that- and not to feel that, at times, the law may be too harsh. But what Marlowe did was murder, and unless we are prepared to say that everyone is free to decide for themselves when someone else should die, there is only one verdict you can bring back, and that verdict is guilty."

Roberts had spoken for an hour and a half; Darnell spoke for nearly three. He took the jury from the beginning of Marlowe's life to the day the Evangeline set sail on its ill-fated voyage around Africa. He quoted from memory and at great length the testimony of Benjamin Whitfield, reminding the jury of the lies he had told and how, on every crucial point, his testimony had been contradicted by the man who had designed and built the Evangeline and by the woman he had betrayed and abandoned, the woman who only because Marlowe had saved her life could now have Whitfield's child.

"I've gone back through all of this, started at the very beginning, because it is important to see that it is only a long series of random chances that we look back on and call fate. Things take on a meaning at the end that they did not have at the beginning. What do we know of the future? How much can we really know about anything?

"What did Marlowe know in the middle of the south Atlantic, except that they were thousands of miles from shore with no food or water, and that if he did not do something Trevelyn, and others like him, would start to take matters into their own hands. Wait until someone died of natural causes? That is what the prosecution, in the comfort of a courtroom, tells us should have been done. What the prosecution forgets is that it was already too late for that! What the prosecution forgets is that Trevelyn, and not just Trevelyn, was demanding that someone had to be killed, and that they should choose the boy. They said it was because the boy was the closest one to death; it seems more likely that it was because he was a boy and less able to resist. What the prosecution does not want you to think too hard about was that Marlowe brought a kind of civilization to what would otherwise have become the law of the jungle, a battle for survival in which, eventually, no one would have been left.

"The prosecution says that there was no necessity for what Marlowe did, because Marlowe did not believe that there was any chance of rescue; that the most he could hope to achieve was to keep the ones he did not kill alive a few days or perhaps a few weeks longer. But even if that were true, it is not clear how that would make what Marlowe did any less necessary. Does the prosecution really wish to insist that the value of a life is measured by how long someone expects it to last? Is it not just as much a murder to kill someone lying in a hospital bed with only a few days or a few weeks left to live?

"You saw Vincent Marlowe, you heard what he had to say. He put his own nephew to death to save him from seeing what he knew he had to do. He did not think there was any chance that any of them would leave the sea alive. You saw the look in his eyes, that awful anguish, when he cried out that he never would have killed the boy if he had thought there was any chance that any of them might come through this alive. You must have believed him when he said it; and you can't possibly have any doubt about it now that we know what we did not know before- that the boy was his sister's child, the closest thing to a son Vincent Marlowe will ever have.

That was what he believed- that there would be no rescue. But he believed something else as well. He believed that human beings endure, that we go on for as long as we can; and that, more than our own survival, we have within us an impulse to do something higher and nobler, to sacrifice ourselves so that others can live. Because as long as any of us are still alive there is always, against all odds, the hope that someone will be left to remember what we did.

"You listened to the prosecution's summation, and you

have listened to mine. Sometime during your deliberations you might remember that there was another summation, one more eloquent than anything either Mr. Roberts or I could say.

It was the simple admission of Vincent Marlowe when he looked you straight in the eye and told you that he does not believe that what he did was right, but that, even now, looking back on it, he would have to do it again. Vincent Marlowe saved six lives, and there isn't anyone in this courtroom who believes that he would not give anything not to have been one of them."

CHAPTER THIRTY

Homer Maitland gave his instructions on the law, leaving until the very end the instruction on the law of necessity. A few minutes after four in the afternoon the jury began their deliberations. A few minutes after six, the bailiff knocked on the jury- room door to ask if they wanted to break for dinner. They asked if, instead of going out, they could have something sent in. At midnight they told the bailiff that they would start again at eight o'clock the next morning.

Darnell knew nothing of this until the jury had already begun its second day of deliberations. He had had an early dinner with Summer Blaine and, mounting only a mild protest, followed her orders and gone straight to bed. He would not admit how tired he was and how much that three-hour summation had taken out of him, but Summer knew. She had been there watching, proud of every word, more certain than she had ever been that nothing could have stopped him, and glad she had not tried. But now it was over, and he was going to do exactly what she told him until, like any normal patient, he was on his way to a full recovery.

"They worked until late last night, and they are already back at it this morning," said Darnell, as he hung up the bedside phone.

"Is that good?" asked Summer, sitting down next to him. "Eat," she said, pointing to a piece of unbuttered toast that had not been touched.

"I used to think that the longer a jury stayed out, the more uncertain they were; and the more uncertain, the greater the doubt- which should be good for the defense. But I've seen juries stay out for days and come back with a verdict that found the defendant guilty on all counts. Who knows what this jury is going to do? I don't know what I would decide.

"Marlowe isn't guilty, and neither is he innocent. If he had killed one person, then maybe- but six? But then if he had not killed them all; if he had stopped at two, or three, or four- no one would be alive. It's what I said at the beginning: there are some situations for which the rules were never made."

Darnell bent his head, a baffled expression in his eyes. He tried to make sense of it all, or at least explain that part of it he thought he understood. "What happened out there was, in a way, almost biblical. It was the way things must have happened in the beginning, before there was any law, when everyone did whatever they had to do to stay alive- until someone had the wisdom to establish a rule and the strength to make everyone follow it.

"Someone had to use violence to stop the violence. How do you then go back and charge them with a crime? That was the real necessity out there- that Marlowe, or some- one like him, impose the law on all the others- but he could not have done that if he had not also given them a reason to believe in it. If it had not been for him, those people would have become half-mad barbarians, killing each other to stay alive. He made them- do I dare say this?- more civilized than they had been before, willing to let chance decide their fate, willing to die so that the others could live.

"It was remarkable what he did, but how many of us are willing to admit it? And perhaps it is better if we do not; better to preserve our own decent illusion that murder and cannibalism can never be right." Darnell looked at Summer to see if he had made his meaning clear, wondering as he did how much of what he had said was true, so much of it still vague and confusing in his mind.

In a way, it did not matter: Marlowe's fate was in the hands of the jury now. Still, it nagged at him, that after all this time, after all the things he had said and heard at trial, there was this terrible doubt about what it meant. With a helpless shrug, he started to get up. The only thing he could do now was get dressed, go the office, and wait.

Summer Blaine would not hear of it. "You need to stay

in bed. They'll call you when the jury has a verdict. You can get to court just as quickly from here. Quicker, actually; I'll drive you."

Darnell waited all day, but the call never came. The following morning, Homer Maitland telephoned to tell him what he would also tell Roberts- that the jury had again worked until close to midnight and again come back at eight. The jury worked all that day and all the next.

Finally, on the fourth morning, Darnell could not take it anymore. "I'm getting dressed," he grumbled when Summer asked him what he thought he was doing. "I need to get down to the office."

"Do you think that will help the jury decide?"

"No, but it may help to stop me from going crazy," he replied as he grabbed a shirt from the closet. He was pulling on his shoes when the telephone rang. Summer took it in the other room.

"They want you back in court at ten-thirty."

Darnell looked up. "They have a verdict?" he asked, just to be sure.

"No. The jury sent a message to the judge saying they haven't been able to reach one."

"That means Maitland is going to give the dynamite instruction. I have to call Marlowe." Homer Maitland did exactly what Darnell had said he would. The jury was brought back into the courtroom and, with the defendant and the lawyers sitting at their places, the judge asked the jury foreman, a balding middle-aged man with gentle eyes, if it were true that they had not yet been able to reach a verdict.

"That's true, your Honor; we have not," he said in a voice that seemed to hint at exhaustion.

Maitland bent forward, a look of quiet confidence in his eye. "You are not to feel bad about this; it shows that you have taken your responsibilities as seriously as you should. Now, it often happens that a jury decides that it cannot decide, and when it does, the law- in all its wisdom- has a remedy."

A smile ran across Maitland's jagged mouth. The

jurors seemed to relax when they saw it. They took it as
a sign that they were not delinquent and that he was not
displeased. "The remedy is that you try again; and that, if
possible, you try harder. I am therefore instructing you to
return to the jury room and resume deliberations.

"Each of you, without sacrificing your own independent judgment, should listen carefully to the opinions of all
the other jurors and try to see things from their perspective.
I am also instructing you to consider the fact that if you do
not reach a verdict, this case will have to be tried again, to a
different jury, and there is no reason to assume that that jury
will be any more capable than you."

With a doubtful look, the foreman said they would
do their best. As the jury headed back to the jury room,
Darnell, with a lawyer's instinct, started to offer Marlowe a
few words of encouragement. One look in his eyes told him
it was useless, that Marlowe was beyond the reach of human
sympathy or help. Darnell patted him on the arm and they
went their separate ways in silence.

The jury was out another day, and another one after
that. Darnell began to feel hopeless and alone, as if the trial
was over and the jury, like the Evangeline, had just disappeared. And then, finally, three days after they had been told
to try again, the jury sent word they were finished. They had
done what Maitland asked and reached a verdict after all.

It was always the quietest time of all, the hush that fell
when the jury filed back into the courtroom with a verdict in
the foreman's hand. Darnell tried to read some meaning into
their averted eyes. They did not look at the crowd of spectators and reporters; they did not look at Roberts and they did
not look at him. They did not look at Marlowe; they did not
look at anyone. They did not even look at Maitland; they sat
with lowered eyes, listening to the silence that echoed like a
final judgment through the room.

"Has the jury reached a verdict?" asked Homer
Maitland in a formal, distant voice. The foreman stood up,
looked across at Judge Maitland and, without a word, held
up the verdict form.

"Would the clerk please hand me the verdict?" The foreman clasped his hands together and waited while Maitland read it over. The lines in Maitland's forehead deepened; his eyes became intense. He looked at the foreman as if he had a question, but then he nodded slowly as if he understood, and not only understood, but approved.

"Give this back to the foreman," he said to the clerk. "Would the foreman please read the verdict?"

The foreman stood as straight as he could. He cleared his throat and began to read:"It is the unanimous verdict of the jury that we cannot decide. We are not a hung jury; we are not split between those who believe the defendant is guilty and those who would vote to acquit. In that sense, we are not divided at all: we all agree that the question of guilt or innocence in the case of the defendant, Vincent Marlowe, is impossible to decide."

The foreman stopped reading. He looked first at Roberts and then at the courtroom crowd.

"We go further still," he said, reading again from the lengthy handwritten note that had been scrawled on the verdict form.

"We understand that this is no legal verdict, and that the case may be tried again. For whatever weight it may carry, we are unanimous in our feeling that it should not. Having listened to all the evidence, having heard the lawyers' arguments, having deliberated among ourselves for the better part of a week, we are each and every one of us convinced that in this matter there is no justice in anything anyone can now do."

Homer Maitland rubbed his chin and then leaned forward on his folded arms. He asked if all the members of the jury agreed with the statement the foreman had read.

"Though this is the opinion of all of you, and though I cannot say the decision you have reached is wrong, the court, as you have rightly anticipated, has now the duty to declare a mistrial. The case is dismissed," he said as he banged his gavel. "The defendant is free to go."

With the crowd swirling all around them, and reporters shouting questions about what it meant and if there was going to be another trial, Darnell fought his way outside. He thought Marlowe was right behind him, but when he turned around the only familiar face he saw was that of Summer Blaine, trying to catch up. She took hold of his hand.

"What does it mean?" she asked.

"It means it's over," said Darnell. He glanced across at Michael Roberts standing on the courthouse steps talking to a crowd of eager reporters. Summer turned around just in time to hear Roberts say that he would not second guess what the jury had done.

"I imagine they came to the same conclusion most people would have come to after listening to everything that was said in that trial: that Vincent Marlowe has been punished enough," said Roberts.

"Does that mean there won't be another trial?" someone called from the back of the crowd. With a weary smile, Roberts shook his head. He looked beyond the circle of faces waiting with blank anticipation to where William Darnell stood with Summer Blaine.

"I was told at the very beginning that taking this case to trial would ruin the lives of people who had already suffered enough. But there was never a choice- a crime had been committed, people had been killed; we had to prosecute. We had to bring what happened out into the open; we could not let it stay a secret.

"We could not allow murder to become a question of someone's private judgment; it had to be brought to a public trial. And now it has. The jury has spoken, and their verdict should be binding on us all. So, no, there will not be another trial. Vincent Marlowe is a free man, and if anyone thinks that this is improper or unfair- if anyone thinks we should keep after him until we find a jury that might be persuaded to convict him- ask yourself this question: do you know anyone who thinks that Vincent Marlowe is a lucky man?"

Summer took Darnell by the arm. "What will happen to Marlowe now?" she asked as they started down the steps.

With a dismal look, Darnell shrugged his shoulders.

Suddenly, he caught sight of a man and woman on the corner half a block ahead. The man held the woman with his arm while she sobbed against his chest. "That's Marlowe," said Darnell in a voice as sad as Summer had ever heard. "The woman is Marlowe's sister."

Summer took Darnell home, and for the next few weeks, while he slowly recovered from the heart attack that had come so close to killing him, never left his side. She insisted that he have perfect quiet, and did everything she could to keep the world away. The telephone calls from reporters- desperate to have a comment about the trial and what the jury had done- she handled with a series of stories that, without quite lying, skirted the edges of the truth.

It was easy to say that he was not available; it was more difficult to say when he would be. All she really knew was that, before he had any business doing it, he would be back in a court of law. She had come to the conclusion that he was right when he said that his work, even if it had almost killed him, was the only thing that kept him alive.

The promise that the Marlowe trial would be his last, that he would go quietly into retirement, had been only provisional, a goal set, an objective to be achieved. Its accomplishment meant only the necessity for another provisional promise, another trial that would give him a reason to live. It was something both he and Marlowe understood, something that she now understood as well, that precisely because it was inevitable, you never surrendered to death. It was not long before the calls stopped coming, not long before the world's attention turned to other things.

The famous people whose lives had been lost or changed forever by the tragedy of the Evangeline were forgotten as other people became famous in their place. But Darnell would never forget any of them. The faces of the survivors, the faces of the witnesses who testified at the trial, remained as vivid and as real to him as they had become when he first saw them, struggling to make sense of what had happened to them- doubting, some of them, that it made any sense at all.

Some evenings Darnell would sit by the window, looking out at the bay as a ship passed under the Golden Gate. He would watch it disappear into the thick, purple night, wondering if Marlowe might be on it, seeking oblivion in the only work he knew. He never heard from Marlowe, not a word; but then he had not expected that he would. Marlowe was the very meaning of solitude. It was nearly a year after the trial when Darnell received a letter, not from Marlowe, but from Marlowe's sister.

It was written in a fine, modest hand on a single sheet of stationery. She thanked him for what he had done for her brother; told him that though a mother's grief was bottomless, she had known when he had first told her what he had done, that he suffered even more than she. Then she told him that she was writing now to tell him that her brother was dead, that he had been reported missing from a freighter on which had taken work as a member of the crew.

He had apparently fallen overboard and was lost at sea. The ship had been in the south Atlantic, she added, close to the very spot where her son had been lost. The name of the ship was the White Rose.

Darnell put down the letter and got up from his desk. He stood at the window, staring down at the busy city street, at everyone going about their busy lives. He could just see Marlowe standing alone on a moonlit night, the ocean vast and miraculous, the way it must have looked when God first touched it and gave it life. He could almost hear the quiet splash of Marlowe's body as the sea welcomed him home.

A Note from the Author:

Thank you for reading <u>Evangeline</u>. Please let me know your thoughts about the book. You can send me email, sign up for my newsletter and get updates about new releases by visiting my website at www.dwbuffa.net.

- D.W. Buffa

OTHER BOOKS BY D. W. BUFFA

The Defense

The Prosecution

The Judgment

The Legacy

Star Witness

Breach of Trust

Trial by Fire

The Grand Master

Rubicon
(Released under pen name
"Lawrence Alexander")

08/11

3×5/13 (2/14)
4× 4/15 (4/15)
5× 08/15 (05/16)
5× 08/15 (9/17)

6× 1/19 (11/22) (5/24)

condition noted
RWL 8/15

6× 1/19 (3/19) (6/20)

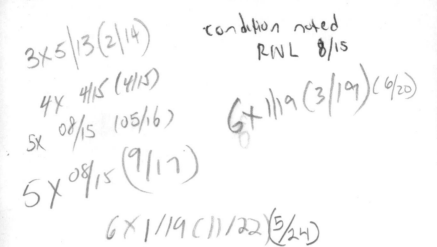

8949671R0

Made in the USA
Charleston, SC
28 July 2011